The Friar's
Lantern

Greg Hickey

ISBN: 978-1-7330937-0-5

For the cowards in Oakland, California who stole the laptop and flash drive containing previous drafts of this book.

The Friar's
Lantern

"Everyone believed that the meeting of the two chess players had been entirely random." -Herbert Quain, *The God of the Labyrinth*

Let t_n be a point in time such that, given t_a and t_b with a<b, t_b occurs subsequent to t_a.

Let $S(t_n)$ be a brain state at t_n.

Let $C(t_n)$ be a choice made at t_n.

Let L be the laws of brain chemistry, which govern how one brain state gives rise to another.

Let D be the claim that determinism exists, or that, given the condition of the universe at some initial time t_0, the way that condition changes thereafter is fixed as a matter of natural law.

1. S(t₁)

The sign on the door reads "Lauterbur State University Functional Magnetic Resonance Imaging Research Laboratory." The broken-down building skulks in the shadow of the university's football stadium at the far north end of this once-prestigious institution whose name has fallen markedly since its late-Cold War Era heyday as a bastion of scientific and technological research. To the east of these two structures, three cars populate a 10,000-space parking lot, little islands of painted steel in a stark, asphalt ocean grid-marked by mottled and faded white lines. The stadium, Ozymandian on the bitumen shore, is beset to the north by woodlands, and here the hard blacktop, the steel girders and thick slabs of concrete devolve into dirt and dead yellow leaves and broken branches overhung by untrimmed trees and dotted with tangled bushes. The little laboratory remains as a mere afterthought, its wearied face shrouded by the sallow, emaciated branches of a willow tree, devoid of leaves even now in mid-May, the tree dead or dying as its limbs sag down in despair to scratch the top of the building.

The laboratory itself is squat and squalid like a red brick bomb shelter, the bricks a departure both from the cement and steel of the stadium that towers above it on one side and the black loam of the wilderness that drags it down from the other. These days, the woodlands' influence has taken hold, smudging the lab's once-crimson bricks a hazy brownish-gray and softening its edges with dirt and erosion. Ivy creeps up the lower right side of the front wall, its leaves splotched with black marks of death, like a zombie hand reaching up from the grave to pry the laboratory away from the force field of the stadium that looms above. Yet all in all, the lab is well-built; the bricks are solid and hold their form, and the few windows are smeared with dust but remain uncracked.

You draw open the frosted glass door and step into a long hallway that veers to the right around a corner fifty feet ahead, and you realize the laboratory is much larger than it looks from the outside. Decades of footprints mopped and waxed into the adsorbent floor have stained the otherwise clean beige tile a murky gray. The walls are sea foam green, drably bright like those of an old hospital room, and you can just make out the flaked scabs of the previous coat of paint under this fresh exterior.

You wander down the hall and around the corner and come to three doors. The ones ahead and to your right are closed, but the door on your left opens into a 12' by 12' anteroom with a desk facing the door and two metal-framed chairs backed with shabby burgundy acrylic. A mid-thirties woman types incessantly on a computer at the desk, her hair tied back at the edges of a smooth face and oval glasses above a trim torso, a white lab coat pulled over her navy business suit. She looks up at you with the scarcest quizzical expression as you enter, the very image of clinical professionalism, all save for the hair's breadth excess of cleavage beneath her lab coat and blouse which conjures up a scene from a cheap pornography.

"I'm here for the study," you say in answer to her expectant gaze. "The MRI…" you pull a folded handwritten note from your pocket, "…about predicting human behavior?"

She lifts a paper-stuffed clipboard from the desk and stands to extend it in your direction. "Fill this out, please."

You retreat to one of the chairs to complete the paperwork, the usual collection of disclaimers, consents and opt-out clauses required for legitimate universities to conduct research on voluntary participants. *A functional magnetic resonance imaging (fMRI) scan will be performed to examine activity in your brain in response to certain stimuli. fMRI scans rely on the interaction of strong magnetic fields with the chemical properties of your body. No radiation will be used, and there are minimal hazards, although possible side effects include headaches, nausea, dizziness, chest pain, back pain, fever, weakness and/or seizures.* You read the last sentence twice to confirm seizures aren't considered a serious hazard. However, *you may end the scan at any time during the procedure.*

You glance up at the receptionist but she ignores you, her flat stare wedded to her computer monitor, her fingers cli-cli-clicking rapidly across the keyboard. No help there. You re-examine the slab of disclaimers, and a touch of doubt creeps into your thoughts. But people have MRIs every day, you remind yourself. This isn't radical new technology anymore. Yet you feel your throat tighten nonetheless.

If you choose to sign the consent form and participate in the study, turn to page 11.

If you choose not to sign the consent form, turn to page 18.

You complete the forms, four pages front and back, signing your name twice and initialing no less than seven times. Yes, *you have read and understood all the information provided in this document.* Yes, *you agree to participate in this VOLUNTARY study.* Yes, *you consent to undergo an fMRI scan.* Yes, *you understand the procedure and are aware of the potential side effects.*

You cross to the receptionist's desk to return your assignment. She takes the clipboard, removes the documents signifying your complicit participation in whatever is in store for you and scans through your work.

"Follow me," she says and leads you through a door behind her desk. "You will need to remove your clothes and wear a gown during the scan. The fMRI is highly magnetic." She indicates the first room on the right of a second hallway almost as long as the first.

You step inside and strip off your clothes, place them in a small square locker and lock it with a non-ferrous key. You don the gown, which covers your body but does little to dispel the feeling of nakedness, and tiptoe back into the hall.

Seven closed doors line the eggshell-painted corridor, three on each side and one at the end. The receptionist leads you through the second door on the left, which bears a sign warning "DANGER: POWERFUL MAGNET ALWAYS ON!"

An 8' by 8' giant donut dominates the cramped room and emits a wheezing, chirping noise that sounds like a goldfinch being forced through an ancient fire bellows. A slender table extends out from its hollow center, its concave surface funneling directly into the hole. The receptionist busies herself with a set of controls on the freshly glazed face of the donut/fMRI machine, Dunkin-artificial-vanilla white against the ivory body of the colossal pastry. Everything else in the room, from the IV stand with its dangling plastic tubes to the trash bin and biohazard container, is frosted with the same antiseptic, colorless plastic. You feel as though you've just stepped onto the bridge of the *Starship Enterprise*.

You scarcely have time to take stock of the room before you hear the door close behind you, and you turn to face a short, slight, balding man in a long white lab coat and glasses.

"Welcome," he says. "I am Dr. Pavlov." He pronounces it "Pahv-love" without the nasal American "a."

You can't decide if you heard him correctly. Dr. Pavlov? That has to be a joke, right? But you recover your senses in time to shake his hand and introduce yourself.

Dr. Pavlov seems just the sort of unassuming man you'd expect to find cooped up in a rundown laboratory next to an abandoned parking lot at the far end of an obscure university. His feet shuffle noiselessly as he walks, and his shoulders round forward in the posture of a man who has spent too many years bent over a computer or a lab bench, and you check yourself as you grasp his hand so as not to crush this poor man's fingers. Yet his grip is firm and steady as he applies just enough pressure to give your unsuspecting palm an uncomfortable squeeze, and as he pumps your hand once and releases, you look up into his green eyes and find them equally unflinching as they bore into yours with a force that registers somewhere between casual curiosity and a penetrating measure of your character.

"Do you know why you are here?" he asks.

You shake your head. "Something about an MRI and predicting behavior, but I don't know all the details."

"Well, you are right so far. It is quite simple, really," Pavlov says with the trimmed precision of a foreign-born tongue. "We will use functional magnetic resonance imaging, or fMRI, to capture images of your brain. During the fMRI scan, I will communicate to you through your headphones and monitor your brain's activity from our control room." He indicates a long, narrow, glass-paned room to his right filled with an array of computer monitors. "You will also view several video sequences and will be asked to perform basic tasks, such as pushing a button. If at any time you wish to end the scan, you merely squeeze the control which you will hold in your left hand."

You cast a wary glance at the ominous donut behind you. The hole seems to have grown smaller since you last looked at it.

"How long will it take?" you ask.

"The scan will last approximately 30 minutes," Pavlov says. "Are you ready to begin?"

"I guess so," you answer.

"Good. Gloria will prepare you for the scan and show you how to use the controls while I initiate the MRI sequence. Do you have any other questions?"

"I don't think so."

"Very well," Pavlov says. "We will start once you are ready."

"Lie down on the table, please," Gloria tells you as Pavlov exits the room.

You take a seat on the edge and swing your legs up to recline into the shallow scooped-out table covered with thin white paper, craning backward to gaze into the mouth of the fMRI as it prepares to swallow you head first. It appears you are about to be launched into some time travel vortex. Gloria gives you two controls: a black plastic rod with a red button at the end to hold in your right hand, just in case you time travel to an episode of *Jeopardy*, and a rubber turkey baster bulb for your left that you can squeeze in panic to stop the scan. She touches a control on the side of the table, and it hums upward until level with the hole. She then wraps a wide cloth strap over your chest and arms and another one over your thighs and anchors them securely on the opposite side of the table.

"You're going to need to remain as still as possible," she explains, as though you had a choice in the matter.

Your head rests on a cheap foam pillow encased in a plastic half-cylinder that surrounds the sides of your face. Gloria slips a pair of big, plastic, ivory headphones over your ears, straps thick, gray, opaque goggles to your eyes and inserts two rectangular pads into the spaces between your head and the cylinder, firmly wedging your skull into place.

"Ready?" she asks, sounding less than concerned for your safety.

You offer a weak thumbs up and a "yes" that is probably louder than necessary given the muffling headphones and your nervous discomfort.

Pavlov's Lady Igor exits the room as you slide into the mouth of the donut. The interior of the tunnel must be about six inches beyond your face, and as you feel its sides disturb the air around your arms, you begin to have a very real understanding of the word "claustrophobia." The machine's screeched ornithic panting would be almost deafening if not for the headphones, but then the poor bird's wheezes are snuffed out by the whir of a bone saw—mercifully brief enough to give you little time to wonder whether you're going to have a cavity drilled or your skull sliced open as part of this whole procedure—and a video monitor on the inside of the goggles comes alive while an androgynous voice crackles through the headphones.

"Welcome to the Lauterbur State University Functional Magnetic Resonance Imaging Research Laboratory, and thank you for your participation in our study on the use of fMRI in predicting human behavior."

An image of the laboratory's dull exterior appears on the video screen, then morphs into a photograph of the lab's MRI scanner.

"Our study builds on previous research in neuroscience, human psychology and MRI technology. In 2008, scientists at the Max Planck Institute for Human Cognitive and Brain Sciences in Leipzig, Germany used fMRI to examine subjects as they engaged in simple voluntary actions. Their research demonstrated that the outcome of an individual's decision may be encoded in the prefrontal and parietal cortices of the brain and detected by fMRI up to ten seconds before that decision enters the individual's conscious awareness. In other words, the human brain is capable of reacting and making decisions in response to external stimuli in advance of the individual consciously articulating a choice."

A cartoon image of a human brain appears on the video screen, with a section at the front of the brain pulsating radioactive red. After a few seconds, the animation expands and the white edges of a human head and body fade in around the brain, in disturbing resemblance to a chalk outline at a crime scene. The letters A and B hover in front of the silhouetted figure, and he (or a hairless, flat-chested she) contemplates the two choices while his brain continues to flash for what must be ten seconds. Then the animation raises its arm to point to the letter B.

"Two years later, a 2010 study by scientists at UCLA demonstrated that fMRI brain scans could be used to predict an individual's choice one week in advance of the resultant action," the voice continues. "In this second study, the researchers showed subjects a video promoting the use of sunscreen while the subjects underwent an fMRI brain scan. Immediately following the scan, subjects were asked to rate the likelihood they would increase their sunscreen use in the subsequent week. A week after the scan, the subjects reported their actual sunscreen use over the course of the week. When compared with subjects' expectations of their behavior, the researchers noted that fMRI-measured activity in the medial prefrontal cortices of the subjects' brains accounted for 23% of actual changes in sunscreen use above and beyond those changes predicted by the subjects themselves. In other words, fMRI was more accurate in predicting changes in subjects' behavior over the course of a week than were the subjects themselves."

The image on the screen melts into a chalk-outline human profile reclining under a white tube with a tiny golden sun on the side, his brain flashing like an industrial fire alarm. The sunscreen fades, and a full-body Mr. Chalky stands and saunters in place as images of the sun and trees appear around him. As the rays beat down in pulsing yellow snakes, he produces a cartoon sunscreen bottle and proceeds to smear the contents over his two-dimensional figure.

"Our research builds on the results of these two studies and others like them by attempting to further identify the decision-making mechanism in the human brain," the ethereal voice continues as the scene fades. "One week from today you will have the opportunity to make a potentially lucrative choice. You will enter a room to find a table holding two closed, opaque boxes."

Beyond the whitewash of the plump headphones, you hear the muffled bone saw interrupted by a harsh, metallic car horn. A pair of two-dimensional cubes labeled "A" and "B" appear on the screen.

"The first box, Box A, will contain $1,000," the voice continues.

A white rectangle with the header "Lauterbur State University" and the text "Pay to the order of _____YOU_____" and "$1,000" levitates out of Box A.

"The second box, Box B, will contain either nothing or $1,000,000."

A second rudimentary check, this one for $1,000,000, arises from Box B, hovers for a moment and then disintegrates into tiny scraps of paper.

"You will have two options from which to choose. You may decide to take both boxes A and B, or to take only Box B but not Box A. If you understand the terms of your choice, press the button on the control in your right hand."

When you are ready, you press the button.

"Based on the fMRI scan taken at this moment in conjunction with a brain state prediction model developed here at the laboratory, a prediction will be made today regarding your choice. If the model predicts you will take both boxes A and B, no money will be deposited in Box B."

The face-outline reappears on the screen, the front of its brain containing the blinking crimson letters A and B. Boxes A and B return, and A opens to release the $1,000 check, while B tips forward to reveal its empty interior.

"If the model predicts you will take only Box B, $1,000,000 will be placed in that box."

The face-outline's brain flashes red once more, this time with just the letter B inside. Box B opens, and the $1,000,000 check flies out.

"If the model predicts you will randomize your choice, such as by flipping a coin, no money will be deposited in Box B. If you understand the terms of your choice in regards to the model's prediction, press the button on the control in your right hand."

You digest the scenario once more and press the button.

"Upon conclusion of this scan, the fMRI data will be encoded into the model, and the model will make its prediction. Based on that prediction, either $1,000,000 or nothing will be placed in Box B."

The person-outline disappears and a "?" leaps in from the upper-right side of the monitor and flies into the open Box B, which closes behind it. A clock materializes, and the hands whip through a few revolutions before the person-outline walks back onto the screen.

"The model will make its prediction, and either $1,000,000 or nothing will be placed in Box B today. You may return to the laboratory one week from today to make your choice. This study has been performed with many other subjects, and the model is currently 91.8% accurate in its predictions, with that rate increasing as our study progresses. If you understand the terms of the entire arrangement, press the button on the control in your right hand."

$1,000,000? You understand that. You press the button, and the voice in your headphones says, "Thank you. This completes the fMRI portion of our study."

The video screen goes dark, and the quiet whir of the table brings you back out of the donut. Gloria removes the goggles, pads and headphones, and you squint in the suddenly bright lights while the fMRI's huff-and-puff chirp rushes back into your ears. She undoes the straps across your body, and you stand as Dr. Pavlov enters the room. He walks with his hands clasped behind his back as though attempting to pull his hunched spine upright. It does not seem a comfortable position.

"Everything okay?" he asks.

"I think so," you say.

"Good. The prediction model is working as we speak. It should be complete in about ten minutes, and then I will place either $1,000,000 or nothing in Box B. You are welcome to wait in the reception area until I am done."

He says "$1,000,000" so coolly, without the melodramatic Dr. Evil fanfare that should accompany any verbalization of such a sum.

Gloria waits by the door as Pavlov returns to the control room and parks at one of the computers. You stare at the calm, diminutive, bespectacled man behind the wall of glass, already engrossed in whatever intricacies of his prediction model are playing out across his monitor. Then you follow Gloria back down the hall, get dressed and return to the waiting room.

She fills a cup from the water cooler in the corner and hands it to you in silence as you take a seat in one of the ragged chairs. You lean back and sip the water and examine the quiet, austere room, the freshly painted, cream-colored walls, the slightly cracked floor tiles, the pert, competent woman perched on the edge of her desk chair, and you try to ascertain exactly where the punchline to this elaborate joke is hiding. You cannot reconcile this ordinarily real 3D world with the crude 2D animations of the video, the blinking red brain, the simple cubic boxes, the bleached white checks for unbelievable sums of money. Yet there was Dr. Pavlov, shuffling out of his glass box with all the vivid truthfulness of the most convincing dream, intimating the same offer made in the video.

This is real. And you don't need to pinch yourself because even as you sit here in this boxy, worn out room in this dumpy, little, derelict laboratory, nothing tangible arises to contradict what you have just experienced. So you sip the last of your water and listen to the oblivious hum of Gloria's fingers on her keyboard until Dr. Pavlov enters the room.

He moves like a ghost, almost hovering, his feet skimming noiselessly across the floor as his hunched shoulders and bowed forehead come at you first. His green eyes sparkle with a gleam you can best describe as triumphant even though none of his features move a millimeter.

"The model is complete," he says. "The prediction has been made, and I have acted accordingly."

You try to read his facial expression, even though you realize from the first glance that it will give you nothing.

"We will see you in a week," he continues. "Next Friday. The same time?"

"Yes," you murmur.

Pavlov extends his hand, and you shake it, careful this time to match his pressure, and then you turn and walk out the door and down the long sea green hallway to the vacant parking lot.

Continue on page 19.

You stand up and return the unsigned paperwork to the receptionist's desk. "I've changed my mind," you say.

She nods perfunctorily. "Okay." She couldn't care less.

You wait for her to say something more but when she resumes her work, you walk from the room, down the long hallway and out into the empty parking lot. For one one-hundredth of a second, you consider turning around and going back in, but decide against it. The study will be going on for a while if you change your mind. You can always come back in a week, a month, a year. It's up to you.

END

2. $\exists L:S(t_1)\wedge L\rightarrow S(t_2)$

On Monday morning you are required to report for jury duty. The county courthouse is a massive granite building, seven stories high and twice as long, a neoclassical monolith fronted with eight fluted Ionic columns capped with scroll volutes. The columns frame the third through sixth story windows set back behind them, each darkened pane separated from the one above by a copper panel engraved with ornamented concentric rectangles. Another set of windows extends beyond the columns on either side, flanked by vertical mouldings crowned with decorative carvings of peaked wreaths that stretch the height of the building. Above the columns, the architrave bears the name "Yetopo County Criminal Courthouse," and this long stone block is capped by another row of nine windows alternating with eight columns in relief, with the whole thing topped off by a cornice bearing a carved ribbon lintel.

The courthouse is Justice epitomized, huge and stony and unflinching as it towers above the shoddy lawn and ragged trees like a lone tank defending a hill against a swarming barbarian horde, the unspoken paternal warning in its cold façade reminding those who dare transgress the Law of the swift severity of the consequences to follow. But inside the heavy wood and brass-plated doors, humanity reigns, humanity in its grossest, shabbiest guise. The line for the metal detectors teems with the lowest elements of society: the pimps, prostitutes, dealers and users, women whose rail-thin ankles sway atop six inch heels, tragicomically supporting cellulite-ridden thighs unhidden by Vegas-length miniskirts, slim but flabby midriffs exposed by glittered tube tops too short in both directions and baring more than a little bra and even more saggy breasts, their clownish faces with wide mouths split open in perpetual sneers, blue and green and lavender eye shadow that seeps into the hollows of rouged cheeks to blend like watercolors on a palette, surrounded by wild, stringy hair effortlessly styled by slinking into bed in the wee hours only to rise shortly afterward, already late for their appearances in court; men whose high-top Jordans and pale blue knock-off Diesel jeans are both two sizes too large, and whose stained white tank tops are one size too small, a combination that forces them to walk with a lame, slouched gait, one hand reaching down with intermittent, lackadaisical spasms to yank up their pants and ebb the creeping tide of white cotton boxer shorts, their arms either skin and bone or thick with powerful strength buried under a layer of fat, their faces drawn and haggard, eyes empty, distant and defeated until they meet the gaze of another and inject a pointed hardness into their flat stares and thin-lipped scowls.

The attorneys assemble in a separate line, some dressed in fine Italian suits, some in disheveled blazers, bright shirts and loud ties, all of them hypnotized by their smartphones. They are not subject to the metal detectors; they flash laminated identification cards and proceed into the great hall beyond. Some carry black patent leather briefcases, some balance stacks of Redweld folders, some push gray, plastic carts overflowing with papers, binders, legal briefs, case notes and research. A Wikipedia article entitled "Gunshot residue" peeks out of a folder on the cart of the woman to your left.

The lawyers rush forward in a stream of perpetual motion as the whole muddy, seething mass of your line oozes forward in parallel, two forks of the same river dragging itself over the scuffed marble floor, with your channel born anew through the silver gates of the metal detectors, only to discover your reincarnations are by some cruel twist just that: repeated incarnations with no change, born into the same grubby world as the one you left behind.

Where are the other potential jurors? Where are the normal people, the every-men and -women, the other yous who inhabit this county of *Yet Opodo*, this land of "one sun" in the language of the indigenous Native Americans? Or have you misjudged these others? Have you misjudged yourself? Is this heaving host the true image of humanity? And are you one of them? You search around you as the human culvert bears you through the metal detector and spills you out to a delta of marble and high fluorescent lights. The others scatter in all directions, and you hesitate in confusion before you manage to find an elevator and ascend to the third floor and Room 3A00.

You enter to find a handful of people interspersed throughout rows of dilapidated, wooden one-room schoolhouse chairs, and in this classroom/boardroom environment, they begin to resemble the jurors you see on *Law and Order*, sensible folk with normal jobs waiting with strained patience in neatly arranged straight-backed seats. Although they'd look a lot more normal if the air of a free health clinic didn't permeate every inch of the Dijon mustard-yellow walls. The mid-morning sunlight casts long, oblique shadows that crawl haphazardly over the scuffed and stained and glaze-peeling hardwood floors. There are few enough of the rectangular fluorescent fixtures to make the incoming sunshine necessary, and these two photon armies battle each other to illuminate the room. The soft, blue-gray rays weep tiny mists of dust in the harsh, bleached, manmade radiation, and each section of the dull yellow-brown paint on the walls gives a different impression of color depending on which light source subdues the other at that point.

You find an aisle seat in an empty row, bury your head in a newspaper and peer around from under downcast brows. The mousy-haired, librarianish woman in front of you sits with legs crossed and one elbow propped on her upper knee, contemplating a compact like poor Yorick's skull as she does her makeup. At the opposite end of the row behind you, a big, sweaty man with a short, unkempt afro and navy t-shirt and jeans picks his fingernails and bobs his head to an impossible rhythm from his iPod. It is 9:13 am, and the room begins to fill. The chairs are precious commodities and for ten minutes, you sit sideways with your knees swiveled outward and the paper pulled up over your face like a parka to beat off the human blizzard that heaves itself over your lap and settles in fleshy drifts on the last of the vacant seats to your left. Before long, the room is SRO, and they still come streaming in. With your nose so deep in a photo of General Petraeus you might as well be the Army's press secretary, you can sense the room beginning to overfill by the warm, bubbling noise and the rich smell of person that drifts over you.

At 10:09, the first bailiffs enter and call off lists of names. Your name isn't called until almost 11:00, which gives you time to read every word of the travel section. Your bailiff, a stolid, working-man type with a brown-gray horseshoe of hair and short-sleeved, beige uniform, leads you and about thirty other people down the hall to a room slightly smaller than the one you just left. You funnel into an aisle between four rows of cracked wooden benches that face what can best be described as a pod. About two feet beyond the first row of seats, a hazy gray bubble stretches from floor to ceiling and wall to jaundiced wall, separating this antechamber from whatever lies within. As the bailiff holds open the pod door and the interior precipitates through the leaden fog, you make out a circular room with several areas sectioned off by curved wooden banisters, some figures seated at two long tables at the front, and a black-robed man perched behind a high podium at the back. It takes you a moment to realize he is the judge and this is the courtroom.

There is an exhibit at the local science museum in which chicken eggs hatch in a glass-enclosed incubation chamber. The attraction is popular with children, who are fascinated by the sight of moist, downy, newborn chicks pecking and stumbling their way out of their shells and into the bright light of their artificial world. Even teenagers and adults become mesmerized by this nativity scene, captivated for up to thirty minutes at a time by the flutter of undeveloped wings, the rapid blinking of newly opened eyes, the shuddered tremors to disengage egg dew that match the spastic quivers of tiny heartbeats. And if such a common occurrence can offer so great a spectacle, then how much more appropriate that human trials are held in this place and not in the grand columned, balustraded and balconied courtrooms of television and film, not in great halls, but in pods like these that line the myriad hallways all throughout one boundless hatchery of Justice, where arguments, counterarguments, examinations and crosses can be brought to heat under watchful, black-cowled eyes, can fornicate a discourse—an intercourse—that leads to a verdict and a sentence, Justice hatched and birthed and burped out of thousands of incubating pods and disseminated into the world of mankind.

The bailiff leads you into the pod, past the attorneys who wait at tables on either side of the central aisle, then on a right turn past the clerk, judge and court reporter and into the wood-paneled arc of the jury box, which becomes noticeably cramped when forced to hold thirty-some jurors instead of twelve.

The judge is a round man, not fat—pudgy maybe—with the general bodily softness that attends most American men of late middle-age. But he is also short, even seated up above you on the bench, and the extra layers of his shapeless black robe add width to his body to match his diminutive height so that he perches upon his pedestal with the stern joviality of a charred marshmallow. His equally spheroid head sits atop a short thick neck, capped off by thin-framed eyeglasses and dense gray hair that droops neatly over his pate.

"Good morning, ladies and gentlemen," he intones. "Thank you for your presence here today. I'm going to ask our court clerk, Ms. Stephenson, to take roll. When she calls your pre-assigned number, please raise your hand and answer 'here.'"

"Criminal Case Number 11-09187, People vs. Dr. David Solon," announces a tall, freckled, blond woman in an equally pale beige business suit who looks like a forty-year-old still stuck in gangly adolescence. "The Honorable Judge Harlan Pitcock presiding. Good morning, jurors."

Ms. Stephenson proceeds to read off jury numbers, and the people around you respond in kind. You are number eighteen.

"Thank you, Ms. Stephenson," says Judge Pitcock, after all thirty-four jurors confirm their presence. "Ladies and gentlemen of the jury, this is a criminal case. It concerns the death of Mr. Damon Belliard on May 3 of last year. The defendant, Dr. David Solon, has been charged with voluntary manslaughter and second-degree murder in connection to Mr. Belliard's death. Has any member of the jury panel read or heard anything about this case or the parties involved?"

No one answers.

"Let the record reflect there is no response," Pitcock announces. "Mrs. Shannon Gray is the attorney for the State. Mr. Kenneth Hines is the attorney for the defendant. Is any member of the jury panel acquainted with either of these attorneys?"

Silence again.

"In accordance with state law, any person serving on a jury must be eighteen years or older, a citizen of the United States, able to read and understand the English language, and a resident of the summoning county, in this case, Yetopo County. Furthermore, a juror cannot have been convicted of an indictable offense in any state or federal court and must not have any physical or mental disability which would prevent the person from properly serving as a juror. Are there any of you who do not meet these requirements?"

No response.

"This trial is expected to last four days. Is there anything about the length or scheduling of the trial that would interfere with your ability to serve?"

What about not wanting to be stuck in this sticky gray pod for thirty-two hours? Does that count? But no one says a word.

The questions continue for twenty-odd minutes. A few panel members answer in the affirmative: yes, they have a relative in the legal profession; yes, they have served on a jury before; yes, they have appeared in traffic court. Judge Pitcock asks them if their past experiences would affect their ability to remain impartial in this trial. Those judged to have legitimate potential for bias are excused, the rest are allowed to stay. Attorneys Gray and Hines pass the time making final preparations for their cases, but it is obvious they hear every word. Shannon Gray flicks through a stack of papers on her desk, her sharp slate eyes darting back and forth between the loose sheets of paper and the jury panel. Her younger male assistant prosecutor frantically scribbles notes by her side. Kenneth Hines and David Solon engage in brief murmured exchanges, whispering from the corners of their mouths in one-word code like professional scouts at a high school baseball game. Dr. Solon watches the jury panel intently, his rapt blue eyes pricking out of his blank face.

Within a half-hour, the panel has been whittled down to seventeen potential jurors.

"Ladies and gentlemen," says Pitcock, "you have, as a group, answered several questions about criminal trials and criminal charges. At this time, I'm going to allow Mrs. Gray and Mr. Hines to ask questions of each of you individually. We'll start with you, Mrs. Gray."

One by one, each of your fellow jurors confesses his or her life to the courtroom. The attorneys ask what type of work they currently do, whether they have ever done any work substantially different from what they do now, their educational history, whether they have served in the military, who else lives in their household and the type of work they do, whether they have any children or parents living elsewhere and the type of work they do, which television shows they watch, what books and magazines they read, any sources from which they learn the news, such as the newspapers they read, the radio stations they listen to, the TV channels they watch, the Internet sites they frequent, and what they do in their spare time. Every so often, the attorneys probe deeper, fixating on seemingly trivial minutiae of ordinary lives. Each juror's story carries an insinuation, a latent prejudice. Surgeons are conservative, in it for the money and especially unsympathetic to killers after seeing the mortal carnage on their tables. Those without college educations can be either wowed or repelled by big words and fancy lawyer tricks. The *CSI* fans think they know more than they do, and their zeal can be advantageous or useless, depending on the lawyer, depending on the defendant, depending on the case.

When Ms. Stephenson calls "Juror Number 18," you state your name, not that it matters, save for any potential tinge of ethnicity and the implications that inherited past might carry. The court is blind to details as you see them, but like forms and textures to the sightless, these details still tell a story, just not the one you had in mind. With clouded eyes, the court runs its hands over your face, your body, senses your emotions like a dog in the air that evaporates from your skin, pricks its ears to catch the inflections in your voice, flicks out a forked snake's tongue to taste the odor of your soul. You struggle to confine your answers to the questions themselves, to the truth, the mundane, the shortest and most efficient way to acquit yourself and get on with this examination. Yet you hear a part of your most closely guarded self cry out in rebellion, insisting you are more than a collection of facts and experiences, and you try to inject your

24

answers with uniqueness, with personality, but even these embellishments remain mere details, sucked up by the court like a digital scanner capturing an old childhood photo, each glorious color, shade and emotion assigned a binary code and bitmapped into a computerized copy, together accented, amplified, articulated in an image that transcends the old bound photo album for a few megabytes of invisible space on a flash drive. And if only you could explain why the two duplicate images are different, why the compressed computer file misses something, even though they remain physically identical in every single way.

Whether or not you had intended to escape jury duty before this moment, the thought of doing so looms large now. The silent judgment bestowed upon your character has left an acrid taste in your mouth, and the thought of four days' confinement to this gray fishbowl looms larger than before. You must appear biased. You must convince one attorney or Pitcock that you cannot impartially adjudicate on this case, and then you will have no further use and will be free to go. The idea is tempting but risky, for if your ruse fails, you will have committed the gravest evil of all in this place where even child rapists are granted the tiniest measure of reprieve for their honesty. Still, even as you finish your speech, your mind begins to concoct a story that will turn you loose from this room.

If you make up a story to get out of jury duty, turn to page 26.
If you do not make up a story, turn to page 29.

You come to the end of your limited biography and fall silent.

"Thank you," Judge Pitcock says from up on his dais. "Is there anything else?"

"No," you answer, then, "well, yes, but it was a long time ago. When I was a little kid."

"Go on," says Pitcock, his bloodhound nose having picked up the scent of further data.

"Well, I had a brother once," you say. "He was a year younger than me—I was four at the time. We were playing in the yard outside our house one morning when this guy in a pickup truck swerved off the road and onto our lawn. A drunk driver maybe, I don't know. He hit my brother and killed him on the spot. Then he just turned back onto the street and took off. The police never caught him. We never heard anything about him again."

"I see." Pitcock grows even rounder, like a pufferfish taking on air. "You didn't tell us about this brother."

"No, he's gone now. Obviously."

"Of course. But I'm surprised you didn't mention this incident earlier."

"I know. I didn't think of it. It was so long ago. He was only three…" And then you realize you've boxed yourself in.

Pitcock rolls on ahead of you. "I understand. And how has your brother's death affected you in your current day-to-day life?"

"I think about him, if that's what you mean."

"I'm sure you do. Yet in your prior answers, you showed no sign of any lasting effects from your brother's death. No trauma, no learning disabilities, no struggles with substance abuse. Isn't that correct?"

"Yes," you admit.

"All right, I'll turn it back over to the attorneys. Mrs. Gray, any further questions for this juror?"

Shannon Gray hinges forward in her seat with a straight back. She is a striking blond woman in her early forties, the kind who could pass for ten years younger with the right makeup, but has instead settled for displaying just how well she has aged. "Juror Number 18, how do you feel now regarding this man who killed your brother?" she asks.

"I think he deserves to be punished," you say, knowing you've entangled yourself in your own lie. You can already hear the counter-questions from Kenneth Hines and Harlan Pitcock.

"Would you like to punish him?" Gray asks.

"I would like there to be some consequence for what he did."

"No matter the cost?"

"I'm sorry, I don't know what you mean."

"I mean, what lengths would you go to in order to see this man punished?"

"I don't know. It was a long time ago. I wouldn't know how to begin looking for him."

"But you still believe he deserves to be punished."

"Yes."

"And how far would you go to see that happen?"

"Well, I wouldn't kill him if that's what you mean."

"I didn't suggest you would," she says. "But you would like to see him punished for his crime?"

"Yes," you answer.

"Your Honor," Gray says to Pitcock, "it seems to me this past incident has ingrained in Juror Number 18 a desire to inflict punishment on wrongdoers who have managed to escape the consequences of the law. I sincerely doubt this juror's ability to deliberate on this case without bias."

Gray's objection seems misplaced, but you're far too awash with silent gratitude at the moment to care.

"Thank you, Mrs. Gray," says Judge Pitcock. "I understand your concern. However, given the time elapsed since the event in question and the absence of any long-term emotional trauma, I believe this juror is perfectly capable of remaining impartial in the case before us. The fact that Juror Number 18 did not even recall the incident until now seems evidence of such." He turns his attention to Hines. "Mr. Hines, do you have any questions for Juror Number 18?"

"No, Your Honor," Hines says.

"Juror Number 18, do you feel you can render an impartial verdict on this case?" Pitcock asks.

What can you say? Your lie has run its course. "I guess so, Your Honor," you answer.

"You guess so?" Pitcock repeats. "Juror Number 18, a man is on trial for murder here. Do you feel you can remain impartial in considering his case?"

There is only one response to this question. "Yes, Your Honor."

"Good," says Pitcock. "Mrs. Gray, you have one remaining strike to use against a member of this jury panel. Do you wish to exclude Juror Number 18?"

"No, Your Honor," Shannon Gray answers.

"Thank you," says Pitcock. "And thank you, Juror Number 18, for your honesty in this matter."

The spotlight passes to the next juror, and you shrink back into your seat. Once everyone has been similarly interrogated and the two attorneys have used all their strikes to exclude undesirable candidates, Pitcock asks Ms. Stephenson to read off the chosen jurors.

"Jurors, please stand as your number is called," she says in a thin, reedy voice that barely fills the pod. "Juror Number 2, Number 5, Number 6, Number 9, Number 12, Number 14, Number 18, Number 23, Number 24, Number 29, Number 32, Number 33."

"Thank you, Ms. Stephenson," says Pitcock. "Is the State satisfied with the jury panel now standing?"

"Yes, Your Honor," Gray answers.

"Is the defense satisfied with the jury panel now standing?"

"We are, Your Honor," says Hines.

"Thank you. Those of you still seated are excused for today. Please call the courthouse after 5:00 pm to see if you are needed tomorrow." The fortunate non-jurors exit the courtroom. "Members of the jury," Pitcock continues, "we will take an hour recess for lunch at this time. Our bailiff, Mr. Gilroy, will show you to the jury room."

You follow the rest of the panel out of the box, and that's it. You're on a jury.

Continue on page 30.

You stick to the truth and finish your autobiography, feeling spent and frustrated as the trivial details of your life dissolve in the thick pod air. A few more harmless questions from Gray and Hines, and you are forgotten once more as the focus shifts to the next juror. After the attorneys have interrogated each potential juror and used all their strikes to exclude any objectionable candidates, Pitcock asks Ms. Stephenson to read off the chosen twelve.

"Jurors, please stand as I call your number," she says in a weak, high-pitched voice. "Juror Number 2, Number 5, Number 6, Number 9, Number 12, Number 14, Number 18, Number 23, Number 24, Number 29, Number 32, Number 33."

"Thank you, Ms. Stephenson," says Pitcock. "Is the State satisfied with the jury panel now standing?"

"Yes, Your Honor," Gray answers.

"Is the defense satisfied with the jury panel now standing?"

"We are, Your Honor," says Hines.

"Thank you," Pitcock says. He addresses the jury box. "Ladies and gentlemen, if your number was not called, you are excused for today. Please call the courthouse after 5:00 to see if you are needed tomorrow." The handful of people not chosen exit the courtroom. "Members of the jury," Pitcock continues, "we will take an hour recess for lunch at this time. Our bailiff, Mr. Gilroy, will show you to the jury room."

You follow the rest of the panel out of the pod, and that's it. You're on a jury.

Continue on page 30.

The trial begins in earnest after lunch. The lawyers march in and make themselves busy at their tables once you and the other jurors have taken your seats. Shannon Gray studies her notes and nods to her assistant's frequent hushed comments in her ear. Kenneth Hines and David Solon assume identical stoic positions, elbows resting on the edges of their chairs, backs reclined against their seats, chins tucked as they gaze into empty space in front of them.

Judge Pitcock enters and calls the court to order, then asks, "Mrs. Gray, are you ready to proceed with your opening statement?"

"I am, Your Honor," Gray replies. "Ladies and gentlemen of the jury," she begins as she strides to the center of the pod, "this trial is the story of two men. The first is the defendant, Dr. David Solon."

She sweeps her arm in his direction. Dr. Solon is a youngish fifty-something with a tall, lean face that dives down to a deep, tapered chin. His light brown hair is tousled boyishly atop his head, and though time has added some heft to a narrow frame, he still looks like a former letterman beneath the hint of silver at his temples and the gray tweed jacket he sports over a robin's egg collared shirt. You imagine it would be easy to pick out his high school yearbook picture. His shoulders alone betray some sign of fatigue or attrition; they descend sharply, limply, from his long neck, a slight defect in his posture that appears out of place with the rest of his figure.

"Dr. Solon holds a Ph.D. in Mathematics and is a renowned professor at Harvey Tech University," Shannon Gray continues. "By all accounts, he is a respected educator, a brilliant thinker and a loving husband. And just over a year ago, on the night of April 26, 2011, his wife was tragically killed during a break-in at their home.

"The second man is the deceased victim, Mr. Damon Belliard. Mr. Belliard was a career criminal, with numerous arrests and convictions over the course of his adult life. It would be all too easy to prejudge this case on these two men's pasts. Indeed, the evidence does suggest that Damon Belliard killed Julia Solon. But you are here today because Dr. Solon killed Damon Belliard one week after his wife's death. So I will remind you that you must set aside any preconceived notions about these two men and judge this case on the facts and the law."

Shannon Gray is not quite beautiful, despite her straight beach-blond hair and slender legs. Her face is all hard lines, long and angular with a high forehead and a large straight-bridged nose, and her trim black skirt suit and the deft curve of her calf muscles atop not-too-tall heels lend to the general severity of her figure. Yet there is a touch of softness to her movements, a certain fluid grace that gives polish to an otherwise stark, ruthless efficiency.

"The circumstances which brought these two men together are undisputed." Gray's crisp voice could fill an opera hall without strain. "Yet the defense also cannot deny that on the evening of May 3, 2011, Dr. David Solon stood over Damon Belliard, who was unarmed. Dr. Solon recognized Damon Belliard as his wife's killer. And Dr. Solon killed Damon Belliard in cold blood. These are the facts of the case, ladies and gentlemen. Now the defense would have you exonerate this man for his act of vigilantism, for avenging the murder of his wife, or perhaps find him guilty of voluntary manslaughter. The law defines voluntary manslaughter as a homicide committed without malice aforethought, such as when the killer acts in a sudden heat of passion in response to some provocation. This crime carries a minimum sentence of one year in prison and a maximum of seventeen years. If you were to find Dr. Solon not guilty of second-degree murder, he might only serve a single year in prison for killing a defenseless man.

"Had Dr. Solon killed Damon Belliard in his home on April 26, that homicide would have met the criteria for manslaughter. Dr. Solon would have acted in a justifiable sudden heat of passion by shooting the intruder who had just killed his wife. However, the definition of manslaughter also states that the passions of the accused cannot cool prior to the commission of the homicide. Furthermore, the accused must not commit the homicide after sufficient time elapses following the incident of provocation to allow the passions of a reasonable person to cool. If either of these conditions obtains, then the accused is guilty, not of manslaughter, but of murder. In the course of this trial, the State will bring evidence to show how Dr. Solon's emotions had cooled in the week between his wife's death and the day he killed Damon Belliard. This was not a crime of heat-of-the-moment passion. Seven days was enough time for Dr. Solon to consider the ramifications of his actions, for his emotions to cool.

"In contrast to manslaughter, second-degree murder describes an intentional homicide committed without deliberation or premeditation, in which the killer intends to cause serious bodily harm to the victim and acts with extreme indifference for human life. Dr. Solon intended to kill Damon Belliard on May 3 and acted with utter indifference for the life of his unarmed victim when he shot him in the head at close range.

"The defense will attempt to convince you that Dr. Solon somehow acted in the heat of the moment a full seven days after the fact. They will trot out a purported expert in neuroscience to try to persuade you that the unconscious impulses of a man's brain can absolve him of moral and legal responsibility. Yet in the end, you need only consider the facts. David Solon killed Damon Belliard. David Solon intended to kill Damon Belliard. And he did so seven days after his wife's death, with coolness of purpose and in full possession of his faculties. Given the facts of the case and the law of this state, you will have the responsibility of finding Dr. David Solon guilty of second-degree murder."

Shannon Gray allows a moment's silence for her words to settle home, then spins on the pointed toe of her ebony pump and whisks back to her table.

"Thank you, Mrs. Gray," Pitcock rumbles. You can tell he enjoys these performances, as though watching two grandchildren engage in a game of his teaching. "Mr. Hines?"

Kenneth Hines rises deliberately, but without a trace of a man putting on a show, and his audience indulges him as he takes his time buttoning his suit jacket and circling to the front of his table.

"Good afternoon, ladies and gentlemen," he begins. His voice pours from his throat with the warm suede texture of a fine cognac. "You have just heard Mrs. Gray tell you many things about my client, Dr. David Solon. Some of them are true. At least one of them, however, is not. David Solon is not a murderer.

"On the night of April 26, a man broke into the home of David and Julia Solon while they slept. Mrs. Solon heard a noise and went to investigate. Dr. Solon awoke a few moments later, saw his wife's side of the bed empty, removed his handgun from the safe in their bedroom and followed her downstairs. As he neared the living room at the bottom of the staircase, he heard two gunshots. He entered the room to find his wife dead on the floor with her killer standing over her. The killer saw Dr. Solon and fled. Dr. Solon fired two shots at the man as he ran from the house, but missed. Evidence presented in the course of this trial will demonstrate that it was, in fact, Damon Belliard who murdered Julia Solon that night."

Hines begins to pace toward the front end of the jury box, his slow, soothing gait like the placid rhythm of a rocking cradle. Whereas Shannon Gray moved quickly and precisely but without hurry, Kenneth Hines drifts with the certainty of an old seaman who knows exactly where he is headed. His deep brown eyes hold the glint of a kind old uncle's secret, and his wavy hair is still thick, though much grayer than his client's. His face is gentle and full, and while his body has succumbed to the fleshiness of healthy middle age, his legs and voice have lost none of their strength.

"That night, David Solon acted intentionally when he fired his gun at Damon Belliard after Belliard killed Julia Solon," he continues. "He acted in a sudden heat of passion, provoked by the sight of his wife's murderer. I think everyone here will agree that any reasonable person would have reacted as Dr. Solon did. Had Dr. Solon killed Damon Belliard on April 26, that homicide would be, at worst, consistent with voluntary manslaughter.

"One week later, on the evening of May 3, Dr. Solon came upon a man in an alley attempting to rob a woman at gunpoint. Dr. Solon raced down the alley and knocked the assailant to the ground, disarming the robber and rescuing the victim. As the assailant rolled over, Dr. Solon instantly recognized him as his wife's murderer. Without hesitation, Dr. Solon shot and killed him."

Hines comes to a stop at the edge of the jury box, rests his left arm on the railing and gazes down the two rows of jurors.

"Again, on May 3, Dr. Solon acted intentionally when he shot the man who murdered his wife," he says. "He acted in a sudden heat of passion, sudden because he did not expect to encounter Damon Belliard in that alley and because he did not recognize him until a split second before he fired. And he acted in a heat of passion because he was looking into the face of his wife's murderer. Had Dr. Solon shot Damon Belliard on April 26, he might stand accused of manslaughter. And when he shot him a week later, it was still a spontaneous reaction to the discovery of his wife's murderer. In the course of this trial, the defense will produce an expert witness in neuroscience and human behavior who will testify to the power of brain chemical reactions to subconsciously influence decisions up to one week after some initial stimulus, independent of the cognitive decision process. Given these unconscious reactions, we should not expect Dr. Solon's passion, or the passion of any other reasonable person, to cool in just one week.

"Second-degree murder carries a maximum sentence of fifty years in prison and a minimum of ten years. So ask yourselves, ladies and gentlemen of the jury, whether you feel justified in sending Dr. Solon to prison for the rest of his life for reacting to the murder of his wife. Are you willing to allow such a sentence based on subjective judgments of Dr. Solon's emotional state, when scientific data indicate the likelihood of long-term unconscious reactions?

"Dr. Solon was provoked by the murder of his wife. He reacted on the night of her murder by attempting to shoot Damon Belliard. He reacted one week later when he discovered Damon Belliard in that alley and shot and killed him. He did not expect to encounter Damon Belliard a second time. He did not plan to kill Damon Belliard. And unless the State can show his reaction was a malicious act of calculated vengeance—which I assure you they cannot—you must find Dr. Solon not guilty of murder."

. . . . .

"So? How was it?" your friend Eve asks as the two of you sit down to dinner that evening.

"Interesting."

The interior of Joy's Noodles, the local pan-Asian café specializing in riffs on classic pad thai, udon and ramen, can best be described as wood—wood floors, wood chairs, unclothed wood tables and carved wood walls. It's a saloon out of a rice noodle Western.

"So you got a case then?" she asks.

"I did. A murder trial."

"Oh, wow. A murder."

You and Eve have been friends since you met in high school. She's short and smart, the daughter of a German father and a Korean mother, a match which produced her straight black hair, almond-shaped eyes and the American melting-pot upbringing that allows her to frequent a place like Joy's without the slightest upturned nose toward the bastardized cuisine.

"What's the case?" she asks.

"Well, they haven't even called any witnesses yet. It was just the jury selection and opening arguments today. The defendant's name is Dr. David Solon. He's a professor at Harvey Tech. Mathematics, I think. Brilliant, good teacher, great husband. He definitely doesn't look like a killer. But one night last year, he and his wife were asleep in bed when a burglar broke into their house. His wife woke up first and went to investigate. He followed, just in time to see the burglar kill her. The police never caught the guy, but a week later Solon saw the killer holding up another woman on the street. He knocked away the guy's gun, picked it up... and shot him dead."

"No way."

"Yeah. The State is really pushing hard for murder. The prosecutor said enough time had elapsed since Solon's wife's death for him to cool off. That there wasn't any more question of the killing being in the heat of the moment." You open your menu, even though you already know what you'll order.

Eve makes a similar show of perusing her dinner options. "So, what do you think?"

"Come on. You know I can't talk much about it." In fact, you've probably already said more than you should.

"Okay." Eve grins and ducks her face into her menu. She won't press you more now. Yet you know from experience that she's an expert interrogator and will learn everything she wants to know about this case no matter how long it takes. She once got you to admit to secretly liking "Escape" by Enrique Iglesias after catching you twitch when someone changed the station as the song came on the radio.

A waiter in a white Dwight Shrute shirt and black slacks takes your long-since-determined order in cracked English. You exchange sips of water before Eve speaks again.

"So what about that study? The MRI. You can talk about that, right? Did you get paid?"

"Not yet. I have to go back on Friday. It was… interesting too."

"You have an astounding vocabulary."

"Prodigious, I know." You explain the scenario of the experiment to Eve.

"Whoa, that sounds like a Borges story. Well, at least you're accurate. You haven't disappointed yet. So are they for real? Where are they going to come up with a million dollars?"

"No idea. I honestly don't know if Pavlov is serious or not. Everything looked reputable once I got inside the lab. The building's a little decrepit, but all the equipment seemed relatively new. Maybe they're funded by an eccentric billionaire. But it's still hard to believe there might be a million dollars waiting for me inside a box in that tiny laboratory."

Eve smirks as the waiter returns and sets down your drinks. She sucks up a huge tapioca ball from her beige taro boba tea.

"So you've decided to take one box then?"

You chuckle at Eve's speculation. "I didn't say that."

"You said there might be a million dollars waiting for you. That means you think you're going to take one box."

"I said 'might be.' I haven't made up my mind yet."
"Okay, so what's your gut instinct?"

If you plan to take only one box, turn to page 37.
If you plan to take both boxes, turn to page 40.

"I guess I am leaning toward one box," you say. "But I still have a few days to think about it."

"You do think you're going to get a million dollars!" Eve crows.

"Yeah, I suppose so," you admit. "I mean Pavlov said—"

Eve rolls her eyes. "I can't believe his name is Pavlov, by the way. Sorry, go on."

"The MRI model is supposed to be 91.8% accurate in its predictions, and its accuracy has improved over time. So if I think I'm going to take one box now, then the model probably predicted I would take one box, which means Pavlov put a million dollars in that box."

"Yeah, I guess so." Eve doesn't sound convinced.

"What, you disagree?"

She frowns. "I'm not sure. It's like looking at one of those Magic Eye images. When you look at it one way, it all makes sense. But as soon as you blink, everything looks blurry again."

"Well, look at it this way," you reply. "Let's say the model is 90% accurate. I have two choices: either I take one box or I take both. Based on past experiments, if I take one box, there's a 90% chance I get the million dollars. But there's a 10% chance that the model was wrong and I get nothing. So my average winnings from taking one box would be 0.9 times one million plus 0.1 times zero. That's $900,000. If I take both boxes, there's a 90% chance the model predicts correctly and I just get the $1,000. So that's 0.9 times 1,000, or $900. There is a 10% chance that it's wrong and I get the million dollars plus the thousand dollars on top of that. 0.1 times 1,001,000 equals $100,100. So my average winnings for two boxes is only $101,000. On average, I would get almost $800,000 dollars more if I took one box than if I took both."

"I see you've been doing some thinking." Eve sucks a machine gun stream of black shells through her flesh-colored drink. "Okay, I see your point."

You can tell she doesn't agree. "But…?"

"Well, everything you said makes sense. If you think you would take one box, then the model probably predicted you would take one box, and so it put the million in that box. But then why wouldn't you take both boxes?"

"What? I just told you—"

"I know, I know, the average winnings. But the model already made its prediction. If the million dollars is in the box, then you might as well take both boxes. You'd still get the million, plus another thousand on top of that."

"No, but—"

"Okay, what if I went with you when you made your decision?"

"What do you mean?" Your tightly woven logic is unraveling fast.

"Let's say that when you go back in four days, I go with you. And let's say the back side of the mystery box is open. You can't see what's inside, but I can. If I could tell you what to do, what would I say?"

"But the boxes are closed," you insist. "No one can see what's inside them."

"I know," Eve says, "but it doesn't really matter. My seeing into the boxes doesn't change what's inside them. The million dollars is already there or not there. And if I could see inside the boxes, I would tell you to take both of them. If there was nothing in the first box, I would want you to take both so you'd at least get the thousand dollars. And if there was a million in the first box, I'd still want you to take both so you'd get the million plus the thousand. And then you could share some of it with me." She smiles, and her teeth flash like bleached seashells amidst her sandy face.

"Yes, but—"

And at this moment, as if to relieve you from the burden of attempting a coherent counterargument, the waiter sets your food down on the table: two identical, white, porcelain bowls filled with steaming noodles. You wonder if you'd ever realize if they mixed up your orders. You dig in, glad to have this shield of food in front of you. Eve follows suit.

You eat in silence, your mind preoccupied with the problem of the boxes and the quantum fortune, there and not there in that nebulous second box. Yet you know Eve is right, that there is no "and." The million dollars is either there or not there at this very moment, even as you slurp a pale brown, oily noodle from a meal you could buy 100,000 times over with your potential winnings. But still the little devil on your shoulder confirms in whispers the deep-seated sense that you have been weighed and measured by that wheezing bird in Pavlov's MRI, that your actions four days from now are merely a *déjà vu* that has yet to reoccur and that you can capitalize on this shared secret between your deepest subconscious and some mysterious model if you just act accordingly and play along.

And when the two of you have finished your meals and resumed your small-talk with the unspoken agreement not to discuss this problem any further tonight, you find yourself no closer to fully defusing Eve's straightforward logic in your own mind, and you suspect that, despite your convictions about the soundness of your own calculations, you never will.

Continue on page 44.

"I guess right now I'm leaning toward both boxes," you say. "I still have a few days to think about it though."

"Really?" Eve's eyebrows jump with shock. Then again, her face is always so animated that you can never be certain it's not an elaborate act. "I was sure you were going to say one."

"I thought about it," you say. "But the million dollars is already in the box or it's not. So I might as well take both boxes and get the extra thousand dollars as well."

"The extra thousand?"

"Yeah. If I take both boxes, I'm guaranteed a thousand dollars either way. If the computer predicted correctly, then a thousand dollars is all I get. But if it was wrong, then I get a million dollars on top of that. Either way, the model has already predicted, and the million dollars is or is not in the second box right now. Whatever is there is there no matter which box I choose, so I might as well take the extra thousand on top of whatever is in the second box."

"Okay, I get that," Eve says. "But I bet lots of people have had the exact same thought. And over 90% of the time, all they got was $1,000."

"But the money is already there or not there," you insist. "There's no reason to take just the one box now."

Eve runs her hand up and down her glass of boba tea. Condensation pours down its sides like sweat on a marathoner. "Think of it from a statistical standpoint," she says. "Of all the people that did it before you, the model correctly predicted their choice 91.8% percent of the time."

"Right, but—"

"So let's say you take one box," she continues. "Of all the people who picked one box before you, about 91.8% ended up with $1,000,000. Of everyone who took both boxes, 91.8% of them ended up with only $1,000. Don't ask me how it's so accurate. But if Pavlov is telling the truth—by the way, I can't believe his name is Pavlov—then the odds seem pretty good that if you take one box you'll end up with a million dollars."

"I guess." You feel like you're staring at a fixed object with one eye. It's in one place when you've got your left eye on it, and then when you switch to your right it jumps an inch to the left.

"And if you take both boxes—"

"Yeah, I know," you say. "Odds are I'll only get $1,000."

"Right. Let's say the model is 90% accurate. Based on past experiments, if you take one box, there's a 90% chance you'll end up with the million dollars. But there's a 10% chance the prediction was wrong and you get nothing. So your average winnings from choosing one box would be 0.9 times one million plus 0.1 times zero, or $900,000. But if you choose both boxes, there's a 90% chance the model predicts correctly and you only get the thousand dollars. 0.9 times $1,000 equals $900. There is a 10% chance the model is wrong and you get the million dollars plus the thousand dollars on top of that. 0.1 times $1,001,000 equals $100,100. So your average winnings from both boxes would only be $101,000. On average, you'd win $800,000 dollars more if you took one box than if you took both. Presumably more, if the model has been almost 92% accurate."

You don't bother to check Eve's mental math. You've never known her to be wrong in that department. She inhales an eruption of tapioca balls like air through a snorkel while you try to absorb her logic. The waiter sets your food down on the table: two blue clay bowls filled with steaming noodles. As usual, you're tempted to switch dishes with Eve when she's not looking just to see if she'll notice. But she dives in right away while you continue to ponder Pavlov's dilemma.

"Wait a minute," you say. Eve glances up and slurps a stray noodle. "You said of all the people who picked one box before me, 91.8% ended up with $1,000,000, and of all the people who picked two boxes, 91.8% of them ended up with only $1,000."

Eve swallows and dips her chopsticks in for another bite. "Yeah, so?"

"But what if no one picked one box? Or no one picked two boxes? Or what if the model picks one box every time and people pick one box only 91.8% of the time?"

"You mean if the model really isn't that good at all."

"Yeah, or if everyone ends up picking one box."

Eve rolls her mouthful around and mulls this possibility. "So you don't think Pavlov is being completely honest," she says.

"I don't know what to think," you answer. "The way it was explained made it sound like the model is really trying to guess which box the subject will pick.

And since there seem to be good reasons for both choices, we assume the subjects are divided in their decisions. But it's possible that's not the case."

Eve sets down her chopsticks. "So that would give us four other possibilities. One, everyone picks one box and the model guesses one box 91.8% of the time. Two, everyone picks two boxes and the model guesses two boxes 91.8% of the time. Three, the model always picks one box and 91.8% of the subjects also pick one box. And four, the model always picks two boxes and 91.8% of the subjects also pick two boxes. Right?"

"Yes." Your stomach growls at the sight of the untouched bowlful in front of you, and you take advantage of Eve thinking aloud to snatch your first bite.

"Options three and four fall in your favor," Eve admits. "If the model always picks one box, then it always puts $1,000,000 in the second box and you should take both boxes. If the model always picks two boxes, then it always puts nothing in the second box and you should still take both boxes."

"Agreed." You reach for the soy sauce.

"But options one and two are no different from the scenario where you assume people make different choices and the model actually tries to guess their decision," Eve continues. "You don't know whether people always pick one box or always pick two boxes, or whether some pick one and some pick two."

"So we're back to square one," you say. "Can the model guess what I'm going to do a week in advance? I say it doesn't matter. The money is there or not there when I sit down to choose."

"But 91.8% of the people who thought the same thing ended up with only $1,000," Eve insists. "Unless you're sure the model always picks one box or always picks two boxes, your expected winnings are still far greater if you just take one box."

You lift up a fresh mouthful, careful to take a proportionate amount of meat and veggies so you aren't left with just noodles at the end. "I don't think we're going to agree on this tonight," you tell Eve.

"I know," she says. "You're much more stubborn than I anticipated. Well done."

"Thanks," you say, "although that sounds like a backhanded compliment."

"Meaning you're usually such a pushover?"

"That's what it sounds like."

Eve shrugs and resumes her meal. "You said it, not me."

"True." You let the comment go and tackle your dinner. Yet you still cannot shake the quandary of Pavlov's boxes and the (dis)appearing fortune, even though you know the million dollars is either there or not there, with no more appearing or disappearing to occur. It's there or not there already, right now, even as your mind wanders and you fumble your chopsticks against the tangled brown mass in your bowl, and you have merely to reach out and take both boxes, pluck the thousand dollars and come whatever may, like latching onto a cluster of noodles with your sticks and drawing them toward your parted lips. If only it were that easy.

Instead, you can hear the whispers of the little devil perched on your shoulder who seems to know your own mind better than you do and tantalizes you with the possibility that Pavlov's machine can and has read your every move. *Deus ex machina*. Or is it *Diabolus*? The devil from the machine? Can the MRI read your thoughts in greater detail than you can? Have you been weighed and measured, your deepest desires nailed squirming to the wall? You know your mind now, it seems, but you do not know it as it was then, at the inception of an idea, of a choice, the spark that may grow into a raging wildfire or shudder and die for lack of air. And it is this diabolical secret that haunts you now, that clouds your mind with doubt.

And when your bowls are empty and your stomachs filled and you begin the post-dinner pleasantries and formalities of polite chit-chat and payments and good nights, you are still no closer to fully disarming Eve's argument in your own mind, and you begin to suspect, despite your certainty about your own reasoning, that you never will.

Continue on page 58.

3. $S(t_2) \leftrightarrow C(t_2)$

"The State calls Detective Leon Hubert." The words snap off Shannon Gray's tongue on the morning of the second day of the trial of Dr. David Solon.

Beyond the murky pod, the pale brown, pockmarked door fires a leaden torpedo through the sickly yellow audience chamber, a human missile that hesitates at the pod door with a mushroomed explosion of silver and black fabric and glass, then barrels straight through the center of the courtroom and into the witness box. Leon Hubert is a slim man with a smooth face, save for the deep pouches under his eyes, a shaved head and a faint mustache thinner than the edge of the razor used to trim it. He has the air of someone destined to either enforce the law or proudly flaunt it. The swagger of his right hand as he raises it to swear to the whole truth and nothing but is scarcely contained by his steel gray pinstriped jacket and his gold tie is already loose at the neck in its failed struggle for confinement.

Shannon Gray approaches the box and the two of them size each other up like prizefighters before a bout. "Detective Hubert, would you please tell the jury about the incident you investigated on the night of April 26, 2011?" she asks.

"Yes, ma'am. On the night in question, I received a call regarding a break-in and a homicide at the home of Dr. David Solon at 843 College Avenue," Hubert says in a flat, gravelly voice. "I was met there by Dr. Solon, who told me his wife had been murdered."

"Would you describe to the jury the statement Dr. Solon made about the events surrounding his wife's death?"

"According to Dr. Solon, he heard a noise in the middle of the night and awoke to find his wife's side of the bed empty. He removed his handgun, a Glock, model 19, 9 mm Luger caliber, semiautomatic pistol, from the safe in his bedroom closet and went downstairs to investigate. As he descended, he heard gunshots and rushed down into the living room in time to see a man run across the room and out the front door of the house. Dr. Solon fired two shots at the fleeing intruder, but both missed. He reentered his home to find his wife dead in their living room from two gunshot wounds to her chest."

"Did Dr. Solon pursue the intruder on foot?"

"He told me he chased the intruder out of the house and fired at him. But he did not pursue him as he fled down the street."

"Was he able to describe the man he saw fleeing the house?"

"Yes. We called the department's sketch artist over immediately. Dr. Solon provided a near-complete description of the suspect."

"Thank you." Shannon Gray retrieves a manila envelope from her table and passes it under Hines's gaze, then returns to the stand and sets it in front of Hubert. "Detective Hubert, I'd like to show you what has been marked as Exhibit 1," she says. "Do you recognize this exhibit?"

Hubert opens the envelope and withdraws a white sheet of paper. "Yes," he says, "this is a composite sketch made of the suspect in the murder of Mrs. Solon, based on the description given by Dr. Solon on the night of April 26."

"Detective Hubert, I'm now going to show you what has been marked as Exhibit 2," Gray says as she grabs a second envelope from her assistant. "Detective, would you please identify this photograph?"

Hubert scans the image. "It's a mug shot," he says. "According to the notations on the bottom of the picture, it was taken of Damon Belliard after his arrest on the charge of breaking and entering on October 2, 2009."

Gray turns toward Pitcock. "Your Honor, I'd like to offer Exhibits 1 and 2 into evidence and publish them to the jury."

Pitcock bobs his head once, his eyelids drooping over his pupils. "You may proceed, Mrs. Gray."

Gray takes the sketch and photo from Hubert and hands them to the jury foreman, who examines them and passes them down the two rows of jurors. The composite's rough colored pencil strokes depict a thin-faced, dark-complexioned man with kinked, close-cropped hair peeking out beneath the edge of a hood. Damon Belliard's mug shot matches it down to the hollows in the cheeks.

"Detective Hubert, did you search Dr. Solon's house for any other evidence that night?" Gray asks.

"Yes," Hubert answers, "the department's crime scene investigators conducted a thorough search of the premises. They recovered four fired cartridge cases—two Magtech 32 Auto caliber and two Winchester 9 mm Luger caliber—and lifted three latent fingerprints. The Medical Examiner later removed two bullets from the decedent's body."

"Thank you, Detective," Gray says. "No further questions, Your Honor."

Pitcock fluffs his tail feathers and turns to the defense table. "Your witness, Mr. Hines."

Hines ambles toward the witness box where Hubert waits, fighting back a smirking disdain for defense attorneys. "Let me get this straight, Detective Hubert," Hines says. "On the night of April 26, Dr. Solon told you he witnessed his wife murdered by an intruder in their home. As the killer fled, Dr. Solon fired two shots at him. Upon investigating the crime scene, you discovered four cartridge cases, two of 9 mm Luger caliber, the same caliber as Dr. Solon's gun, and two more of 32 Auto caliber, which were fired in an unknown gun of a different caliber than the one owned and fired by Dr. Solon. Is that correct?"

"Yes," Hubert answers.

"And on the night of April 26, did Dr. Solon answer all your questions regarding the break-in at his home and the murder of his wife?"

"Yes, he did."

"He didn't volunteer any other information in addition to these answers?"

"No, he did not."

"He didn't make any comment regarding his wife's murderer?"

"No."

"So other than answering your questions, did Dr. Solon say anything else to you on that night?"

"He thanked me for my help as we left."

"That's it?" Hines asks. "So all in all, he was very quiet then?"

"Yes," says Hubert.

"Brooding?"

"Brooding?" Hubert repeats. "No, I wouldn't say so."

"Vengeful?"

"I really couldn't say."

"Did he appear distraught? Shocked? Grief-stricken?"

"I suppose so."

"Thank you, Detective," Hines says. "No further questions, Your Honor."

Pitcock swivels his neckless head across the pod. "Mrs. Gray, would you care to redirect?"

"Detective Hubert, I'm sure you've encountered many criminals over the course of your career," Shannon Gray says as she stands behind her table. "Do they often confess to you crimes they plan to commit in the future?"

"No," answers Hubert.

"No further questions, Your Honor," says Gray.

Hines declines to recross, and Pitcock excuses Detective Hubert, who exits the pod in a smart swirl of silver.

"The State calls Mrs. Judith Alethea," Shannon Gray announces.

The anteroom door opens timidly, and a pale, fleshy smudge appears behind the gray pod like a smeared daub of oil paint. Judith Alethea, as she tiptoes through the pod door, is scarcely less blurry inside the sooted glass. Her face is a pink-white smear of makeup applied with inexpert and desperate exaggeration that exacerbates her middle age instead of hiding it. She wears a decade-old, flesh-colored, polyester suit and pulls a taupe clutch to her chest like a life preserver as she toddles into the witness box and shrinks down in the seat. The bailiff swears her in as the court reporter cranes forward to hear and Shannon Gray rests a hand on the edge of the witness box as if commiserating with a kindly old aunt.

"Mrs. Alethea," Gray begins, "would you please describe the incident you were involved in on the evening of May 3, 2011?"

Judith Alethea leans into the microphone and says, "I was walking to the bus stop from the Walmart on 15th and Jackson. I passed an alley—somewhere on Jackson, between 12th and 13th I think—and as I passed, a man grabbed me and pulled me down into it." Her voice gains in volume as she falls into the rhythm of storytelling, but begins to warble as she recalls the terrifying memory. "He pointed a gun at me and told me to take off my jewelry and empty my purse onto the ground. I was so scared I could barely undo the catch, and he screamed at me to 'hurry up!' and jabbed his gun at me."

Her voice peters out again, and Shannon Gray, slightly sway-backed in her tailored suit, prompts her, "And what happened next?"

Judith Alethea flicks her black-rimmed eyes toward David Solon before finding solace in the front edge of the witness box. "A man came charging down the alley and knocked the thief to the ground."

"A man?" Gray pursues. "Mrs. Alethea, is that man in the courtroom today?"

"He is," Alethea admits.

"Would you please identify this man for the jury?"

Alethea gestures reluctantly in the direction of the defense's table.

"Let the record show the witness has indicated Dr. Solon," Pitcock says to the court reporter.

Gray retrieves one of her photo exhibits from the clerk's evidence table and holds it casually in one hand, the face of the picture pressed against her waist. "And Mrs. Alethea, would you recognize the man who was trying to rob you if you saw him again?"

"I certainly would," Alethea answers, a sudden self-righteous sharpness to her voice.

Gray flips the photo around and holds it aloft in one hand for all to see, speaking more to the jurors than to Alethea. "Is this the man who threatened you that day?"

"Yes, it is." The image is the mug shot of Damon Belliard.

"Thank you. Now you said this man pulled you to the end of the alley and aimed his gun at you. How close was he to you?"

"I don't know. Close. Just a few feet away, I think."

Gray advances toward the stand. "Like this?" she asks. "Or closer?"

"Closer," says Alethea. Gray steps forward. "A little more. Yes." Gray stops within arm's length of Alethea.

"And how did he hold his gun?" Gray asks. "Like this?" She tucks her right elbow to her hip and brandishes her hand from her stomach like a pistol.

"Yes, yes, like that," Alethea agrees.

Gray swivels her body to put Alethea on her left and the jury on her right, her finger aimed into the rear hollow of the pod. She pauses, then swings back to Alethea, turning her back to the jury. "Like that?"

"Yes," says Alethea.

"And at this point, Dr. Solon charged down the alley and knocked Mr. Belliard to the ground. What happened next?"

"I ran. I ran to the end of the alley and—"

"Did you look back into the alley?"

"Yes."

"And what did you see?"

The pink blush and white powder switch their colors and turn Judith Alethea's cheeks a warm, splotchy rouge flecked with rosy ashes. "I saw Dr. Solon standing over the thief lying on the ground. Dr. Solon was holding the gun and aiming it at the thief."

"What happened next?"

"Dr. Solon yelled at me to call the police."

"And did you?"

"I was about to, but the man on the ground turned over onto his back. And

Dr. Solon... he shot him."

"Let me get this straight, Mrs. Alethea," Gray says. "Dr. Solon knocked Mr. Belliard to the ground and retrieved his gun. Is that right?"

"Yes."

"So Mr. Belliard was unarmed at this point?"

"Yes."

"And when Mr. Belliard turned over, just before Dr. Solon shot him, did you see him threaten Dr. Solon in any way?"

"No," Alethea mutters to her lap. "No."

"Thank you, Mrs. Alethea. No further questions."

"Your witness, Mr. Hines," intones Pitcock.

Hines ambles to the stand and stops with his back to Pitcock, almost leaning on the witness stand so that he can address Judith Alethea intimately while giving the jury a peep show of this touching tête-à-tête.

"Mrs. Alethea, when you were in that alley, Damon Belliard threatened to kill you," he says. "Is that right?"

"Yes, he did," she answers meekly.

"Did you believe him?"

"Yes."

Hines steps back and raises his voice to bring the jury into their conversation. "So you were prepared to do whatever he demanded of you?"

"Yes."

"You were prepared to give him your money, your jewelry, your credit cards, everything?"

"Yes."

"And you were just about to do so when Dr. Solon intervened?"

"Yes."

"So Dr. Solon saved you from being robbed of your possessions?"

"Yes, yes, he did."

"And indeed, he may have saved your life?"

"Objection." Shannon Gray will let Hines get only so far.

"I'll withdraw it," Hines concedes, having made his point. "Mrs. Alethea, you testified that after Dr. Solon interceded on your behalf, you fled the alley and looked back to see Dr. Solon pointing a gun at this man who had been about to rob you. Dr. Solon yelled at you to call the police, and then you saw Mr. Belliard turn over, and Dr. Solon shot him. Is that correct?"

"Yes."

"So Dr. Solon didn't shoot Mr. Belliard right away. In fact, it was only after Mr. Belliard turned over that Dr. Solon fired. Is that correct?"

"Yes, it is."

"Thank you, Mrs. Alethea." Hines crooks his head over his shoulder, says "no further questions, Your Honor," and gives Judith Alethea a final reassuring smile before strolling back to his seat.

Gray declines to redirect, and Pitcock excuses Judith Alethea, who creeps down the two steps from the witness box, her hands gripping the railing and her clutch with equal firmness. Her blond perm droops, her ankles shudder above her high heels, and her makeup has finally melted into the creases of her face as she disappears behind the gray pod door.

●　　　●　　　●　　　●　　　●

The trial breaks for lunch, during which you and your compatriots retreat to the jury room for a choice between catered chicken sandwiches or chicken salads. You eat in a chair against one wall, dig out your phone and key up the chess app. You're a few moves into a game when another juror pulls up a chair in front of you and peeks at your phone.

"Does it bother you?" he asks.

"What do you mean?"

You look up into a soft, rectangular face. Drooping bags under his squinted eyes frame a long nose that descends dramatically to a downturned point and shades a pinched mouth.

"The computer letting you win," he says. He wears a brownish green polo shirt unbuttoned to his collarbones and parts his thin, wavy, unkempt hair down the middle so that it wilts over his ears.

"It's on Intermediate," you tell him.

"Right. What do you think happens between Intermediate and Advanced? The Joe Schmo program gets replaced with the Bobby Fisher version?"

"No."

"Of course not," he says as he unwraps his sandwich. "The Beginner Level is like a dad playing with his son for the first time. He could Scholar's Mate the kid every game but he plays it out to make his son feel a little better and learn how to play. As the kid improves, the dad makes him work a little harder. So are you playing a game or getting a lesson?"

Taken aback, you stare at the guy until he flashes a cynical smirk and extends an unveined, ivory hand.

"Sorry, I'm John," he says. "John Mann."

You shake his hand cautiously and introduce yourself.

"I guess I came on a little strong there," he says. "I work in IT. Studied programming in college." He inclines his head toward your phone. "Are you good?"

"So-so," you say. "I win at the Intermediate level every now and then. But I suppose that just makes me a little kid, huh?"

John Mann lays the ankle of one long leg atop the opposite knee and folds his wide-spaced fingers in his lap. "We all are," he says. "A human hasn't beaten the top computer chess program in over fifteen years."

Your game appears to substantiate that assertion. You've left a pawn unprotected, and the computer's black knight has captured it to fork your rook and queen.

"No one?" you ask.

Mann wipes a drop of pesto aioli from the corner of his mouth. "Not even the highest-rated Grandmasters."

"And I'm guessing this is just a watered-down version," you say, raising your phone from your lap.

"Something like that. I doubt your app uses the same code as Deep Blue."

"What's Deep Blue?"

"The top computer chess software," Mann answers. "It can search over 200 million positions per second to determine the optimal move."

"Wow."

"Yeah. Humans have no chance. Chess is about making the best move possible given the conditions on the board. The player who can string together more optimal moves wins."

"And a computer that can search 200 million positions per second can do that faster than a human."

"Not just faster," Mann says. "Better. Even if you could imagine every possible outcome of every potential move, you couldn't remember them all in order to compare them. At this point, computer programs have basically solved the game of chess."

"What do you mean, solved chess?" you ask.

"The top programs out there have found the set of moves guaranteed to be unbeatable."

"You mean there's a cheat sheet floating around on the Internet?"

"Not exactly. And strictly speaking, we don't know for certain that chess has been solved. Just like we don't know the sun will rise tomorrow. But the fact that no human can beat the best computer chess program suggests the computer is playing an unbeatable strategy. There must be a reason the computer never loses."

"But that doesn't mean there's a 100% foolproof strategy," you say. "Even if chess is only 90% solved, the odds still favor the computer. Could we tell the difference just because a computer hasn't lost to a human in however many years?"

"You're right," Mann concedes. "But let's say chess is only 90% solved. Think of how the model works. The computer takes a particular scenario, examines all the possible moves and all the possible outcomes of those moves and picks the move with the best outcome. And the more scenarios it encounters, the more iterations of the model it runs, the better the strategy. So even if chess is only 90% solved today, it could be 91% next week, 92% the week after. It's just a matter of time."

"I guess so," you say. The prospects for future human chess supremacy indeed look bleak as you sacrifice your rook to save your queen and maneuver to trap the computer's knight behind your ranks. You don't imagine you'll ever progress beyond the Intermediate level. But there are people out there playing Advanced. And surely a few of them must win some of the time. It seems impossible for any entity to be 100% perfect. Then again, maybe you only think that way because you're limited by your human imperfections and shortfalls of knowledge.

"Besides," John continues, "you said it yourself: even if the computer plays the optimal move in 90% of all scenarios, the best human player would probably never approach that success rate."

"But a human could," you insist. "It's at least possible."

"Of course it's possible. For one move or ten moves. But it comes down to following the solved strategy for the whole game. That's what determines the outcome. Whichever player adheres more closely to the solved strategy wins. The computer's software and its memory capacity just make it far better equipped to do so."

"But the computer's not invincible. It's not perfect."

Mann offers a thin-lipped smile. "And that very thought is what leads to your downfall," he says. "The best any human can hope to do against a computer is play it to a draw. And if you think you can beat the computer, that you can actually win, that's when you'll lose. Victory is a mirage, a will-o'-the-wisp, *ignis fatuus*. The light that leads you astray. You think you have a bright idea, you think you've seen the brilliant move that will beat the computer, but unless you're playing the solved strategy... poof, you're wrong." Mann blows out an imaginary flame on his fingertips. "And your mistake costs you the game. Humans suffer from the illusion of deliberation. The computer has no illusions. It reads the situation on the board and makes the best possible move in that situation."

"Still... "

"Look, from start to finish, the game is set up according to a sort of script. There's an optimal move in every situation. Say you play first. Pawn to e4, or whatever. Your move causes the computer to play the best possible countermove. You play again, and that new move causes the computer to play the best possible move given this new scenario. The computer follows the script dictated by the solved strategy. And as soon as you deviate from the script"—his hands flare out of his lap, his bony fingers explode like nails from a pipe bomb—"you lose."

"But why couldn't a human just happen to play the optimal move when the computer doesn't?" you ask. "Just once. One in a billion times. Someone like Rain Man."

Mann runs a hand through his greasy brown hair. "But they haven't. No one has. Not in hundreds, maybe thousands of games between the best humans and the best computers in more than fifteen years. And maybe they can't."

Your phone buzzes. Checkmate.

"Besides, you're no Rain Man," Mann says. "None of us are."

"Not today, at least," you admit.

"Well, maybe the sun will stay down tomorrow." He checks his watch. "Almost 1:00. Back to work, I guess."

You exit the chess game and follow Mann into the courtroom.

•　　　•　　　•　　　•　　　•

Following the break, Shannon Gray calls her next witness, Detective Isabel Aliba, a young officer in a trim navy blue uniform, who wears her dark hair pulled into a tight ponytail with a single wispy curl escaping around her smooth, cinnamon-colored face. She has wide, brown, thick-lashed eyes and soft, parted lips and ascends to the stand with a curt precision that belies her girlish face.

"Detective Aliba," Gray says, "would you please describe for the jury the incident you investigated on the evening of May 3, 2011?"

Isabel Aliba pivots her chair to face the jury. Her faint black eyebrows are neatly edged strips. In fact, everything about her features appears smooth and controlled, save for the faint gray shadows that descend from the inner corners of her eyes to the tops of her cheeks. "Witnesses reported hearing a gunshot in the 1200 block of Jackson Avenue," she says. "I arrived on the scene along with several other officers to find Dr. Solon in an alley at 1238 Jackson, along with the body of a man later identified as Damon Belliard."

"What did you do when you arrived at the scene?"

"My unit photographed the scene, collected evidence and placed Dr. Solon under arrest. We then transported him to the station, where I reiterated his Miranda rights and questioned him about the circumstances of Mr. Belliard's death."

Gray hands Aliba a manila envelope. "Detective, I'd like you to examine this item, which has been marked as Exhibit 3. Do you recognize these documents?"

Aliba's stubby fingers prize open the clasp of the envelope, and she scans the papers inside, her lips opened in a gentle O, her manicured brows creeping a millimeter closer together. "Yes, I do. It's a copy of the statement Dr. Solon made to me on May 3."

"Your Honor, I'd like to offer Exhibit 3 into evidence," Gray says to Pitcock.

"You may proceed." Pitcock seems a bit bubblier after lunch, the drowsiness gone from his thick-browed eyes.

"Detective, would you please read aloud the highlighted section on the third page of Exhibit 3?" Gray asks Aliba.

"I asked Dr. Solon 'what happened after you disarmed Mr. Belliard and retrieved his firearm?" Aliba answers. "To which Dr. Solon replied, 'I aimed the gun at him and shot him.'"

"And Dr. Solon admitted this freely? Without any coercion?"

"Yes," Aliba says. "I asked him to explain to me what happened and he told me everything immediately of his own free will."

"Where was Dr. Solon going prior to entering that alley?"

"He told me he had just met a friend for coffee. He was returning to his car to drive home."

"Did you speak to Dr. Solon's friend?"

"Yes. A Dr. James Adalwin. He confirmed Dr. Solon's story."

"According to Dr. Solon's statement, Mr. Belliard was in possession of a handgun which Dr. Solon used to shoot him. Did you recover this weapon from the alley on Jackson?" Gray asks.

"Yes, we did," Aliba answers.

"What type of gun was it?"

"It was a Bryco, model 38, 32 Auto caliber, semiautomatic pistol."

"Detective Aliba, is the Bryco model 38 a magazine-fed firearm?" Gray asks.

"Yes, it is."

"And in such a firearm, the cartridges are loaded into a container called a magazine, which is inserted into the grip of the firearm. Each pull of the trigger then fires one cartridge and loads the next cartridge from the magazine. Is that correct?"

"Yes."

"How many cartridges does the magazine of this firearm hold?"

"The magazine holds seven cartridges."

"And how many cartridges remained in the magazine when you found it?"

"There were five cartridges in the magazine and a sixth in the chamber of the gun."

"Did you recover any fired evidence?"

"Yes, we found one cartridge case at the scene, and the Medical Examiner removed one bullet from Mr. Belliard's body."

"And what did you do with this evidence?"

"We submitted these items to the Yetopo County Forensic Science Laboratory for further testing."

"And what did you do with Dr. Solon after you took his statement?" Gray asks.

"We transported him to the Yetopo County Detention Center," Aliba replies.

"Did you treat Dr. Solon for any injuries?"

"No. Beyond a few minor scrapes, he sustained no serious injuries."

"Did you commend him to psychiatric treatment?"

"No."

"Why not?"

"He didn't seem to need it. When I spoke to him, Dr. Solon appeared perfectly lucid and in full possession of his faculties."

"Thank you, Detective," Gray says. "No further questions."

Hines stands behind his table. "Detective Aliba, did you ask Dr. Solon why he shot Damon Belliard?" he asks.

"Yes," Aliba answers. "Dr. Solon said 'because he killed my wife.'"

"Thank you, Detective," Hines says. "No further questions, Your Honor."

Gray declines to redirect, and Pitcock excuses Detective Aliba and asks "Mrs. Gray, do you have any further witnesses at this time?"

"No, Your Honor," Gray answers. "However, the State does have an additional exhibit to enter into evidence." She holds aloft a thin folder. "This is a stipulation to the testimony on the forensic analysis of firearms and latent fingerprints evidence from this case as performed by Mr. Brian Thomas of the Yetopo County Forensic Science Laboratory. It is my understanding that the defense has agreed to stipulate to the contents of Mr. Thomas' report and to the testimony he would have given had he appeared in court today."

"Is that so, Mr. Hines?" Pitcock asks.

"Yes, Your Honor," Hines replies. "The defense has agreed to so stipulate."

"All right, Mrs. Gray," says Pitcock. "Ladies and gentlemen of the jury, in place of a witness testifying in person, the parties may agree and stipulate to what a witness would testify. In this case, both the State and the defense stipulate that if Mr. Brian Thomas were called to testify, he would testify to the following. You may proceed, Mrs. Gray."

"Thank you, Your Honor," Gray says. "Both parties stipulate that had Mr. Thomas testified before this court, he would have testified that he performed forensic firearms and latent fingerprints examinations on the evidence recovered from 843 College Avenue on April 26, 2011, and from 1238 Jackson Avenue on May 3, 2011. That the two Winchester 9 mm Luger caliber fired cartridge cases recovered on April 26, 2011, were fired in the Glock, model 19, 9 mm Luger caliber, semiautomatic pistol, serial number CFU262US, owned by Dr. David Solon. That the two PMC 32 Auto caliber fired cartridge cases recovered on April 26, 2011, were fired in the Bryco model 38, 32 Auto caliber, semiautomatic pistol, serial number 294798, recovered on May 3, 2011. That the two fired bullets recovered from the body of Julia Solon by the Yetopo County Medical Examiner on April 26, 2011, were fired from the same Bryco firearm. That one of the three latent fingerprint lifts recovered from a laptop computer at 843 College Avenue on April 26, 2011, was made by the same source as the left thumbprint on the ten fingerprint card marked Damon Belliard."

You observe David Solon as Shannon Gray reads. Even with Hines at his side, the table seems too large; the pod swells around him and diminishes him. It is inconceivable to imagine all that weighs upon him during these proceedings. Yet his face remains entirely devoid of emotion. Only after hearing this new evidence, which all but guarantees Damon Belliard murdered his wife, can you discern a slight relaxation that draws his shoulders millimeters farther away from his ears, and the air in the room feels suddenly lighter.

"That the one PMC 32 Auto caliber fired cartridge case recovered at 1238 Jackson Avenue on May 3, 2011, was fired in the aforementioned Bryco firearm," Gray reads. "That the one fired bullet recovered from the body of Damon Belliard by the Yetopo County Medical Examiner on May 4, 2011, was fired from the same Bryco firearm. That examination of the Bryco firearm revealed three suitable latent fingerprints. That one of these fingerprints was made by the same source as the left thumbprint on the ten fingerprint card marked Damon Belliard. That the second fingerprint was made by the same source as the right index fingerprint on the ten fingerprint card marked Damon Belliard. That the third fingerprint was made by the same source as the right index fingerprint on the ten fingerprint card marked David Solon. And it's stipulated that Mr. Thomas is qualified to perform forensic firearms identification and latent fingerprint analysis, including the tests described above."

Gray advances toward the bench. "Your Honor, I'd like to enter this report into evidence as Exhibit 4."

"You may proceed, Mrs. Gray," he says, and Gray passes the stipulation to the clerk. "Ladies and gentlemen of the jury," Pitcock continues, "you should consider this stipulation as evidence in the case, just as if the witness Mr. Brian Thomas had testified in front of you in this courtroom. Mrs. Gray, you have no further witnesses?" he asks.

"No, Your Honor," Shannon Gray answers. "At this time, the State rests."

Pitcock teeters back in his high chair and says "Very well. Ladies and gentlemen, this court will adjourn for the day and resume tomorrow morning at 9:00 am."

Pitcock shuffles back to his chambers, the attorneys file out and you and your fellow jurors edge out of the double-rowed jury box as the second day of the trial comes to an end.

Continue on page 73.

3. $S(t_2) \leftrightarrow C(t_2)$

"The State calls Detective Leon Hubert," Shannon Gray announces on the morning of the second day of the trial of Dr. David Solon.

Beyond the haze of the pod, the wooden anteroom door swings open to propel a streak of silver down the aisle of the audience chamber, clipping along with all the somber gumption of the champion sperm kicking down the home stretch to the egg as the befogged pod membrane opens to suck him in with a great vaginal slurp that draws him through the center of the courtroom and into the witness box.

Leon Hubert is young in the face and ten years older in his eyes, a well-built man with a shadow of close-trimmed black hair and a sharply concave mustache that gives him a perpetual frowning sneer. He utters his oath of honesty without closing his lips between words, his canines bared in a Doberman grin. He could be a gang leader or ruthless lawman in his steel suit and gold tie, his face both hard and shrewd, a man equally capable of brute violence and patient cunning.

"Detective Hubert," Gray begins, "would you please tell the jury about the incident you investigated on the night of April 26, 2011?"

"Yes, ma'am. On the night in question, I received a call about a break-in and homicide at the home of Dr. David Solon at 843 College Avenue." Detective Hubert speaks with a deep rolling bass that rises slightly in tenor at the conclusion of each sentence. "When I arrived, Dr. Solon told me his wife had been murdered."

"What did Dr. Solon tell you about the events leading to Mrs. Solon's death?"

"Dr. Solon said he awoke to a noise in the middle of the night and found his wife's side of the bed empty. He removed his Glock model 19, 9 mm Luger caliber, semiautomatic pistol, from the safe in his bedroom closet, and went downstairs to investigate. As he descended the stairs, he heard gunshots and rushed into his living room in time to see a man flee past him across the room and out the front door. Dr. Solon fired two shots at the man as he ran down the street, but both missed. He returned to his house to find his wife dead in their living room with two gunshot wounds to her chest."

"Did Dr. Solon pursue the intruder on foot?"

"He told me he chased the intruder out of the house and fired at him. But he did not pursue him as he fled down the street."

"Was he able to describe the man he saw fleeing the house?" Gray asks.

"Yes," Hubert answers. "Dr. Solon provided a thorough description of the man he saw to the department's sketch artist."

Shannon Gray loops back toward her table. "Detective Hubert, I'd like to show you what has been marked as Exhibit 1." She grabs a manila folder and flashes its contents for Hines's approval, then returns to the stand and lays the folder in front of Hubert. "Detective, would you please identify Exhibit 1?"

Hubert withdraws a sheet of paper and says, "This is the composite sketch made of the suspect in the murder of Mrs. Solon, based on the description given by Dr. Solon on the night of April 26."

"I'm now going to show you what has been marked as Exhibit 2," Gray says as she retrieves a second folder from her table. "Detective, would you please identify this photograph?"

Hubert gives the image a practiced once-over. "This is a mug shot of Damon Belliard, photographed on October 2, 2009, following Mr. Belliard's arrest on the charge of breaking and entering."

Gray turns toward Pitcock. "Your Honor, I'd like to offer Exhibits 1 and 2 into evidence and publish them to the jury."

Pitcock bobs his head. "You may proceed, Mrs. Gray."

Gray hands the two images to the jury foreman to your right. The composite is a rough sketch in colored pencil depicting a gaunt face with kinked, close-cropped hair peeking out from under the edge of a hood. The mug shot of Belliard, a thin, sallow-skinned black man staring blankly into the camera, hardly requires a side-by-side comparison. If ever there was a true-to-life composite sketch, it is this one.

"Detective Hubert, did you find any other evidence at Dr. Solon's house that night?" Gray asks as she retrieves the images from the last juror and passes them to the court clerk.

"Yes," Hubert answers, "the department's crime scene investigators recovered four discharged cartridge cases: two Winchester 9 mm Luger caliber and two PMC 32 Auto caliber. Two bullets were later removed from the decedent's body during her autopsy. CSIs also lifted three latent fingerprints from a laptop at the house."

"Thank you, Detective," Gray says. "No further questions, Your Honor."

Pitcock turns to the defense table. "Your witness, Mr. Hines."

Kenneth Hines eases toward the witness box like a long carpet unrolling down a flight of stairs. Hubert waits, fighting back a general contempt for defense attorneys.

"Detective Hubert," Hines says, "those four discharged cartridge cases your CSIs recovered on April 26—two were 9 mm Luger caliber, the same caliber as Dr. Solon's Glock handgun, while the other two were 32 Auto caliber, a different caliber than Dr. Solon's gun. Isn't that right?"

"Yes," Hubert answers.

"And on the night of April 26, did Dr. Solon answer all your questions about the burglary of his home and the murder of his wife?" Hines asks.

"Yes, he did."

"He didn't volunteer any other information in addition to these answers?"

"No."

"He didn't make any other comment regarding his wife's murderer?"

"No."

"That's it? So all in all, he was very quiet then?"

"Yes."

"Brooding?"

"Brooding?" Hubert has probably never heard this word spoken aloud. You're not sure you have either. "No, I wouldn't say so."

"Vengeful?"

"I really couldn't say."

"Was he distraught? Shocked? Grief-stricken?"

"I suppose so."

"Thank you, Detective. No further questions, Your Honor."

Pitcock ducks his neckless chin, owl-like, down into the puffed-up folds of his robe. "Mrs. Gray, would you care to redirect?"

"Detective Hubert, I'm sure you've encountered many criminals in the course of your law enforcement career," Gray says from behind her table. "Do they often confess to you crimes they plan to commit in the future?"

"No," Hubert answers.

"No further questions, Your Honor."

Hines declines to recross, and Pitcock excuses Detective Hubert, who briskly exits the pod.

"The State calls Mrs. Judith Alethea," Gray announces.

The anteroom door inches open and a blurred daub of oil paint materializes behind the frosted lens of the pod. Yet Judith Alethea is hardly more distinct as she tiptoes out of the glassy smog, her face a spilt cream smudge of makeup caked on and cracking at the corners of her eyes that intensifies her middle age instead of hiding it. A hesitant and excitable slap of putty, thoroughly kneaded by life and imprinted with its multilayered, multicolored narratives like transposed comic strips, she wears a thick, bunchy, ecru suit and hugs an equally bland oversized purse to her hip as she slowly minces into the witness box and huddles down in the seat. The big-boned, moon-faced court reporter leans forward to hear as Alethea swears her oath, while Shannon Gray hovers by the witness box as if attending to a senile aunt.

When Alethea has finished, Gray steps back to capture her witness and jury in a single glance. "Mrs. Alethea, would you please describe the incident in which you were involved on the evening of May 3, 2011?" she asks.

Judith Alethea hunches forward and speaks haltingly. "I was walking to the bus stop from the Walmart on 15th and Jackson. There was an alley—somewhere on Jackson, between 12th and 13th, I think—and as I passed, a man grabbed me and pulled me into it." The volume of her voice ebbs and flows as she wavers between self-consciousness, excitement and fear at recalling the terrible event. "He aimed a gun at me and told me to take off my jewelry and empty my purse onto the ground. I was so scared I could barely undo the catch, and he screamed at me to 'hurry up!'"

Her voice trails off and she stares down at her lap and squinches her eyes together. "I often think that if I hadn't been walking down that street on that day… You know I usually go for groceries on Friday, but I ran out of flour over the weekend so I had to go on Tuesday. And if I had just waited one day, maybe—"

"Thank you, Mrs. Alethea," Shannon Gray interrupts. "Please tell the jury what happened after the assailant ordered you to give him your valuables."

"A man came charging down the alley and knocked the thief to the ground," Alethea answers. Wrinkled pouches of skin show through the crusts of makeup under her eyes.

"A man?" Gray pursues. "Is that man here in the courtroom today?"

"Yes," Alethea mutters.

"Would you please identify him for the jury?"

Alethea hesitates a moment and then inclines her head toward the defendant's table. "Let the record show the witness has indicated Dr. Solon," Pitcock tells the court reporter.

"What about the man who was trying to rob you?" Gray asks as she retrieves a folder from the clerk's evidence table. "Would you recognize him if you saw him again?"

The flutter disappears from Judith Alethea's voice, replaced by an indignant edge. "I most certainly would."

Gray pulls the mug shot of Damon Belliard from the folder and holds it aloft. "Is this the man who threatened you that day?" she asks, her eyes on the jury.

"Yes, it is."

"And when this man pulled you into the alley and aimed his gun at you, how close was he to you at that point?"

"Close," Alethea says. "Just a few feet away, I think."

Gray sweeps toward the witness box. "As close as I am now?" she asks. "Or closer?"

"Closer," says Alethea. Gray steps forward. "A little more. Yes, like that." Gray could reach out and touch Alethea on the stand.

"And how did he hold his gun?" Gray asks. "Out in front of him? Or against his body, like this?" She tucks her right elbow against her hip and wields her index finger, pistol-like, at her stomach.

"Like that," Alethea answers. "Against his body."

Gray pivots to put Alethea on her left and the jury on her right, her finger-gun aimed into the back recesses of the pod. She pauses there, then swivels back toward Alethea. "Like that?"

"Yes," says Alethea.

"And as you stated earlier, Dr. Solon ran down the alley and knocked Mr. Belliard to the ground. What happened next?"

Judith Alethea squeezes her clutch and presses her crimson-red lips into a thin line. "I ran. I ran down the alley to the street."

"Did you look back into the alley?"

"Yes."

"And what did you see?"

Alethea's face reddens, briefly melting through the ivory deposits of powder and cover-up. "I saw Dr. Solon standing over the thief as he lay on the ground. Dr. Solon was holding the gun and aiming it at the thief."

"What happened next?"

"Dr. Solon yelled at me to call the police."

"And did you?"

"I was about to, but the man on the ground turned onto his back. And Dr. Solon… he shot him."

"Let's take a step back, Mrs. Alethea," Gray says. "You said Dr. Solon knocked Mr. Belliard to the ground and retrieved his gun. Is that right?"

"Yes."

"So Mr. Belliard was unarmed when Dr. Solon shot him?"

"Yes."

"Did you see Mr. Belliard threaten Dr. Solon in any way before Dr. Solon killed him?"

Judith Alethea rubs one palm against the back of her other hand. "No," she says softly. "No, I didn't."

"Thank you, Mrs. Alethea. No further questions."

"Your witness, Mr. Hines," says Pitcock.

"Mrs. Alethea, Damon Belliard threatened to kill you in that alley," Hines says as he strolls to the witness stand. "Isn't that right?"

"Yes."

"And you believed him?"

"Yes."

"So you were prepared to do whatever he demanded of you?"

"Yes."

"You were prepared to give him your money, your jewelry, your credit cards, everything?"

"Yes, I was."

"And you were just about to do as he demanded, to empty your purse, and drop your jewelry on the ground when Dr. Solon intervened?"

"Yes."

"So Dr. Solon saved you from being robbed of your possessions?"

"Yes, yes he did." Judith Alethea sets her purse on the ledge in front of her and seems to rise a few inches out of her seat.

"And indeed, he may have saved your life?" Hines asks.

"Objection," Shannon Gray calls before Alethea can answer.

"I'll withdraw it," Hines concedes. He waits to let the jury absorb the impact of his unanswered question and rests his left hand on the rail of the witness box, standing close enough to Alethea to make the jury feel they are watching an intimate conversation between two lifelong friends. "Mrs. Alethea," he says, "you testified that after Dr. Solon disarmed your assailant, you fled the alley and looked back to see Dr. Solon pointing a gun at the man who had tried to rob you. When you reached the street, Dr. Solon yelled at you to call the police, and then you saw Damon Belliard turn onto his back, and Dr. Solon shot him. In other words, Dr. Solon didn't shoot Mr. Belliard right away. In fact, it was only after Mr. Belliard turned onto his back that Dr. Solon fired. Is that correct?"

"Yes, it is."

"And Dr. Solon shot Mr. Belliard immediately after he turned onto his back?"

"Yes."

"Thank you, Mrs. Alethea. No further questions, Your Honor." Hines gently pats the edge of the witness box as though it was Judith Alethea's hand before he returns to his seat.

Alethea's eyes flash toward the door of the pod, but Judge Pitcock rolls his ponderous head away from Hines and intones "Mrs. Gray?"

Shannon Gray stands in place, calves pressed against her pushed-back chair as she leans into her fingertips splayed upon the tabletop. "Mrs. Alethea, when you reached the end of the alley, you said you turned back and saw Dr. Solon aiming a gun at Damon Belliard?"

"Yes," Alethea exhales.

"And Mr. Belliard was lying on the ground, unarmed, while Dr. Solon stood over him. Is that correct?"

"Yes, it is."

"No further questions, Your Honor."

Pitcock calls for Hines, who demurs, and then excuses Judith Alethea. She tiptoes down the steps from the witness box, perhaps doubting her ankles' preparedness for the strain of her high heels, her blond curls slightly fizzled, her makeup burrowing into the wrinkles of her drawn face. She crosses the floor of the courtroom as fast as she can while still keeping up appearances, a murky, fleshy pulp that fades into obscurity as the pod door swings shut behind her.

•   •   •   •   •

Pitcock grants you and your fellow jurors an hour-long recess for lunch, during which you retire to the jury room for six-inch Subway sandwiches and bottled water. You eat in a chair against one wall and pull up a chess game on your phone. You're already down a knight to the computer app set to Intermediate and almost too distracted to notice the man who pulls up a chair in front of you.

"Does it bother you?" he asks. "The computer letting you win?" He parts his hair down the middle to expose a large forehead, high, well-defined cheekbones and wide, flat, penetrating eyes. His features under the hard fluorescent ceiling lights have the shape of an upside-down triangle: the pinched eyes split by a long imperial nose just wider than his narrow mouth.

"What do you mean?" you ask.

"It's like a dad playing with his son for the first time," he says. "The dad could Scholar's Mate the kid every game, but he plays it out to make his son feel a little better and learn how to play. So are you playing a game or getting a lesson?"

You stare at the pale, hairless skin of his upper chest visible under a wrinkled, dark green polo shirt.

"Sorry," he says in response to your blank look. "I'm a computer scientist. I'm doing research over at Lauterbur State on autonomous systems." He extends a milky hand with long tapered fingers. "I'm John," he says. "John Mann."

You shake his hand and introduce yourself. His grip is steady, but nothing like Pavlov's.

"So I'm just a little kid," you say with a forced smirk.

He shrugs. "We all are. A human hasn't beaten the top computer chess program in over fifteen years."

"Really? Not even once?"

Mann shakes his head, and his dark brown curls flop from side to side. "Not even the highest-rated Grandmasters."

You glance back at your phone to see the computer's black knight has leapt forward, threatening to fork your king and rook. "Doesn't look good for me then," you say.

"Don't take it too hard," he replies. "We built them that way." He leans in and rests his forearms on his thighs. His breath reeks of phosphate-soaked ham. "And between you and me, I think they've done it."

"Who's done what?"

"Solved chess. The computers."

"What do you mean, 'solved chess?'"

"Computers have figured out the optimal move to play in every situation, creating a strategy no one can beat. The best anyone could do is play one of them to a draw."

"A perfect chess strategy? Is that even possible?"

Mann crosses one surprisingly limber leg over the other knee and eases back in his chair. "Sure it is. It exists for almost every game. Checkers has one. Chess is just the next level."

"So how do you know we've found it?"

"Humans haven't. But I bet a computer has. Imagine you're playing craps and the dice keep coming up snake eyes. Wouldn't you begin to suspect they were loaded? Same thing with chess. The more times a human fails to beat the best computer, the more it looks like the computer can't be beat. And why can't it be beat? Because it's unbeatable. Because it plays the solved strategy, the best possible move in every situation from the beginning of the game to the end."

"But how would you really know?" you ask. "Is there a list of the moves or something?"

"Not yet," Mann says. "Chess is fairly complicated. But we do know computers have solved checkers, and they've solved all chess endgames involving three to six pieces. From there it's just a matter of back-extrapolation. What's the best way to get from seven to six pieces? From eight to seven? Pretty soon you're back to all thirty-two pieces and the computer just starts whittling yours away."

"I guess so," you admit. "It makes sense, at least in theory."

"It's a simple recursive model. Take all the known endgames, come up with all the possible situations that could have led to them, find the best possible move in each situation to produce the endgame. Keep going back, scenario after scenario, iteration after iteration. No human could do it. We don't have the time or the memory to compare all those scenarios. But chess has a defined set of rules and a finite number of positions, and the top computer can search over 200 million positions per second to determine the optimal move."

"Wow." You've staved off the computer's knight, but now the queen has started picking off your pawns one by one. "So where do we stand?" you ask.

"Well, the proof, as they say, is in the pudding," Mann answers. He brushes some crumbs off his pant leg. "How do you know when you've found the solved strategy? When you've got a computer that can't lose."

"I guess so."

"For today's computers, chess is just a simple programming script," he continues. "Say you're white and you go first. Pawn to e4, or whatever. That's just an input for the computer; it knows the best countermove to play in response. You play again, and that new move causes the computer to make the best possible move given the new scenario. The computer follows the blueprint determined by the solved strategy. And as soon as you deviate from the script"—his hands flare out of his lap, his bony fingers explode like nails from a pipe bomb—"you lose."

"But still, couldn't a human play the optimal move?" you ask

John grins like a high school teacher dealing with a promising but mistaken student. "Sure he could," he says. "For one move. Or a few. But if you think you can beat the computer, you're finished. The best you can hope to do is draw, and that's if you follow the solved strategy the whole way. Winning is a mirage, a will-o'-the-wisp, *ignis fatuus*. The light that leads you astray. You think you have a bright idea, you think you've seen the brilliant move that will beat the computer, but unless you're playing the solved strategy, you're wrong. And your mistake costs you the game. Humans suffer from the illusion of deliberation. The computer has no illusions. It reads the situation on the board and makes the best possible move in that situation."

"But a human could conceivably follow the solved strategy," you say.

"Conceivably. And he or she could force a draw. But no human has as good a chance to play the optimal move every time for ten, twenty, thirty moves or more as a computer programmed to do so."

The computer's queen swoops in to nab the bishop you've been too distracted to guard.

"No," you say, "but he could—"

"Look," says Mann, "programmers design a computer to find the best possible move to win the game. That's the computer's sole purpose."

"But when she plays chess, a human's purpose is still to win the game."

"It's not the same thing. Each time the programmer simulates a new scenario, the computer gets conditioned to play the optimal move in that scenario. Instantly. Permanently. Over and over and over again. Humans just aren't equipped to undergo that kind of extensive conditioning."

"But—"

"It comes down to this: however good a human is, she doesn't have the solved strategy. The computer's moves are determined by that programmed script. It knows what the human's going to do, or rather what she should do, in every situation. But humans suffer from that illusion of deliberation, trying to outthink what is already set down in circuits and chips. Our wiring is imperfect. And given the parameters of the game and the situation on the board at any given moment, the computer spits out the best move every time. That's its job, that's what it was set up to do. Repeated simulations condition it to play the solved strategy automatically."

"And I'm not a computer."

"No, you're not."

You look down at your phone to see the ebony queen sweep aside a pawn and plant herself squarely in front of your king, protected by her bishop. "CHECKMATE."

"Obviously," you add.

Mann peeks at your game. "Yeah. Sorry." He rises from his chair. "Well, see you in there."

"Yeah, see you." You close the chess app and prepare to return to the courtroom.

•   •   •   •   •

Following the recess, the State calls Detective Isabel Aliba, a cappuccino-skinned policewoman with big, dark, doe-y eyes who mounts the stand with the same military crispness as Detective Hubert, but with a trace less swagger, a hint more self-awareness in her motions. Her soft face, small, downturned nose, and thin, perky lips perpetually parted to reveal her front four sun-white teeth combine to a delicate prettiness, yet her silky black hair is pulled into a utilitarian ponytail that strains the skin of her forehead into a constant appearance of guarded vigilance.

"Detective Aliba," Shannon Gray begins, "would you explain to the jury the events leading to Dr. Solon's arrest on May 3, 2011?"

Isabel Aliba swivels her chair to face the jury box. She has waxed her dark eyebrows into thin strips that peak above her chocolate irises and descend and widen toward the bridge of her nose, and when she speaks, her voice is soft but sure. "Witnesses reported hearing a gunshot in the 1200 block of Jackson Avenue. I arrived on the scene with several other officers to find Dr. Solon in an alley at 1238 Jackson, along with the body of a man later identified as Damon Belliard. The attending officers arrested Dr. Solon and brought him into the station. I reiterated his Miranda rights at that time, and then questioned him about his involvement in Mr. Belliard's death."

"Would you please summarize for the jury the contents of this interview?" Gray asks.

"I asked Dr. Solon to explain how he came to be at the crime scene," Aliba replies. "He told me he was walking along Jackson when he saw a man holding a woman at gunpoint in the alley. Dr. Solon approached the assailant from behind and threw him to the ground. The fall knocked the man's gun from his hand, and the woman fled the scene. Dr. Solon retrieved the gun and aimed it at the assailant. He told me he intended to hold the man there until the police arrived to arrest him. However, when the assailant rolled over to face him, Dr. Solon said he recognized him as the man who had killed his wife. He fired the gun, and killed him."

"And Dr. Solon admitted this all freely? Without any coercion?"

"Yes, he did. I asked him to tell me what he was doing in the alley and he told me everything."

"Did he tell you where he was going prior to entering that alley?"

"He said he had just met a friend for coffee. A Dr. James Adalwin—he corroborated Dr. Solon's story. Dr. Solon told me he was returning to his car to drive home."

Gray retrieves an envelope from her table and passes it to Aliba. "Detective, I'd like you to examine this item, which has been marked Exhibit 3. Do you recognize these documents?"

Aliba opens the envelope and reads the papers held inside, her smooth brow pinching slightly. "Yes, I do," she says. This is the record of the statement Dr. Solon made to me on May 3."

"Your Honor, I'd like to offer Exhibit 3 into evidence," Gray says to Pitcock.

"You may proceed." Pitcock seems more chipper after lunch. He reminds you of the sultan from Disney's *Aladdin*.

"Detective, would you please read aloud the highlighted section on the third page of Exhibit 3?" Gray asks.

"I asked Dr. Solon 'what happened after you disarmed the decedent and retrieved his firearm?' to which Dr. Solon replied 'I aimed the gun at him and shot him.'"

"Detective Aliba, did you find any physical evidence in the alley at 1238 Jackson?"

"Yes. Crime scene investigators recovered a Bryco model 38, 32 Auto caliber pistol and one 32 Auto caliber cartridge case. The Medical Examiner also removed a bullet from Mr. Belliard's body."

"And the Bryco model 38 is a magazine-fed firearm, right?"

"Yes, it is."

"How many cartridges does the magazine of this firearm hold?"

"It can hold seven cartridges."

"And how many cartridges were in the magazine when you recovered it on May 3?"

"There were five cartridges in the magazine and one in the chamber of the gun."

"Thank you, Detective," says Gray. "No further questions, Your Honor."

Hines, unruffled, wafts toward the stand and settles himself just below Pitcock's roost to face the jury and Aliba.

"Detective Aliba," he says, "when you interviewed Dr. Solon after his arrest, didn't he tell you he intended to guard Judith Alethea's assailant until the police arrived to arrest him?"

"Yes, he did."

"And it was only after the assailant turned over and Dr. Solon saw his face that he recognized him as Damon Belliard, the man who had killed his wife. Isn't that right?"

"Yes, that is what Dr. Solon told me."

"So Dr. Solon told you he did not recognize Damon Belliard when he entered the alley, and in fact did not recognize Mr. Belliard until a split second before he shot him?"

"That's correct."

"Thank you, Detective. No further questions, Your Honor."

"Mrs. Gray?" asks Pitcock.

"No further questions."

Pitcock excuses Detective Aliba, and Shannon Gray announces "Your Honor, the State has no further witnesses at this time. However, we do have an additional exhibit to enter into evidence." Gray hefts a slim folder. "This is a stipulation to the testimony of Mr. Brian Thomas, a forensic scientist at the Yetopo County Forensic Science Laboratory who performed forensic firearms and latent fingerprints analysis on the evidence in this case. The stipulation is signed by Mr. Hines, agreeing to the contents of Mr. Thomas' report and to the testimony he would have provided had he appeared in court."

"Is that correct, Mr. Hines?" Pitcock asks.

"Yes, Your Honor," Hines replies. "The defense will stipulate to the contents of Mr. Thomas' testimony."

"All right," Pitcock says. "Ladies and gentlemen of the jury, in place of a witness testifying in person, the parties may agree to what a witness would have testified. In this instance, the State and the defense agree that if Mr. Brian

Thomas were called to testify, he would testify to the following. Go ahead, Mrs. Gray."

"Thank you, Your Honor," Gray says. "Ladies and gentlemen, both parties have agreed that if Mr. Thomas had testified today, he would have testified that he performed forensic firearms and latent fingerprints analysis on the evidence recovered from 843 College Avenue on April 26, 2011, and from 1238 Jackson Avenue on May 3, 2011. He would have testified that the two Winchester 9 mm Luger caliber fired cartridge cases recovered on April 26, 2011, were fired in the Glock, model 19, 9 mm Luger caliber, semiautomatic pistol, serial number CFU262US, owned by and recovered from Dr. David Solon on April 26, 2011. That the two PMC 32 Auto caliber fired cartridge cases recovered on April 26, 2011, were fired in the Bryco model 38, 32 Auto caliber, semiautomatic pistol, serial number 294798, recovered on May 3, 2011. That the two fired bullets recovered from the body of Julia Solon by the Yetopo County Medical Examiner on April 26, 2011, were fired from the same Bryco firearm. That one of the three latent fingerprint lifts recovered from a laptop computer at 843 College Avenue on April 26, 2011, was made by the same source as the left thumbprint on the ten fingerprint card marked Damon Belliard."

You glance at Dr. Solon as Shannon Gray reads, but his hard, flat face betrays nothing. He watches this trial for his life with the same academic detachment he might display at a lecture given by one of his colleagues. Yet at this pronouncement, which all but certifies Damon Belliard did indeed murder his wife, you can just make out the slight separation of his long fingers held interlaced and clenched on the table, and the relaxation of the tiny facial muscles at his temples, loosening his skin so that it subsides into soft wrinkles around his cool blue eyes.

"That the one PMC 32 Auto caliber fired cartridge case recovered at 1238 Jackson Avenue on May 3, 2011, was fired in the aforementioned Bryco firearm," Gray continues. "That the one fired bullet recovered from the body of Damon Belliard by the Yetopo County Medical Examiner on May 4, 2011, was fired from the same Bryco firearm. That examination of the Bryco firearm revealed three suitable latent fingerprints. That one of these fingerprints was made by the same source as the left thumbprint on the ten fingerprint card marked Damon Belliard. That the second fingerprint was made by the same source as the right index fingerprint on the ten fingerprint card marked Damon Belliard. That the third fingerprint was made by the same source as the right index fingerprint on the ten fingerprint card marked David Solon. It is further stipulated that Mr. Thomas is qualified to perform forensic firearms identification and latent fingerprint analysis, including the tests described above."

"Thank you, Mrs. Gray," Pitcock says when Gray finishes. "Ladies and gentlemen of the jury, you should consider this stipulation as evidence in the case, just as if Mr. Brian Thomas had testified in front of you in this courtroom. You may place whatever weight on it as you see fit. Mrs. Gray, you have no further witnesses at this time?"

"No, Your Honor," Gray answers. "The State rests."

Pitcock rocks back in his chair. "Ladies and gentlemen," he says, "at this time we will adjourn for the day. This trial will resume tomorrow morning at 9:00 am."

Pitcock trundles daintily to his chambers, and you and your fellow jurors shuffle out of the box as the first day of the trial winds to a close.

Continue on page 78.

Greg Hickey

You grab a quick dinner at a local restaurant on your way home. It is still early and the place is empty save for you and one man at the bar. You sit at a four top in the middle of the open room and rehash the day's events in your head. There seems to be no doubt about the basic facts. David Solon killed Damon Belliard. It appears all but certain that Belliard killed Solon's wife. The composite sketch and the forensic evidence leave little room for further speculation. David Solon killed the right man, and with pretty good reason. Yet even so, can you justly acquit him of murder?

The restaurant is cut from the same mold as every sports bar across the country. Jerseys, pennants and photos of the local teams plaster the walls. The service is prompt and the food is reliable and decently priced. But you don't have to be a fan of anything to fit in here, especially at 5:08 on a Tuesday evening. Besides, it's amazing how hungry sitting in a jury box for six hours will make you. Not that it matters—you could eat this place's roast chicken after a full Thanksgiving dinner.

The man at the bar wears a Boston cap and Josh Beckett jersey. Red Sox Nation is everywhere these days. A late afternoon Sox-Yankees game is in the bottom of the seventh on ESPN above the bar.

Beckett's portly doppelganger is pulling out all the stops. He's switched to the shark fin rally cap (hat folded in on itself and perched atop his head with the bill pointed straight up like a dorsal fin), and he nurses a beer with his left hand while his right hand busies itself by furiously rubbing some talisman near his throat (Ted Williams's left thumbnail or something—you can't tell from behind him). When the bartender serves him a new glass, he leans over and reaches across his body to grab it with his left hand, never once releasing his mysterious amulet with his right.

The bartender, a trim, balding man whose single-rolled shirt sleeves and black vest are a touch too hip for his age and surroundings, just shakes his head. "Are all Sox fans as crazy as you, Larry?" he asks.

"Carl, all I know is the Sox have won two Series in the last seven years," Larry replies. "That's good enough for me. And look," he gestures to the TV, "they've got a rally going even now."

You squint at the scoreboard in the bottom corner of the screen. Larry's right: the Red Sox, down by two, have runners on first and second with one out. A tall young waiter with short brown hair gelled into flattened spikes delivers your chicken.

"C'mon, Big Papi!" Larry cheers, thumping his free left hand on the bar. Sadly, the restaurant lacks the long mirror opposite the bar to show Larry he's the only fan in the joint. "Hey Carl, gimme a straw," he clamors.

"A straw?"

"Yeah, a straw. C'mon, hurry up. Please."

With bemused reluctance, Carl slaps a paper-coated straw in front of Larry. Larry bites off the tip of the disposable sleeve and slips the plastic cylinder into his beer.

"You must be shittin' me," Carl says, glaring at the obvious offense.

"Just watch."

Larry turns his attention to the game as David Ortiz, a.k.a. Big Papi, digs in. Little rivulets of chicken juice trickle out under your knife as you cut into your half-bird. It smells like a hookah distilled from a French chef's garden. Larry adjusts his fin, pumps his necklace and sips his beer through the straw. Carl compulsively wipes down the counter, but can't take his eyes off the game. Ortiz fouls off a high fastball that had Pesky's Pole written all over it, then obliges Larry's superstitious gesticulations by hammering a double off the Green Monster to score a pair. Larry erupts with glee, cheering and slapping the bar and bouncing on his stool like a four-year-old birthday boy.

"Yeah, Big Papi felt your mojo," Carl mutters as he turns his full attention to shining his already pristine bar. "The Force was with him."

"Doesn't matter how it happened," says Larry. "Just that it did."

"But you think you had something to do with it."

"I do my thing and Papi drives in two. I don't ask why. I just go with it."

"But you think these things happen because of you. If you don't suck beer through a straw, Ortiz strikes out."

"Yeah, so?"

"Do you hear yourself right now?" Carl is incredulous. "That's—"

"Hold on, man." Larry silences Carl with a raised hand. "Drew's up. Back to work."

"Yeah, I guess you'd better," Carl deadpans. "He needs all the help he can get."

Larry resumes his manic routine, and sure enough, J.D. Drew, the Red Sox much-maligned right fielder, laces a single up the middle to drive in Ortiz. Larry almost falls off his stool.

"Yes! Yes! I told you," he screams, stabbing his finger in Carl's direction. "J.D.! My man."

Carl just shakes his head and turns away. Larry bounces around on his stool in some kind of victory dance and sucks on his beer. You opt to tackle your drumstick bare-handed. Even without your mother around, eating with your fingers still makes all food taste better.

"What did I tell you, Carl?" Larry shouts from the bar. "What did I tell you? We are on tonight!"

Carl mutters something with his back to Larry.

"Yeah, we've got it working tonight," Larry continues.

Carl steps into the kitchen as a double play ends the Red Sox rally.

"Crap, I missed it," Larry says. "Oh well, we got three. You hear that, Carl?" he calls into the back. "We got three. Howdja like them apples?"

Larry relaxes as the game goes to commercial and turns his cephalo-dorsal fin back into a baseball hat. Carl re-emerges with a tray of clean glasses.

"Larry, let me ask you something," he says. "Were you this nuts before the Sox won the '04 Series?"

"What do you mean?"

"I mean, when did you start doing your… routine?"

"Game 4 of the 2004 ALCS," Larry answers without hesitation. "We were down 3-0 in the Series and down one in the game. Kevin Millar was up. I turned my hat to the shark's fin. To be honest, I thought it looked dumb at the time. But then Millar walked and Roberts stole second and—"

"I know, I know. And they tied the game off Rivera and came back and won that game and the next seven after that for their first World Series since 1917. That's great. My question is, did the Sox become good because of your routine or did you start your routine because the Sox became good? I mean if Millar had struck out and the Yankees had won Game 4, would you still be drinking your beer left-handed through a straw?"

You polish off the drumstick, lick your fingers clean and dry them on your napkin before you cut into the remainder of the breast.

"Are you saying it's just a coincidence?" Larry asks.

"I'm saying it's a coincidence the Sox happened to win Game 4 the night you started wearing your hat sideways on your head," Carl replies. "After that,

I'm saying the Red Sox spent their money wisely, drafted well and their players delivered. Your act got crazier and crazier as they kept winning, but they won because they were good, not because of you. You wearing your hat like a mohawk has nothing to do with it."

"That hurts, Carl."

"Sorry. Just my opinion."

"I know. You gotta be a fan to get it. All I know is I do my thing and the Sox keep winning. That's good enough for me."

"Okay, Larry. Whatever you say." Carl stacks glasses on a shelf opposite the bar. After a moment, he turns back to Larry. "No, wait. Do you actually think you control the Sox's fate? I mean that your beer-drinking and necklace-rubbing have some telekinetic power that transcends space to control baseballs and bats?"

"I don't know, man," Larry sighs. "It just works, okay?"

"And you never wonder how? When they lose a game, you don't think 'hey maybe this routine I've got going doesn't actually have any effect at all?'"

"No."

"So you think it's like a video game or something? *MLB: The Show* with really odd controllers? And Ortiz and Drew and Beckett and all the rest are just real-life flesh and blood pawns that you somehow manipulate? You control them like a god? Is that it?"

"Look, Carl." Larry raises his voice and thumps his glass on the bar, the amber liquid sloshing onto his hand. "I know it's crazy. But I'm not insane enough to think I actually control the team. I just love the Sox, and this is how I like to watch the game, okay? It's not hurting anybody. I'm not stabbing a Jeter voodoo doll or anything. I like to see them win and I like to feel a part of it. That's all."

"Okay, okay," Carl backs off. "I'm sorry."

"Yeah, no problem," Larry grumbles.

"Next one's on me, okay?"

"Yeah, sure." The game resumes, and Larry shifts his beer to his right hand and takes his necklace in his left as Carl looks on.

"The Sox are in the field. I gotta switch it up," he explains.

"Go Sox," Carl sighs.

You finish up your chicken as Larry settles back into his routine and the Sox dispatch the Yankees in order. Eve texts you to ask about the trial as the waiter drops off the bill. You tell her you'll be home soon. You take one last look at Larry on the way out. He's downed his beer and orders another, along with a fresh straw, as the game breaks for commercial. Despite his half-hearted denial, what does he really think? Does each win reinforce his delusion that he can actually affect the game? You recall John Mann's description of computer chess domination. Does Larry believe each game is just a feel-good movie he's directing? You wonder what Ortiz, Beckett and the rest of the Sox would think about that. Or other fans for that matter, whether Yankees, Red Sox or otherwise. But it seems to keep Larry happy. Maybe you do have to be a fan to get it.

•   •   •   •   •

Back home, you park yourself in front of your computer to catch up on the day's emails while the tail end of the evening news plays on the TV in the background. A chat window pops up on the monitor as soon as you sit down. evenso77; Eve.

evenso77: howd it go today?"

You peruse the day's Groupons (manicure/pedicure, unknown Mediterranean restaurant, tire rotation, one month of unlimited yoga classes) before you answer.

JQP47: good

    states witnesses etc

evenso77: cool

    anyone interesting?

You wait a second, then begin to type without thinking, the letters flickering onto the screen at the soft commands of your fingertips.

JQP47: not if you havent seen them

evenso77: ooh…intriguing!

    tell me more

You delete the Groupons. Nothing to sucker you in today.

JQP47: sorry

    cant do it

evenso77: :(

    youre no fun

    what about your box problem?

JQP47: nothing yet

    i still have until friday to decide

evenso77: well? still leaning toward 1 box?

If you still plan to take only one box, turn to page 86.
If you plan to take both boxes, turn to page 90.

It is not even 4:30 when you step outside. Must be nice to be a judge. The surrounding streets lie empty, except for a woman setting up a Three Card Monte scam on the far corner. Pretty bold, a block away from the courthouse. She calls to you, her first mark of the evening. You hesitate for a moment, but decide it can't hurt to just look.

"That's it," she sings out as you turn in her direction. "Come try your luck against the quickest hands around."

You always thought Monte dealers worked with at least one or two shills, faux players who conspire with the dealer to swindle the real marks out of their bets. Seeing this woman alone makes you a bit more comfortable.

"Welcome to Lucky Lady," she says as you stop in front of her set-up. "That's me." She flashes a single gold tooth amidst a row of pearly whites.

"How much is it?" you ask.

"That's up to you, sugar," she says. "You can bet as much as you want." She sits atop a blue plastic crate and lays three red-backed playing cards face up on the cardboard box that serves as a table. "Here, we'll play one for free. You got your two black jacks and the queen of hearts. Find the lady and you're a winner."

She flips the cards over and jazz-hands ten dexterous fingers to show she isn't hiding anything. Her lavender t-shirt barely covers her shoulders and exposes smooth, light-brown arms with the outline of a heart and the name "Jamal" tattooed on her right biceps. Nothing up those sleeves. Her short hair looks like a thousand little Slinkies bobbing atop her head.

"Ready?" she asks.

"I guess so," you say, your eyes boring into the back of the queen.

"Here we go." Her slender arms come alive in a blur of motion, hands snaking out to shift and swirl the cards as she calls out a steady stream of encouragement. "Where's that lady? Stay with her. Lucky lady. You got it now. Eyes on the lady, eyes on the lady, and…" Clap! She sweeps her hands up off the box and brings them together with a loud smack. "Now you just point out the lady, put your money down and we'll see if you're a winner," she says.

"This one's free, right?" you ask.

"That's right, honey. So normally you say 'I bet $10,' put your money down and pick your card. But this game's just for fun."

"Okay, I pick this one," you say, indicating the middle card.

"If you want it, take it," she says. "I don't touch the cards. This ain't no scam."

You bend down and turn over the middle card. It's the queen.

"Ooh, look at you!" she crows. "Beginner's luck. We gonna play for real this time?"

The game does seem fairly legitimate. You just have to follow the cards and hope you can keep pace with her hands. And you've never lost a Jumbotron game of find-the-ball at any sporting event you've ever attended.

"All right, I'll play," you tell her.

"That's what I like to hear, sugar." She shuffles the three cards in one hand. "What you doing out here anyway? You in trouble or something?" She points at the courthouse with her free hand.

"No, I'm a juror on a case."

"Oh, jury duty. That's like that movie with what's-his-name—Paulie something."

"Paulie Shore?"

"That's it. *Jury Duty* with Paulie Shore."

You force a chuckle. "I guess so. Kind of like that."

Lucky slides the cards face down onto her makeshift table. "He's just got one of those faces. A funny face. I don't know if he's really funny. He just looks it. Not ugly, just funny. Like you look at him and you want to laugh. Guess he's lucky that way. You ready, honey?"

"I think so."

She flashes you the queen once more, then turns it face down. "You know what to do now. Just follow the lady."

And then her hands explode to life, zig-zagging wildly over the cards faster than seems humanly possible. To your eyes, she doesn't even touch the cards; they dance like Etch-a-Sketch dust millimeters beneath her fingertips, whirling around the box in a blur of motion. Your eyes unfocus, the box and her hands fade and smudge, and the edges of the cards go a bit fuzzy. But when everything comes to a sudden stop and her hands are raised and clapped, you think you still know where to locate the queen.

"Well baby," she says, "you gonna find her?"

"I'll try," you answer. "I bet $10."

"Money first," she says. You drop two fives on the box. "All right, where is she?"

"Right here," you say, picking up the card on your left. It's the jack of clubs.

"Sorry, honey. You lost her that time. Try that one." She slides your money off the table with one hand as she points to the card on your right with the other. You turn it over—it's the queen. "You want to try again, or is that it for today?" she asks.

"I'll try again. But can I bet a dollar this time?"

"Sure can. That's the minimum bet." She shuffles the cards and asks, "What do you think? If you're born looking like Paulie, you gonna be anything but a funny man?"

"I suppose he did have a head start," you admit.

"That's for sure. All of them, they all had one. You look at those magazines. *People*'s most beautiful people. You s'pose Brad and Denzel and Angelina and Janet were ever going to be someone other than what they are? With those faces?"

"Do you think they were always beautiful?" you ask.

"What, you mean like they were those kids in high school with the big glasses and bumps all over their faces? Maybe. Late bloomers. Doesn't matter though."

"Why not?"

"Cause it was written in them all along, just waiting to get out. It's not like they weren't going to become beautiful. And all a sudden they take off their glasses and some talent scout sees them and they're in magazines and movies the rest of their lives. Don't even have to think about it. Just follow along."

"But it's not like they don't have talent," you say. "Angelina and Denzel have won Oscars."

"You can teach someone to act," says Lucky. "You can't teach a pretty face. Once someone first saw that face, they were off to acting school or doing photo shoots and life was set. End of story, happily ever after. All because of their faces. All because of their genes. It's in them from the start." She spreads the cards face down on the box. "You ready?"

You tighten your gaze on the queen's back. "Yes."

Her hands take off, and her mouth follows with a hyperspeed flood of advice that skips across the twirling cards. But when everything slides to a stop, you are once more convinced you know the location of the queen. And once more you are wrong. Yet you play again. And again. And again. And within the space of five minutes, you're out $15.

"Another one?" she asks after your sixth straight defeat.

Forget chess; you're beginning to think no human alive can beat Lucky at Three Card Monte. But you acquiesce anyway. "One more."

"You got it. Double or nothing?"

You've played six games already. If you had picked cards at random, you should have won twice by now. It's not just that you've lost the queen amidst the shuffle. The deception runs deeper. Lucky Lady here has baited you into taking the wrong card each time. Either that or she's cheating somehow. Yet you've only seen three cards this whole time, there's nowhere for her to hide an extra card, and she always lets you handle the cards when you make your choice. Although the "quickest hands around" must be capable of substituting a jack for a queen without you noticing. You decide you'll just have to watch for something like that.

"Okay," you say. "Double or nothing."

"Here we go."

The dance begins. Each game the partners seem to move even faster, the cards reeling around her hands at greater and greater speeds while she sings out encouragement at a breakneck polka pace. But now you know what to look for. You concentrate on the interaction of the cards and her hands and force yourself not to blink. And then, at the end of the whole sequence, just before she dashes the cards to the cardboard table and throws her hands into a resounding clap, you spot what you're looking for. For a brief instant, shorter than the flash of a bullet from a gun, her right hand snatches two cards at once, passes lightly over the box and drops them in sequence, one next to the other. As far as your eyes can tell, the queen should be in the middle, the other card on the left. Yet your eyes have already deceived you six times before. This must be the trick in the whole game—to make you think she dropped the queen instead of the jack she laid in its place.

"So sugar, double or nothing?"

You stare at the backs of the cards.

"C'mon now," Lucky prompts. "I may be fast but I'm only human. Not some freaky computer."

"Okay," you concede as you pull out a wrinkled twenty. "You have change?"

She hands you back your first five as you lay the twenty on the table.

"All right, where is she?"

If this were any other game of the sort—find the football under the three helmets, et cetera—you would take the middle card in a heartbeat. But you've seen how Lucky might make you believe the queen is in one place when she's not. Maybe it's time to suspend rational judgment for a moment. Maybe what you think you see is just an illusion. If she's intentionally deceiving you, perhaps you should pick the left card, even though you have no concrete evidence it's the queen.

"Well, baby? What do you think?"

If you decide to pick the card on the left, turn to page 83.

If you decide to pick the middle card, turn to page 84.

"This one," you say, as you turn over the left card. It's the queen.

"There you go!" crows Lucky. "Well done, honey."

"Thank you." You take back your twenty as she returns your five and five ones.

"You wanna go again?"

"No thanks. I'll quit while I'm still ahead. Or even. You weren't kidding about the quickest hands around."

"Thank you, honey. You come back anytime you want now. I'll be waiting."

"I will." But not anytime soon. You walk away fortunate to have escaped without losing $30.

"Say hi to Paulie for me," Lucky calls. You turn and wave, and she flashes a gold-toothed grin.

Paulie Shore. The man with the funny face destined for comedy. Was Lucky destined for Three Card Monte? All you know is had you played a few more games, you'd almost certainly be back in the hole again. The thought of winning $1,000,000 three days from now seems even more unreal. You decide it's time to head home for the day.

Continue on page 85.

"This one," you say as you turn over the middle card. Jack of spades. You stare at his mocking profile in disbelief. Lucky quickly pockets your twenty while you turn over the left card. Queen of hearts. You should have known.

"Sorry, sugar."

Your head reels a little. It was just $30 but it went so fast. You allow yourself a rueful smirk at the still unbelievable thought that you might end up a millionaire in three days. "I think I'm done for today," you tell Lucky.

"Okay honey," she says. "You come back anytime. Your luck's bound to change."

"Thanks."

"Say hi to Paulie for me," she adds.

"Paulie, right. See you around," you say. She waves as you turn to go.

Paulie Shore, born with a face for comedy. What were you born for? $1,000? $1,000,000? Whatever it is, it's definitely time to go home. You spend the commute trying to rationalize blowing $30 on ten minutes' worth of entertainment.

Continue on page 85.

When you arrive home, you order Chinese food, turn on the TV and plop down at your computer to check your email while the evening news runs in the background. You quickly scan today's Groupons—Swedish massage, unknown sushi restaurant, car wash, teeth whitening—and delete the email without viewing the latter half of the deals.

A chat window from Eve pops up on your monitor.

evenso77: howd it go today?

You clear out the remainder of your inbox before responding.

JQP47: good

    states witnesses etc

evenso77: cool

    anyone interesting?

You burn 30 seconds checking your Facebook News Feed.

JQP47: not if you havent seen them

evenso77: ooh…intriguing!

    tell me more

You opt for retreat instead, too tired, confused, contemplative or brain-sore to rehash your day. Avoidance is so much more convenient when a shield of Youtube videos, profile updates, and tweets hovers eighteen inches in front of your face.

JQP47: sorry

    cant do it

evenso77: :(

    youre no fun

Eve lets you duck behind the Great Wall of Chrome for now and tries a different tack.

evenso77: what about your box problem?

JQP47: nothing yet

    i still have until friday to decide

evenso77: well? still leaning toward 2 boxes?

If you still plan to take both boxes, turn to page 93.

If you plan to take only one box, turn to page 96.

JQP47: yeah i think so
    1 box
You cue up a game of Minesweeper.
evenso77: really?
JQP47: yeah
    i understand your side but i still think the model is that good
    if i were one of the people before me and i picked 1 box theres a 91.8%
    chance it would have $1M inside
evenso77: ok i get where youre coming from
    but just bc the model has been accurate in the past doesn't mean its
    going to keep being accurate
You haven't tried your hand at Minesweeper in a while, but you need a break from chess right now. It's one of those games that's entertaining but only pseudo-addictive, like some rare seasonal fruit that everyone gorges on for the few desperate weeks following its harvest, then forgets as they slip back into the everyday routine of apples and oranges and bananas.
JQP47: but still
    take 2 baseball players, one hitting .300 the other hitting .100
    who do you want up in the bottom of the ninth?
evenso77: depends on their history, their matchups
JQP47: say those are their career averages
    and they hit 300 and 100 against the current pitcher
evenso77: the 300 hitter obviously
    but their averages dont mean one of them is more likely to get a hit
    theyre records, not probabilities for the future
You select the Advanced level of Minesweeper. Each level has its own challenge. Beginner is all about speed. Figure out how to clear the most space on the board as quickly as possible. Advanced is all about patience. And luck.
JQP47: but the averages suggest the 300 guy is better
    better hitter = more likely to get a hit
evenso77: no better average = has gotten more hits

id take a 100 hitter in the majors right now over hank aaron

JQP47: right bc aaron isnt a better hitter right now

he was a better hitter than a 100 hitter is currently

evenso77: ok what about a current .050 hitter? him or aaron right now?

JQP47: i dont know

You wonder what Larry would have to say about all this. Would Big Papi be wallowing in the minors without his help?

evenso77: why not? how would you measure them?

JQP47: well batting average obviously

but also age, recent at-bats, injuries

there could be lots of factors

evenso77: exactly

which is why batting averages arent strict predictors

You don't remember Minesweeper's mouse controls at first, but then the buttons come back instinctively, without conscious thought, just some deeply ingrained and all-but-useless muscle memory. Left-click to reveal the hidden contents of a square. Right-click to mark a mine. Right-and-left to show potential mine locations.

JQP47: but theyre at least good indicators

and im not saying pavlov's model will always be 91.8% accurate

but the fact that it has been suggests its pretty good

look i cant say for sure the sun will rise tomorrow but the fact that it

has every day of my life leads me to believe it will

evenso77: but sunrise is a natural phenomenon

you have no say in the matter

in your problem you get to choose which box you take

and this model has never been used on you before

The game is deceptively easy to start. Your first square expands into an overgrown Tetris blob that occupies a third of the board and gives you plenty of options. You flag the known mines and left-click to send right-angled tentacles creeping across the screen to section off corners of the display. When you're stuck, you just move onto the next tucked-in "1" square and feel a small palpitation of excitement when another limb shoots out from the main body.

JQP47: yeah but its been used on other people

they must be somewhat like me

evenso77: but thats like saying all pitchers are alike

if you want to know the chances a certain player gets a hit, his batting average matters but so does who hes facing

hes got a better shot against a minor league scrub than roger clemens right?

JQP47: true

evenso77: so if you dont know who the pitcher is you dont know the batters chances to get a hit

there are just too many variables

same thing in your case

the model has never encountered you before

maybe it got all its hits off scrub brains

JQP47: haha

There comes a point in every Advanced game where you have to guess. Sometimes you can make educated guesses, figure it's more likely to have one mine in contact with several high-numbered squares than to have multiple mines doing the same work. But you can only play the percentages to a point before you reach an uncertain leap of faith. You can know how many mines exist, but not where they are, and you always postpone this moment of truth, even though facing it early on can either set you up for a win or blow you up and keep you from wasting your time delaying the inevitable.

evenso77: seriously

you keep comparing yourself to the other 91% of the subjects

but youre a completely different person

like theres probably some guy who hit 100 for his career but was 15 for 20 off clemens

JQP47: whats your point?

evenso77: my point is everybodys different

individualities matter, not just how other people did in the past

and what matters is whats in those boxes right now

You've cleared about two-thirds of the Minesweeper board and sectioned off a couple pockets to attend to later when you reach your dead end. Two of them in fact. You reluctantly flag the remaining deducible mines and then decide to go big, leaving a small edge section for a potential victory lap in order to confront the big chunk of uncharted territory that looms on the left side of the screen.

evenso77: just think about it

hey i gotta run

my mom just called for her weekly chat

You imagine Eve's obligatory eye roll whenever her notoriously overbearing mother enters the conversation.

JQP47: ok say hi for me

evenso77: will do

have fun tomorrow

JQP47: thanks

bye

You start small, try to figure out the most probable mine location and give it a tentative left-click. It's a 3. You're safe, but not for long. Another random do or die guess presents itself in short order. You hover for a moment, then switch squares and click before you can change your mind. The mine explodes under your mouse, and you close the game in frustration.

Continue on page 99.

JQP47: no, i think i may take 2 boxes now

    evenso77: wow!

        what changed your mind?

JQP47: i dont know

        i guess i just looked at it differently

    evenso77: well i think i changed my mind too

JQP47: oh yeah? 1 box?

    evenso77: i think so

        i know the money is already there when you make your choice

        but i think you were right: if you were one of the people before you and you took 1 box theres a 91.8% chance youd get $1M

        if you took 2 boxes theres a 91.8% chance youd just get the $1K

Your old argument still has a ring of truth to it, yet some other notion has dampened the force of this logic.

    JQP47: but that percentage doesnt say anything about the future

        if im playing craps and i get a 7 on 9 of 10 rolls that doesnt mean theres a 90% chance im gonna get 7 on my next roll

    evenso77: maybe, maybe not

        what if you got 90 out of 100?

        and they were all 3/4?

    JQP47: doesnt matter

        the probability of rolling dice doesnt depend on the past

        each roll is independent

    evenso77: unless the dice are loaded

        and if you got 90 out of 100 7s wouldnt you start to think they might be?

You navigate to Facebook and click on the profile of the first name atop your News Feed, a junior high acquaintance you haven't seen since the third day of high school.

    JQP47: yeah maybe

    evenso77: thats the point

its not that theres a 91.8% chance that pavlovs model is going to guess right

its the fact that its been 91.8% accurate in the past that suggests its a really good predictor

like the craps game: if you started getting lots of 7s you might think the dice were loaded and keep expecting 7s

i just think this model is that good

Apparently, your Facebook pseudo-friend is a doctor now. A pediatrician. You try to recall her as a young teenager. Was she smart? Science-oriented? You have no idea.

JQP47: so why is it good?

evenso77: what do you mean?

JQP47: you said you think its a good predictor

but how? does it read peoples minds? a week in advance?

thats crazy

evenso77: but its doing it

91.8%

JQP47: but how?

if its predictions are that good there must be something for it to predict from

something about peoples brain chemistry that says what theyre going to do before they do it

The chat screen remains blank for a moment. You scroll through the woman's Facebook photo gallery. College, med school, residency. What does a pre-doctor look like? Could you read any signs from a photo? You wonder if she had already chosen her career path when you knew her, if it was a passion she harbored all along.

evenso77: i guess so

never thought about it before but you may be right

like theres some script in peoples brains that maps out what theyre going to do

Some idea you can't quite place catches in your brain. Was it from Pavlov and the MRI?

JQP47: pavlov did mention some other studies

like this kinda thing had been done before

evenso77: like what?

JQP47: something about sunscreen

like the MRI could tell if you would use it or not
i forget exactly
but youre saying my mind can make decisions im not aware of
evenso77: yeah i guess
but is that so crazy? you dont tell your heart to beat

You place your hand on your chest and try to consciously slow down your pulse. You don't notice much of a change. You return to Facebook's News Feed. Are old acquaintances surprised when they look at you now and see what you've become years later?

JQP47: thats different
this is a conscious decision
evenso77: how do you know?
JQP47: bc im thinking about it right now!
evenso77: you dont think every person b4 u believes they thought about it
for the whole week?
isnt it possible your mind is already made up and you just think youre
making conscious decisions now?

You stare blankly at your computer screen, unsure how to answer. You are rescued by the next line from Eve.

evenso77: hang on someones at the door
She returns a minute later.
evenso77: sorry i have to go
plumbers here—my sinks clogged
but youre not off the hook
JQP47: haha ok
good luck w that
evenso77: thanks
bye
JQP47: bye

Continue on page 115.

JQP47: yeah i guess so
    2 boxes
  evenso77: still?
JQP47: yeah
  evenso77: ok i see where youre coming from
    i know the money is already there when you make your choice
    but if you were one of the people before you and you took
    2 boxes theres a 91.8% chance youd get just the $1K
    if you took 1 box theres a 91.8% chance youd get $1M
JQP47: but those numbers dont say anything about the future
    lets say im flipping a coin and i get 9 of 10 heads
    that doesnt mean theres a 90% chance ill get heads on my next flip
  evenso77: maybe, maybe not
    what if you got 90 out of 100?
JQP47: doesnt matter
    the probability of flipping a coin doesnt depend on the past
    each flip is still 50-50
  evenso77: unless its weighted
    and if you got 90 out of 100 heads wouldnt you start to consider that possibility?

You ponder this suggestion while perusing the top picks on YouTube. Music videos, movie trailers, cute puppies, late night talk shows. Lucky was right. Even Internet stars are beautiful people capable of incredibly amazing or hilarious feats. You try to think of any attractive and unsuccessful people you know.

JQP47: maybe
    but it could still be random chance
  evenso77: it could be
    but that looks less likely with every heads
    the point is not that theres a 91.8% chance pavlovs model will correctly predict your choice
    its the fact that its been 91.8% accurate in the past that suggests its a really good model

93

like the coin flip: if you started to get lots of heads you might think the coin was weighted and start betting on heads

You watch thirty seconds of a Leno monolog on the latest inept politician before switching to a compilation of absurd human feats: people blowing bubbles into an intricate sculpture, executing complex ping pong trick shots, parkouring over cars and in and out of their clothes. How do these people ever discover they can do this stuff?

JQP47: so why is the model so good?

evenso77: what do you mean?

JQP47: you said you think its really good

but at what? reading peoples minds? a week in advance?

thats crazy

evenso77: but its doing it

91.8%

JQP47: but how?

it must make its predictions from something

like something about peoples brain chemistry tells what theyre going to do before they do it

Your stomach begins to churn, reminding you that you haven't had anything to eat since that six-inch sub at lunch.

evenso77: i guess so

never thought about it before but i suppose youre right

like theres some script in peoples brains that maps out what theyre about to do

A stray thought comes back to you now. Something John Mann said earlier. Or Pavlov?

JQP47: pavlov did mention some other studies

like this kinda thing had been done before

evenso77: like what?

JQP47: like an MRI could predict whether people would use sunscreen

i forget exactly

but youre saying my mind can make decisions im not aware of

evenso77: yeah i guess

but is that so crazy? you dont tell your heart to beat

JQP47: thats different

this is a conscious decision

evenso77: how do you know?

maybe you just think youre thinking about it

There's a muffled knock at your front door. Your stomach utters a vicious growl in response, drowned out by a two-year-old putting Aretha Franklin to shame on your computer.

JQP47: but you could say the same for any decision

maybe i just think im thinking about everything

what am i supposed to do with that?

evenso77: duh

1 box

: P

JQP47: thanks

The knock repeats itself, louder this time. Chinese delivery men wait for no one.

JQP47: sorry eve i have to go

my dinners here

evenso77: cop out

JQP47: bye

Continue on page 115.

JQP47: no i think im gonna go w 1 box now

    evenso77: really!

        what changed your mind?

JQP47: i guess i just looked at it a differently

    evenso77: well i think i changed my mind too

JQP47: youre a 2 boxer now?

You've never known Eve to change her mind. And her stubbornness is not born of blind ignorance. More often than not, she's anticipated all counterarguments to her position from the outset and has made a fixed, informed decision while anyone else would still be weighing her options.

    evenso77: yeah i think so

        it all depends on the difference between probability and past occurrence

JQP47: you mean just bc the model has been accurate in the past doesn't

    mean it will continue

    evenso77: exactly

        its not the same thing

JQP47: but take an A student and a D student

    who do you expect to score better on the next test?

    evenso77: probably the A student

        but its not set in stone

JQP47: say theyre in high school and theyve gotten those grades their

    whole life

    evenso77: their grades alone dont mean the A student will get a better

        grade on the next test

        its not like picking colored marbles out of a bag

        there arent a fixed number of scenarios and outcomes

JQP47: but their grades suggest the A student is a better student than the D student

    better student = more likely to test better

    evenso77: no better grades = has tested better in the past

        what if the A student gets mono and misses a month?

        now the D student has a better chance to score higher

Your stomach grumbles. You check the clock on your computer—nine minutes 'til kung pao. On TV, a heavyset Asian weatherman with wire-framed eyeglasses gestures blindly at the mapped-over green screen behind him. Sunny and warm tomorrow, high of 78°. Aside from race, all weathermen look the same, like chubby, myopic American Girl dolls.

JQP47: maybe

> but youve just stacked the deck
> the A student is a better student and will likely score higher on the test unless
> something happens, e.g. she gets hit by a bus and ends up brain dead

evenso77: aha!

> so circumstances matter

JQP47: of course they do

> to some extent
> but maybe they don't
> maybe the A student parties the night before, shows up to the test hung over and
> still aces it just bc shes that smart

evenso77: so how do you know? how do you predict how student will score on a test?

JQP47: grades and previous test scores to start

> but also health, interest in the subject, unforeseen circumstances, etc.
> there could be lots of factors

evenso77: exactly

> so past test scores arent strict predictors

JQP47: not perfectly no

> but theyre at least very good indicators
> you have to introduce some special explanation as to why a D student will
> outscore an A student on a test
> and im not saying pavlovs model will always be 91.8% accurate
> but the fact that it has been leads me to believe its a pretty good model

Convex lavender curves bearing alternating semi-circles and jagged triangles sweep relentlessly across the TV satellite map like giant invading bacteria. It's amazing how much data must go into meteorology, and yet the experts still seem to get it wrong fairly often.

JQP47: look i cant say theres a 99.999% chance the sun will rise tomorrow, but the fact

> that it has every day of my life leads me to believe it will do so again

evenso77: but sunrise is a natural phenomenon

> you have no say in the matter
> in your problem you get to choose which box you take

other factors exist

and this model has never been used on you before

JQP47: yeah but its been used on other people

they must be somewhat like me

evenso77: but not exactly

just like all tests, all subject matters arent alike

if the D student spends all his time playing video games he might do better on a

computer programming test than the honors english student

JQP47: true

The news wraps up with the prediction of unseasonably hot weather for the weekend. Global warming indeed. The female anchor stumbles over a bad pun, and the male anchor forces a laugh as a peppy adult contemporary riff rounds out the show.

evenso77: same thing in your case

the model has never encountered you before

maybe it was just really comfortable with the previous brains

you could be its "computer programming" test

JQP47: haha

evenso77: but again your choice doesnt change the prediction

you cant think "if i were 1 of the 91%" before you

bc youre not

youre you

just like how certain students do better in certain subjects

it doesn't matter what other people did before you

JQP47: i guess so

You hear a muffled knock at the front door. Your stomach roars.

JQP47: ok thats my dinner

gotta go

evenso77: ok talk to you later

have fun tomorrow

JQP47: bye

Continue on page 99.

"Your Honor, the defense calls Dr. Franko Pavlov," Hines announces as the trial resumes on Wednesday morning.

Your initial reaction is to try to recall the first name of the Dr. Pavlov from the MRI experiment. The coincidence seems too incredible. Yet it could not be anyone else waiting beyond that dimpled wood door. And though you struggle a bit to picture him outside the confines of his decrepit laboratory, to imagine him other than as a hunched Frankenstein laboring over his monster, the thought that he might be here, now, at this very trial, begins to feel entirely natural, in the way of Hercule Poirot uncovering the most implausible suspect as the only one capable of committing the crime.

The anteroom door eases open to emit a splotchy apparition that materializes into the form of your Dr. Pavlov as he enters the pod. He drifts forward, bent like a listing question mark, much the same as you left him in his worn beige pants and button-up shirt, though he has replaced his lab coat with a well-used gray blazer for his appearance in court. He alights on the edge of the witness chair, his kyphotic spine and unflinching jadeite eyes offering his customary mélange of frailty and rigor.

"Dr. Pavlov," Hines begins, "would you please introduce yourself to the members of the jury?"

"My name is Dr. Franko Pavlov," he says as he rolls his shoulders toward the jury box. "I am the Alexander J. Solomon Professor of Neuroscience at Lauterbur State University and the director of the Lauterbur State Functional Magnetic Resonance Imaging Research Laboratory."

"Would you please summarize your formal education?"

"I received a Bachelor of Science in Biochemistry from Pomona College in 1983 and a Ph.D. in Neuroscience from the University of California, Los Angeles in 1988. I served as an Assistant Professor of Neuroscience from 1989 through 1996 at the University of California, Los Angeles, and as Associate Professor and Professor of Neuroscience from 1997 through the present at Lauterbur State University. In 2001, I assumed directorship of the Functional Magnetic Resonance Imaging Research Laboratory at Lauterbur State."

"What is the subject of your research at the laboratory?" Hines asks.

"Our research is primarily concerned with the brain's unconscious responses to external stimuli," Pavlov answers. "We know that presenting the brain with a choice triggers a chemical response in the brain which leads to a decision. Our research attempts to characterize the nature of that initial response—how and where it occurs in the brain, how quickly, and to what extent the human subject is aware of this response as it occurs. We conduct most of our work using Functional Magnetic Resonance Imaging, or fMRI for short. With fMRI, we can take a picture of a subject's brain as it is presented with some external stimulus. The fMRI will indicate the areas of the brain that receive the most blood flow, which are the areas most affected by the stimulus and subsequent decision. Our research follows many previous studies in demonstrating that most of this activity occurs in an area of the brain called the prefrontal cortex, or PFC.

"fMRI also allows us to learn more about the exact nature of the PFC response in a subject's brain. A 2008 study by Soon, Brass, Heinze and Hayes demonstrated that fMRI can detect a chemical response in the PFC indicating a subject's decision up to ten seconds prior to the subject articulating that decision. In a 2010 study, Falk, Berkman, Mann, Harrison and Lieberman showed that the result of an fMRI brain scan can be used to predict an individual's future decision above and beyond that individual's own prediction. In our current research at the laboratory, we are attempting to determine the extent of the predictive power of fMRI brain scans. While undergoing an fMRI scan, subjects are presented with a scenario and a decision they will make a week later. We use the fMRI results in a model to predict each subject's decision before they make it the following week. As of now, our model is 93.1% accurate in its predictions."

"Thank you, Dr. Pavlov," Hines says. "Your Honor, I'd like to tender Dr. Pavlov as an expert in neuroscience and human behavior."

"Mrs. Gray?" Pitcock asks.

"Dr. Pavlov, you stated that you are currently employed by Lauterbur State University," Gray says. "But your research there is financed by a grant from another organization, isn't it?"

"Yes, that's correct."

"And what organization is that?"

"Science Applications Corporation, a private science and technology firm."

"Isn't Science Applications Corporation a government defense contractor?"

Pavlov's lips widen into a thin smile. "Some of their work is intended for military use, yes."

"And in what way is your work intended for military use?"

"Objection, Your Honor," Hines says. "Is this line of questioning relevant to Dr. Pavlov's body of knowledge and the findings of his research?"

"Your Honor," Gray says, "I would argue it is imperative to know the source of funds for any scientific research in order to determine the extent of potential bias."

"Your objection is overruled, Mr. Hines," Pitcock says after a moment's consideration. "However, Mrs. Gray, please confine your questions to a determination of possible bias. Dr. Pavlov, you may answer the question."

"Our work is not intended for military use, Mrs. Gray," Pavlov says.

"But it could be, right?" Gray asks. "Your research aims to create a model to determine what an individual will choose when presented with a particular scenario. And if that's possible, then you could simply introduce a certain external stimulus to create a desired response in the individual. Isn't that correct?"

"Brain responses in terms of PFC activity are not nearly so simple, Mrs. Gray," Pavlov replies.

"Is it possible the United States Department of Defense thinks they might be so simple?" Gray asks. "Your research is financed by a private science applications company that doubles as a defense contractor for the United States government, and it sounds like your work could have amazing applications in the field of psychological warfare. Is it ludicrous for me to imagine our government has a hand in financing your work and intends to use your results—if positive—in some such military capacity?"

"I'm sorry, Mrs. Gray," Pavlov says, "but whatever you may imagine, I do not know of any government influence on our laboratory's current funding."

"Of course not," Gray smirks. "Dr. Pavlov, have you received any offers for future grants from Science Applications Corporation?"

"No, we have not."

"Have you received offers for future grants from any other entities?"

"No."

"So as of this moment, when your current grant expires your research will no longer have funding. Is that correct?"

"Yes. However—"

"Thank you, Dr. Pavlov," Gray cuts him off. She turns to Judge Pitcock.

"No further questions, Your Honor."

"Mrs. Gray, do you have any objections to Dr. Pavlov's testimony?" Pitcock asks.

Her assistant whispers something in her ear, but Gray waves him off. "No, Your Honor," she answers.

Pitcock sighs. "In that case, the court recognizes Dr. Franko Pavlov as an expert in the fields of neuroscience and human behavior. You may proceed, Mr. Hines."

"Thank you, Your Honor." Hines advances toward the witness box. "Dr. Pavlov, you said you have developed a model to make predictions of human behavior based on fMRI brain scans, and that these predictions are over 93% accurate. Is that correct?"

"Yes, that is the subject of our current research."

"Can you explain how you manage to achieve such a high degree of accuracy?"

Pavlov adjusts his glasses and settles back in his chair. "As I stated earlier, an external stimulus that requires a decision causes significant activity in the prefrontal cortex of the human brain. Using fMRI, we are able to observe such activity. Our model then characterizes this PFC activity based on a variety of factors, such as intensity, duration and specific location within the PFC, in order to make its prediction. Extensive research in this field, by myself and the other scientists I mentioned earlier, indicates that the type of PFC activity that occurs in response to a given stimulus serves as a reliable indicator of the nature of the subsequent decision. Because humans are not consciously aware of this chemical activity in their own brains, it is often possible to predict a subject's choice with greater accuracy than the subject's own prediction about that choice."

"In other words, a decision can arise in a person's brain without that person's conscious awareness," Hines says. "Is that correct?"

"Yes, that is correct."

"And the brain response which leads to such a decision could occur a week prior to the actual decision being made?"

Pavlov folds his hands across his belt buckle. "Yes, the preliminary findings of our current research and the 2010 study I mentioned earlier both show evidence of PFC activity up to one week in advance of a conscious choice."

As the hour approaches midday, the temperature inside the pod begins to climb. Bulletproof glass does not exactly encourage ventilation. You can feel the onset of a sweat mustache, and the jurors around you surreptitiously wipe at their temples and the backs of their necks. Kenneth Hines unbuttons his suit coat and lightly fans his torso with its flaps as he speaks.

"So based on your research, it's possible for a subject to encounter a scenario which causes a particular response in his brain unbeknownst to the subject, and for that brain response to generate a decision a week later that is different than the decision the subject predicted he would make," he says. "Is that correct?"

"Yes, it is."

Hines waits a moment to let this idea settle, then says, "Thank you, Dr. Pavlov. No further questions, Your Honor."

Shannon Gray is out of her seat before Pitcock can announce "your witness." She strides to center court of the soot-glassed arena and faces Pavlov with her head thrown back. "Dr. Pavlov, the 2010 study you referred to—that one measured sunscreen use among the participants, didn't it?" she asks.

"Yes," Pavlov says, "in the 2010 study, Dr. Falk and her colleagues conducted an fMRI scan on subjects' brains while they viewed promotional videos about the benefits of sunscreen use. The researchers found that the fMRI results more accurately predicted subjects' future sunscreen use than did the subjects themselves."

"And the fMRI-based predictions were made a week in advance of the subjects' decisions?"

"Yes."

"So some people incorrectly predicted they would use more sunscreen while the fMRI correctly predicted they would use less, and other people incorrectly predicted they would use less sunscreen while the fMRI correctly predicted they would use more. Is that an accurate assessment of the results?"

"Yes, it is."

"And does your current research generally support these findings?"

"Yes, it does."

Shannon Gray paces between Pavlov and Pitcock, her steps short and exact. "Let's take the first case from the sunscreen experiment then—the people who wrongly predicted they would use more sunscreen while the fMRI predicted they would use less. Can you explain how such a result came about?"

"As I stated earlier, subjects underwent an fMRI scan while viewing a promotional video about sunscreen use," Pavlov answers. "In the cases you described, the fMRI results likely identified something in the subjects' PFC response to indicate they were not persuaded by the video. As a result, the researchers predicted these subjects would be less likely to use sunscreen over the course of the subsequent week. After the fMRI, the subjects were asked to estimate their expected sunscreen use for the next week. In the case you described, these subjects would have thought themselves more likely to use sunscreen. A week after the fMRI, the subjects returned to the laboratory and tabulated their sunscreen use over the previous week in comparison to past use. The subjects you described would have reported less sunscreen use, in accordance with the fMRI results but contrary to their own predictions."

"I see," Gray says. "So in other words, the brains of these subjects displayed an adverse, unconscious chemical response to the promotional video which suggested decreased sunscreen use. Is that correct?"

"Yes, it is."

"And this unconscious response occurred after the video stimulus provided in the experiment. Is that correct?"

"Yes, it is."

"Dr. Pavlov, are you suggesting the researchers in this experiment were responsible for giving these subjects sunburn?" Gray asks with feigned disbelief.

"No," Pavlov answers with a constrained grin, "I said nothing about responsibility. I merely stated that a chemical response leading to the decision to not use sunscreen could have occurred in these subjects' brains without their conscious awareness."

"And how did such a chemical response arise?" Gray asks.

"It arose as a result of the stimulus provided by the video promoting sunscreen use."

"Which the researchers presented to the subjects."

"Yes."

"So these researchers were responsible for playing the video. They caused it to be played. Is that correct?"

"Yes."

"And after they viewed this video, certain subjects decreased their sunscreen use over the course of the following week."

"That is correct."

Shannon Gray flexes her right arm and cocks her index finger toward the perforated tile ceiling of the pod. "Dr. Pavlov, imagine I stand in a large crowd of people and fire a loaded gun into the air. The bullet from the gun comes down and strikes a man in the head and kills him. Would you hold me responsible for the bullet released from that gun?"

"I would."

"And that bullet, which is my responsibility, kills a man. Would you hold me responsible for that man's death?"

Pavlov's smile fades, and his crooked spine appears to unfurl slightly. "Mrs. Gray," he says, "you have ventured into the realm of philosophical speculation. Unfortunately, my expertise is limited to the field of neuroscience."

"And human behavior, I believe."

"Yes, and human behavior."

"So how would you judge my behavior of firing a gun into the air while in the midst of a large crowd of people?"

"Objection, Your Honor," Kenneth Hines protests. "Not only is this hypothetical scenario outside the witness's area of expertise, but I fail to see the relevance of the current line of questioning to the evidence presented under direct examination."

Pitcock shifts in his high chair and leans onto his right armrest. "Sustained," he says. "Mrs. Gray, please limit your questions to the scope of direct examination and the extent of the witness's expertise."

"Yes, Your Honor," Gray acquiesces.

She and Pavlov sweat inhumanly—Gray hardly at all, her straight, golden hair matted against the edges of her forehead and above her ears to give her a slight helmeted appearance, though no moisture darkens these locks. Pavlov glistens like Michael Jordan, a fine mist on the bald skin of his pate that evinces disdain for the mere mortals who must sacrifice pints of bodily fluid to even approach his capacities. In contrast, twin rivulets have started their course down your breastbone and spine.

"Dr. Pavlov," Gray says, "in the course of our *voir dire* you told me, and I quote, 'brain responses in terms of PFC activity are not nearly so simple.' So you admit some complexity exists in the relationship between external stimuli and human brain response in the form of PFC activity?"

"Yes, I do," Pavlov answers.

"And since in your current research your model has only been 93.1% accurate, your imperfect results would seem to support that fact."

"Yes," Pavlov agrees, "we still have much to learn about human brain chemistry as it relates to external stimuli, deliberation and decision-making." He seems a touch dismayed, not in having to admit his failure to Shannon Gray, but out of genuine disappointment that he has not yet unlocked the secrets of the human brain.

"So in your research, 6.9% of people acted just the way they expected to act and your model got it wrong," Gray presses. "Am I right?"

"As I said, we have encountered subjects where our model did not accurately predict their decisions," Pavlov answers.

"Thank you, Dr. Pavlov," says Shannon Gray. "No further questions, Your Honor."

"Mr. Hines?" Pitcock intones.

Hines stands and rests his fingertips on the table in front of him. His jacket hangs like a curtain around the slight bulge of his midsection. "Dr. Pavlov, do the results of your experiment indicate that it is possible for an individual to make a decision without conscious awareness of that choice?" he asks.

"Yes."

"And in your experiment, does that unconscious decision occur a week in advance of the subject's conscious choice?

"Yes."

"And how often has your model accurately predicted such a decision a week in advance?" he asks.

"93.1% of the time," says Pavlov.

"Thank you, Doctor. No further questions."

Gray declines to recross, Pitcock announces, "The witness is excused," and Pavlov glides down from the witness box and out the pod door.

· · · · ·

The trial recesses for lunch. Today it's Arby's roast beef sandwiches. Variety is the spice of life. As you plow through a blob of mayonnaise, you ponder the least offensive condiment one could order for somebody else. You settle on mild salsa. Slightly adventurous, yet tame enough for the weak-tongued; just enough kick for the heat seekers. The Goldilocks of condiments. Maybe not on a sandwich though. You try to imagine roast beef and salsa as John Mann sits down next to you.

"No chess today?" he asks.

You shake your head, having literally bitten off more than you can chew. People invariably choose this exact moment to ask a question.

Mann notices your plight and waits for you to gulp down your mouthful of thick white bread and minimal fillings. "You know him, don't you? Pavlov?"

"Yes," you acknowledge.

"I thought so," Mann says. "I was watching you when he was called. I could tell you recognized his name."

You set your sandwich down and watch a thick bead of mayo ooze onto the paper wrapping. "I'm a subject in his research," you say.

"Really? What's it about? He never did say."

You explain the experiment to Mann as he listens in attentive silence.

"So you're going to take just the one box then," he says when you've finished.

"I think so."

"Because Pavlov's model has been 93% accurate."

"Yeah, that seems pretty good to me. It was only 91.8% when I first went."

Mann flips open his sandwich and douses the limp rusty lettuce with three packets of yellow mustard. "Do you think his model determines your choice?" he asks.

"What do you mean?"

"Well, you're making your decision based on the accuracy of Pavlov's model. You've decided to take one box because you believe the model already predicted you would and has put $1,000,000 in the box."

"Right."

"So could you change your mind? I mean could you actually decide here and now to take both boxes?"

"Of I course I could," you say, frowning. "But why would I?"

"If your decision is based on the accuracy of the model, you must think there's a reason the model has been so accurate," he says, his wavy, brown hair bobbing as he gets excited. "It can't have guessed right 93% of the time by luck. So the MRI must have read something in your brain last Friday on which the model based its prediction. In other words, if everything goes the way you think it will, if you take one box and it has a million dollars inside, then something in your brain last Friday must have told the model you would take one box. And if this model is really that accurate, then you can't take two boxes now. Because if you did, something in your brain would have told the model you were going to take two boxes."

"But that's ridiculous," you say. "Of course I could take both boxes on Friday. Just like I could jump out that window." You indicate one of the narrow panes that line the opposite wall. "I just choose not to."

"Maybe," he says. "But you won't take two boxes. Or if you do, you would have all along. Because if you take two boxes, the model would have seen that a week ago and it will guess right and you'll only get $1,000. So you can't really change your mind now. It's already been decided. If you believe the model is really that good, then you believe your mind has already chosen what you'll do. Your so-called choice on Friday just confirms what was already determined last week."

"But I can choose otherwise," you insist. "I could jump out that window. I could have worn brown shoes instead of black today. I could have—" The half-chewed bite you had tucked in your cheek finds its way into your windpipe. You start to cough, but fortunately the bread pretty much disintegrates in your throat.

John eyes you with concern until you stop hacking. "Prove it," he says.

"What?"

"Prove you could have worn brown shoes," he says as he pinches off a morsel of his own sandwich.

"What do you mean? I can't go back to this morning and put on new shoes."

"Exactly. Just like you can't go back to Friday and rewire your brain. If you pick one box because you believe in Pavlov's model, you think you don't have a choice now. You think there's some unconscious signal in your brain that said 'one' last week. You didn't mean for it to say 'one.' But you know the model is very accurate. You know if you pick one box, it will have guessed one box. Because you never chose in the first place. It was just a chemical reaction, predetermined from the moment you slid into the MRI and the video started to play. You didn't choose then and now you're just guessing what the model predicted. So don't pretend you actually get to make a decision. Either the model is so accurate because of your unwilled, unconscious brain chemistry, or it's just really, really lucky. But you can't have it both ways."

This notion churns through your mind like a greasy burrito after a night of dry heaves. But then a brighter idea breaks through. "Maybe," you say. "But I'll still have a million bucks."

Mann leans back and smiles. "I guess so," he says. "You'll find out soon enough."

•   •   •   •   •

By the time you return from lunch, the courtroom is brutally hot, and everyone is in that kid-stuck-in-a-classroom-in-the-last-week-of-school mode, even Judge Pitcock, who rolls back and forth in his high chair like a chubby, hyperactive pre-teen. Condensation forms on the smoky walls of the pod and a palpable electricity simmers in the air as Dr. David Solon climbs into the witness stand with the measured gait of a man who has ascended to hundreds of lecterns and faced far bigger crowds than the one assembled today in this meager capsule. He utters his oath of honesty while perched on the edge of his seat, and you can easily imagine him leaning against a desk in a university classroom in much the same manner as he sits here now.

Kenneth Hines positions himself between Dr. Solon and the jury, close enough to show commiserative support for his client yet still leaving a sufficient buffer to allow Solon some airspace. "Dr. Solon," he begins, "would you please introduce yourself to the members of the jury?"

Dr. Solon turns and fixes you with his azure gaze. "My name is Dr. David Solon," he answers. "I am currently a Professor of Mathematics at Harvey Tech University."

"Would you please summarize your formal education and employment history?"

"I received a Bachelor of Science in Mathematics from the University of California, Berkeley in 1985 and a Ph.D. in Mathematics from the University of Chicago in 1990. I served as Assistant Professor of Mathematics from 1991 through 1995 at the University of Chicago, and as Associate Professor and then Professor of Mathematics at Harvey Tech University from 1995 through the present."

"And by now I think everyone here knows of your wife, Julia. How long were the two of you married?"

"We met in college in 1984 and married in 1988. We would have celebrated our twenty-third anniversary last October."

"Were you ever divorced or separated?"

"No."

"Do you have any children?"

"No, we never had any."

"And prior to this trial, had you ever been accused or convicted of a felony in any court of law?"

"No."

"Thank you. Now would you please describe what happened in your home on the night of April 26, 2011?"

"Julia and I went to bed around 11:00 on April 25," Dr. Solon answers. "At approximately 3:15 the next morning, I was awakened by some noise that seemed to come from the ground floor of our house. Julia was not in bed. I became suspicious and retrieved my handgun from the locked safe in our bedroom closet and went downstairs to investigate. As I came down the steps, I heard a scream and some gunshots and ran down the rest of the way. When I got to the bottom I saw Julia lying motionless on the floor in the middle of the room. A man stood over her, and when I entered the room he ran past me and out the front door of our house. I chased him to the door and fired two shots at him as he fled. Neither shot hit him, and he escaped down the street."

"What did you do then?" Hines asks.

"I called 911 immediately. But it was apparent that Julia was already... gone."

"And when the police arrived in response to your call, you managed to help them generate a composite sketch of your wife's murderer. How were you able to identify this man?"

Solon slowly spins the white gold band on his left ring finger. "He looked at me briefly when I came into the living room, and I saw his face. I got another look at him as he ran past me on his way toward the door."

Hines tugs at the knot of his tie and takes one step closer to the witness stand. "Dr. Solon, would you now tell the jury about the incident that occurred on the evening of May 3?" he asks.

Solon tilts his upper back off his chair to sit perfectly upright. "I was walking down Jackson Avenue when I heard a commotion in an alley off the street to my left. I looked down the alley and saw a man with his back to me holding a woman at gunpoint. He was speaking loudly to her, although I couldn't make out his words. Seeing no one else around, I began to walk slowly down the alley. When I was about twenty feet from the assailant, I broke into a run in his direction and I managed to knock him to the ground before he could turn toward me. He dropped his gun when I hit him, and I picked it up before he could retrieve it. The woman fled down the alley. I stood over the man and pointed the gun at him and yelled back to the woman to call the police. Then he rolled over, and I saw his face. It was the man who shot Julia. Something came over me at that moment. I saw his face and I remembered him standing over Julia in our living room. And I shot him."

"Dr. Solon, would you please expand upon your previous statement?" Hines asks. "In particular, why did you kill this man, Damon Belliard?"

Solon answers without hesitation. "He killed my wife. I stood over him in that alley and I saw the man who killed Julia. I didn't think about it."

"And on the night of April 26, why did you fire your gun at Damon Belliard?"

"Because he had just killed my wife."

"Did you think about it then?"

"No. I saw him standing over Julia. He ran for the door, and I fired."

"Thank you, Dr. Solon," says Hines. "No further questions, Your Honor."

Pitcock turns to Shannon Gray. "Mrs. Gray?"

Gray steps around her table and circles toward the stand. Dr. Solon watches her patiently, his suntanned skin drawn tight across his cheekbones, his blue eyes tinged with pink.

"Dr. Solon, do you admit to shooting Damon Belliard on the evening of May 3, seven days after your wife's death?" Gray begins.

"Yes, I do."

"You testified under direct examination that you fired twice at Mr. Belliard as he fled your home on April 26. You didn't pursue him after those shots missed?"

"No, I went—"

"After April 26, what did you expect to happen to Mr. Belliard?"

"I imagined the police would arrest him and charge him with murder. I did not anticipate seeing him again until he appeared in court."

"And when you imagined seeing him in court, did you also imagine shooting him?"

"No."

"So after the incident on April 26 when you actually shot at Mr. Belliard, you no longer expected to shoot him," Gray says. "Is that correct?"

"Under the circumstances I expected to encounter Mr. Belliard—"

"Please answer the question, Doctor."

"When I imagined seeing Mr. Belliard in court, I did not image shooting him there."

"So between April 26 and May 3, when you imagined your next encounter with Damon Belliard, did you expect to shoot him at that encounter?" Gray asks.

"No, I did not," Solon answers.

"But you did shoot him on May 3?"

"Yes."

"And you intended to shoot him on May 3?"

"Yes, I did." Dr. Solon casts a glance over his left shoulder toward the jury, but Gray recalls his attention with her next question.

"Did you intend to kill him?"

"I'm sorry, Mrs. Gray, but I did not take the time to form any intention about the fate of Mr. Belliard. I simply—"

"Please answer the question, Dr. Solon," Gray says. "Did you intend to kill Damon Belliard?"

Dr. Solon stifles a sigh. "Again, Mrs. Gray, I cannot say for certain what I intended to befall Mr. Belliard in the few seconds I had to act."

"But you are aware it is quite possible for a person to die of a gunshot wound?"

"Yes."

Gray grabs a sheet of paper from her assistant and holds it aloft to Dr. Solon. "The Medical Examiner's autopsy report states Damon Belliard died from a gunshot wound to the brain. So you shot Mr. Belliard in the head?"

"Yes," answers Solon.

"Were you aiming for his head?"

"Yes."

"Dr. Solon, based on evidence found in the alley on May 3 as well as previous eyewitness testimony, it appears you only fired one shot at Mr. Belliard," Gray says. "Is that your recollection?"

"Yes, it is."

"You didn't shoot him, or attempt to shoot him, more than once?"

"No," Dr. Solon says, his voice even and without emotion.

"Why not?"

"Because he was dead after the first shot."

"You were sure of that?"

"I didn't check his pulse. The shot hit him and he fell back to the ground and didn't move."

Gray walks slowly toward the jury box. "How much time passed from the moment you recognized Damon Belliard to the moment your shot struck him?"

"I don't know," Solon answers. "Less than a few seconds, I would imagine."

"So before you recognized Mr. Belliard in that alley on May 3, you no longer expected to shoot him. Then in less than a few seconds, you realized who he was, flew into a rage at the thought of your wife's death, shot him and decided he was dead. Dr. Solon, schizophrenics don't have mood swings that erratic."

"Objection, Your Honor," says Hines. "Badgering the witness."

"Sustained," Pitcock agrees.

"Dr. Solon," Gray continues, "you are claiming that just after acting rationally to help apprehend a criminal, you lost all control of yourself, shot him and then returned to your senses at once in order to examine him and conclude he was dead. Is that correct?"

"I shot Mr. Belliard one time," Solon reiterates. "I do not know why I should have shot him more than that."

"Did you recognize Mr. Belliard before you entered the alley that day?"

"No, I did not."

"You testified that you saw a man with his back to you holding a gun to a woman in the alley. Is that correct?"

"Yes, it is."

"You were sure this man was holding a gun?"

"Yes."

"Mrs. Alethea testified that Mr. Belliard held his gun like this." Gray tucks her hand into her stomach, index finger extended toward Dr. Solon, then pivots to face the jury, her back to the witness. "Dr. Solon, can you see my face?" she asks.

"No, I cannot," he answers.

"Can you see my right hand?"

"No."

"Thank you, Dr. Solon. No further questions, Your Honor."

"Mr. Hines?" Pitcock asks.

Hines remains seated and tugs at the lapels of his suit jacket to settle it farther back on his shoulders. "Dr. Solon, you stated that between your encounters with Mr. Belliard on April 26 and May 3, you only expected to see him when he was put on trial for your wife's murder," he says. "Is that correct?"

"Yes," Solon answers.

"And when you imagined seeing Mr. Belliard in court, you did not intend to shoot him. Is that correct?"

"Yes, it is."

"Did you expect to encounter Damon Belliard in an alley holding up a woman at gunpoint?"

"No."

"Did you give any consideration as to what you might do if you met him in such a situation?"

"No, I did not."

It seems Solon and Hines are two men cut from the same cloth. In another life, they could have been friends. Yet even if Dr. Solon manages to escape a prison sentence, their relationship will come to an abrupt end after the trial, forever tainted in memory by this event. They are professional acquaintances now, intelligent, capable and mutually respectful, but nothing more. So often the circumstances of our lives define those with whom we share this existence, forcing our kindred souls into typecast, sterile roles like teacher, colleague or client.

"On May 3, did you recognize Mr. Belliard before you entered the alley?" Hines asks.

"No."

"Did you see that he was holding a gun?"

"Yes, I did."

"According to the police reports, forensic analysis on this case and your previous testimony, you fired two shots after your wife's murderer on April 26," Hines says. "Is that accurate?"

"Yes, it is."

"You didn't empty the magazine?"

"No."

"And why not?"

"Because after two shots the killer was out of range, and I was more concerned about Julia."

"Thank you, Dr. Solon. No further questions, Your Honor."

Pitcock's head lolls from Hines to Gray. "Mrs. Gray?"

"No further questions," Gray says.

"The witness is excused," says Pitcock, and David Solon steps down from the stand, his head bowed and hands folded in front of him.

"Your Honor, the defense rests," Hines declares.

"Very well," Pitcock says. "In that case, this court will recess for the remainder of the day. It will reconvene tomorrow morning at 9:00, at which time Mrs. Gray and Mr. Hines will present their closing statements."

Continue on page 132.

"Your Honor, the defense calls Dr. Franko Pavlov," Kenneth Hines announces as David Solon's trial resumes the following morning.

There are so many sights and sounds that sift through human consciousness alone and inconspicuous that it should come as no surprise when one of them is repeated and recalled and granted the special name of coincidence or *déjà vu*. Yet if ever there was a coincidence, this declaration surely counts. At the same time, it seems both completely absurd and perfectly natural that Dr. Pavlov should appear at this trial. For while his lurking specter outside the anteroom is altogether uncanny, the incongruity is so outlandish that it manages to circle the spectrum of credulity to arrive at expectation, and you find yourself hard-pressed to imagine these two events—the MRI study and the trial—coexisting without the presence of Dr. Franko Pavlov.

The outer door opens with a muffled creak, and a roughly ovoid shape floats forward. Dr. Pavlov's gloomy, bespectacled face peers around the edge of the pod door first, followed by his body in its characteristic slow shuffle, his shoulders and forehead pulling him forward, hunched like the ghost of Quasimodo. He has left his white lab coat behind in place of a much-used, dark gray blazer but still wears the same khaki slacks (slightly frayed at the bottoms), the same gray and white checkered shirt. He climbs to the stand and alights on the edge of the seat, his slumped torso and probing gaze offering juxtaposed indications of relaxation and vigilance.

"Dr. Pavlov," Hines begins, "would you please introduce yourself to the court?"

"My name is Dr. Franko Pavlov," he answers. "I am the Alexander J. Solomon Professor of Neuroscience at Lauterbur State University and the director of the Lauterbur State Functional Magnetic Resonance Imaging Research Laboratory."

"Would you please summarize your formal education?"

"I earned a Bachelor of Science in Biochemistry from Pomona College in 1983 and a Ph.D. in Neuroscience from the University of California, Los Angeles in 1988. I served as an Assistant Professor of Neuroscience from 1989 through 1996 at the University of California, Los Angeles and as an Associate Professor and Professor of Neuroscience from 1997 through the present at Lauterbur State University. In 2001, I assumed the directorship of the Functional Magnetic Resonance Imaging Research Laboratory at Lauterbur State."

"Would you please describe the subject of your research at the laboratory?"

Pavlov folds his thick hands in his lap and uncoils back in his seat. "Our research is primarily concerned with the brain's unconscious responses to external stimuli," he says. "We know certain situations trigger a chemical reaction in the brain that eventually leads to a decision. Our research attempts to characterize the nature of those initial reactions—how and where they occur in the brain, how quickly, and to what degree the human subject is aware of these responses as they occur. We conduct most of our research using Functional Magnetic Resonance Imaging, or fMRI for short. With fMRI, we can take a picture of a subject's brain as we present the subject with an external stimulus. The fMRI then indicates the areas of the brain that receive the most blood flow, which are the areas most affected by the stimulus and subsequent decision. Our preliminary findings are consistent with the results of numerous previous studies, which demonstrate that most of this activity occurs in an area of the brain called the prefrontal cortex, or PFC.

"fMRI analysis also makes it possible to learn more about the nature of the PFC response in a subject's brain. A 2008 study by Soon, Brass, Heinze and Hayes demonstrated that fMRI can detect a chemical response indicating an individual's decision in the PFC up to ten seconds prior to when that person becomes aware of the decision. A 2010 study by Falk, Berkman, Mann, Harrison and Lieberman demonstrated that the result of such an fMRI brain scan can be used to predict an individual's future decision a week in advance above and beyond that individual's own expectation. Our current research seeks to determine the extent of the predictive power of fMRI brain scans. We perform an fMRI scan of a subject's brain as we present the subject with a scenario and a choice which they will make a week later. We then use the results of this scan in a model to predict each subject's choice before they make it the following week. As of now, our model is 93.1% accurate in it predictions."

"Thank you, Dr. Pavlov," Hines says. "Your Honor, I'd like to tender Dr. Pavlov as an expert in the fields of neuroscience and human behavior."

Pitcock nods. "Mrs. Gray?"

"Dr. Pavlov, you stated that you are currently employed by Lauterbur State

University," says Gray, striding to the witness stand. "Yet your research there is financed by a grant from another organization. Is that correct?"

"Yes, it is."

"And what organization is that?"

"Science Applications Corporation, a private science and technology company," Pavlov replies.

"Isn't Science Applications Corporation a government defense contractor?" Gray asks.

"I believe some of their work is intended for military use, yes," Pavlov says.

"And in what way is your work intended for military use?"

"Objection, Your Honor," Hines says. "What is the relevance of this line of questioning?"

"Your Honor," Gray breaks in, "knowing the source of funds for a body of scientific research is essential to establish any possible bias that could arise."

"The objection is overruled," says Pitcock after brief contemplation. "Mrs. Gray, I will allow you some leeway in this line of questioning, provided you do not stray from the issue of potential bias. Please answer the question, Doctor."

"Our work is not intended for military use," Pavlov says.

"But it could be, right?" Gray asks. "Your research aims to create a model to determine what an individual will choose when presented with a particular scenario. And if that's possible, then you could simply introduce a certain external stimulus to create a desired response in the individual. Isn't that correct?"

"Brain responses in terms of PFC activity are not so simple, Mrs. Gray," says Pavlov.

"Is it possible the United States Department of Defense thinks they might be that simple?" Gray asks. "It sounds like your research might have incredible applications in the field of psychological warfare."

"I am not aware of any attitude the Defense Department holds toward our research," Pavlov answers over Hines' objection.

"But that would be their attitude, wouldn't it? Provided you give them favorable results."

"Objection, Your Honor," Hines repeats calmly. "I believe we are beyond the question of bias."

"Sustained," says Pitcock.

Gray rolls on without pause. Were they a bit closer in age and background, she and Pavlov might be a classic power couple, each getting off on trying to one-up the other. Even now, their combative exchange has not yet flared with sparks of animosity; they thrust and parry almost cheerfully, like longtime fencing partners.

"Dr. Pavlov, have you received offers for future grants from Science Applications Corporation?" Gray asks.

"No," he answers.

"Have you received offers for future grants from any other entities?"

"No."

"So as of this moment, when your current grant expires your research will no longer be funded. Is that correct?"

"Yes. However—"

"Thank you, Dr. Pavlov," Gray interrupts. "No further questions, Your Honor."

"Mrs. Gray, do you have any objection to Dr. Pavlov's testimony?" Pitcock asks.

Shannon Gray has already returned to her table and is bent over her notes. Her assistant flashes a piece of paper under her nose, but she looks up without reading the message and answers "no, Your Honor."

Pitcock sighs. "In that case, this court recognizes Dr. Franko Pavlov as an expert in the fields of neuroscience and human behavior. You may proceed, Mr. Hines."

"Thank you, Your Honor," Hines says as he ambles toward the witness stand. "Dr. Pavlov, you stated that you have developed a model that makes predictions of human behavior based on fMRI scans of the human brain, and that these predictions are over 93% accurate. How do you achieve such a high degree of accuracy?"

"As I said before, an external stimulus prompting a decision produces a significant response in the prefrontal cortex of the human brain," Pavlov answers. "We use fMRI to record such activity. Our model then characterizes this PFC activity based on a variety of factors, such as intensity, duration, and specific location within the PFC, in order to predict the outcome of a subject's decision. Extensive research in this field, by our laboratory as well as the others I have mentioned, indicates that the type of PFC activity generated in response to a scenario serves as a reliable indicator of the nature of the subsequent decision. However, because humans are not consciously aware of this chemical activity in their own brains, it is often possible to predict a subject's choice with greater accuracy than even the subject's own prediction about the future decision."

"And this model you created to characterize PFC activity and predict a subject's choice—do you modify it over time?" Hines asks.

"Yes," answers Pavlov. "We adjust our model after each subject based on the data recorded during the subject's brain response to the stimulus and the accuracy of the prediction. In all its manifestations, our model has been 93.1% accurate up to this point, but its predictive accuracy has actually increased over time as we make modifications."

"Do you expect the accuracy of the model to continue to improve in the future?"

"Yes. If we adjust the model in response to each data set, we do expect its accuracy to increase over time."

Hines settles in next to the witness stand and rests his left hand on the rail, his body open to Pavlov and the jury. "Do you believe it possible to develop a perfect model, one that is 100% accurate in its predictions?" he asks.

"I believe PFC activity in the human brain serves as an extremely accurate gauge of future decisions," Pavlov answers. "Perhaps even 100% accurate. Whether we will ever develop a model that perfectly captures the predictive power of this brain chemistry remains to be seen."

"But you've done pretty well thus far."

"Yes, I believe we have," says Pavlov.

"And because of the accuracy of your model, is it true that you can often predict subjects' future decisions better than they can?"

"Yes."

Hines paces a deliberate loop past the jury box. "So based on your research, it is possible for a decision to arise in a person's brain without that person's conscious awareness. Is that correct?"

"Yes, that is correct," Pavlov answers.

"And the brain response that leads to such a decision could occur a week prior to the actual decision?"

"Yes, the preliminary findings of our current research, as well as in the 2010 study I mentioned earlier, both confirm that hypothesis."

"So it's possible to present a subject with a scenario that causes a particular brain response unbeknownst to the subject, and for that response to generate a decision a week later that differs from the decision the subject predicted he would make. Is that correct?"

"Yes, it is."

Hines waits a moment to let this idea settle, then says "thank you, Dr.

Pavlov. No further questions, Your Honor."

Shannon Gray bursts out of her seat before Hines can even return to his table. "Dr. Pavlov, in the 2010 study you mentioned, fMRI results proved more accurate in predicting sunscreen use than did the subjects themselves," she says. "Is that correct?"

"Yes," Pavlov replies, "Dr. Falk and her colleagues published research in 2010 in which they conducted fMRI scans on subjects' brains while they viewed videos promoting sunscreen use. The researchers found that the fMRI results more accurately predicted subjects' future sunscreen use than did the subjects themselves."

"So some people incorrectly predicted they would use more sunscreen while the fMRI correctly predicted they would use less, whereas others incorrectly predicted they would use less sunscreen while the fMRI correctly predicted they would use more. Is that an accurate assessment of the results?"

"Yes, it is."

"And does your current research generally support these findings?"

"Yes, it does."

Shannon Gray folds her hands in front of her thighs. "Let's take the first case from the sunscreen experiment then—the people who incorrectly predicted they would use more sunscreen while the fMRI correctly predicted they would use less. Can you explain how such a result came about?"

"As I stated earlier, subjects underwent an fMRI scan while they viewed a video promoting sunscreen use," says Pavlov. "In the cases you described, the fMRI results identified some aspect of the subjects' PFC responses that indicated they were not persuaded by the video. Consequently, the model suggested that these subjects would be less likely to use sunscreen in the subsequent week. After the fMRI, the researchers asked the subjects to predict their sunscreen use over the next seven days. In the cases you described, these subjects would have thought themselves more likely to use sunscreen. A week after the fMRI, the subjects returned to the laboratory and rated their sunscreen use over the previous week in comparison to past use. The subjects you described would have reported less sunscreen use, in accordance with the fMRI results but contrary to their own predictions."

"I see. So in other words, some chemical reaction in these subjects' brains suggested they would use less sunscreen. Is that correct?"

"Yes, it is."

"And because these subjects incorrectly predicted increased sunscreen use, this chemical response must have been unconscious. Is that right?"

"Yes, it would appear so."

"So in the course of this experiment, these subjects had an unconscious chemical response in their brains that prompted them to use less sunscreen in the subsequent week, and this response occurred during the informational video that the researchers played as part of the experiment. Am I right?"

"Yes."

"Dr. Pavlov, are you suggesting the researchers were responsible for giving these subjects sunburn?" Gray asks in mock incredulity.

"No, I said nothing about responsibility," Pavlov replies. "I merely said a chemical response leading to the decision to not use sunscreen could have occurred in these subjects' brains without their conscious awareness."

Shannon Gray steps closer to the stand. "But what caused that decision?"

Pavlov rounds forward in his seat like a vulture eyeing a creature it wishes had died hours ago. "It is hard to pinpoint a single cause from the design of the experiment," he says. "The researchers merely demonstrated the presence of a chemical response in certain subjects' brains indicating reduced sunscreen use when these subjects observed the video. However, it is not entirely accurate to say the video itself caused the subjects to use less sunscreen."

"So there could have been other factors that influenced these subjects' decisions?" Gray asks.

"There could have been. However, this study and our current research still show that decisions can arise—"

"Thank you, Doctor," Gray interrupts. "No further questions, Your Honor."

"Mr. Hines?" Pitcock intones.

"Dr. Pavlov, is it possible for an individual to make a decision without conscious awareness of that choice?" Hines asks.

"Yes, it is," Pavlov answers.

"And can that unconscious decision occur a week in advance of the subject's awareness of the choice?"

"Yes."

"How often has your model accurately predicted such an unconscious decision a week in advance?"

"93.1% of the time."

"Thank you, Doctor. No further questions, Your Honor."

"Mrs. Gray?" Pitcock asks, but Gray declines. "The witness is excused," says Pitcock, and Pavlov glides down from the witness box and out the pod door.

•   •   •   •   •

The trial recesses for lunch. Today it's pizza. You eat alone at the jury table and ponder whether the worst foods you can eat just happen to be vegetarian. Pizza. French fries. No meat in candy or the –itos food group. Vegan ice cream probably isn't any healthier than the full dairy version.

John Mann settles down next to you with a slice of three-cheese on a grease-soaked paper plate. "No chess?" he asks.

"No, not today." In fact, you haven't played since the two of you last spoke.

"You know him, don't you? Pavlov?" Mann folds his slice with one hand and takes a huge bite. His hands are made for pizza-eating. Meaty palms to hold even the biggest slice. Nimble, dainty fingers to make the fold. "I was watching you when the defense called him," he says. "I could tell you recognized his name."

"Yeah, I know him," you acknowledge. "I'm a subject in his research."

"Really? What's it about? He never did say."

You explain the whole experiment—the lab, the MRI, the choice—in as much detail as you can recall.

"So you're going to take both boxes then," John says when you've finished.

"I think so."

"Do you think you'll get the million and the thousand?" he asks.

You shrug. "I don't know."

"Probably not. Pavlov's model seems pretty good. What did he say—93%?"

"Yeah. But it doesn't matter. The money is there or it's not. If the model thinks I'll take two boxes and I take one, I get nothing."

"But if you knew the model was 100% accurate, would you still take two boxes?" John asks. "Even if you knew you'd only get $1,000?"

"It's not 100%," you reply. "Pavlov said so himself."

"It could be," he says. "Pavlov said it gets more accurate each time. Maybe he's tweaked it to perfection by now."

"But I don't know that."

"No. But assume for a second that it is 100%. Would you still take two boxes?"

"I guess not," you admit.

"Right. What if it were 99% accurate?"

"I don't know."

"98%?"

"Maybe."

John lifts his plate off the table and weighs the remainder of his pizza in one hand. "So you *are* assuming the model isn't 100% accurate. Maybe not even 98 or 99%. Because if it were, you'd take one box and the million dollars. But you're okay with 93%?"

"But I don't know what the model predicted. And since it did predict already, I may as well take two boxes."

"Assuming the model isn't perfect."

"Yeah, I guess so."

John shoves the back third of his slice into his mouth. "Let me ask you this," he says, tucking the partially gnawed pizza into his cheek, "do you think you can change your mind now?"

"What do you mean?"

"Well, if Pavlov's model is as accurate as he claims, then you've already decided, because the model has already predicted what you'll do. And if it's perfectly accurate, you can't change your mind now. What you choose Friday only confirms what was already determined last week. So if you take two boxes, whether you think you planned it from the beginning or you think you changed your mind at the last second, in all likelihood your brain said 'two' when you did the MRI last week."

"You're making it sound backward," you say. "Of course I can change my mind. What I choose now doesn't affect what Pavlov put in the box last week."

John gulps down his mouthful and chases it with a swig of Coke from a plastic Dixie cup. "You only think that because we experience time as moving in one direction. Our lives would get very confusing if we couldn't tell the past from the future. But time is just another dimension, like space. Things move forward and backward in space and they can move forward and backward in time. There's no scientific law that says what you choose this Friday can't affect what Pavlov put in the box last week."

"Then why haven't we discovered time travel?" you ask. "Why don't we experience time in reverse more often? If you spilled your drink, it wouldn't leap up off the floor and back into your cup again."

"That's because entropy, or disorder, tends to increase with time," John says. "Spilling my Coke creates a more disordered state, so events in the universe appear to move in that direction. And this ordering of events allows us to make sense of them so that you don't remember the future, when I spill Coke on the floor, only the past, when it's still in my cup on the table. But in regards to

Pavlov's experiment, you have to ask which is a more ordered state: your brain chemistry last week or your brain chemistry this Friday?"

"You mean regarding my decision to take one or two boxes?" you ask. "I would think my brain gets more ordered as I get closer to a decision. If my decision is based on some stimulus, then at the time of the stimulus the decision is in its infancy. Different impulses exist, different options get weighed. But as I near the decision, that chaos starts to coalesce into a single purpose."

"I agree. So based on that reasoning, your brain will be more ordered on Friday when you make your choice than it was when you first went in for the MRI. Given the principle of entropy, time should run backward from Friday to last week. Your choice on Friday would influence your brain state at the time of the MRI."

"But it's possible to decrease entropy," you say. "If I build a table out of scraps of wood, I create a more ordered condition, but I don't go back in time to do so."

"You're right," John says. "When you finish the table, the wood is in a more ordered state than when you started. But the work to build the table produces heat energy, which is disordered. So even putting the wood in a more ordered state increases total entropy because of that release of heat. Making a decision is a similar process, in that brain activity also produces heat energy."

"So if the entropy of my brain state last week plus the entropy of the heat required to reach that state is greater than the entropy of my brain state plus heat on Friday, then time should move backward from Friday to last week."

"Right." John makes a show of swirling the brown liquid in his plastic cup like it's a freshly poured Cab before he polishes it off in one swig. "And that," he says, "is the million dollar question. Pun intended."

Your head hurts. You close your eyes and grind the heels of your hands against your eyelids, then drag one palm down your face. "But you also said we experience time as moving forward. Meaning I don't remember the future."

"True."

"And as time moves forward, I have new experiences. I create more memories. So there's more data."

"All right, ladies and gentlemen," the bailiff announces from the door leading back to the pod, "you're on again."

You stand up but continue talking. "More information for my brain to process. Therefore, more brain activity and more heat energy."

John folds his empty plate and cup together. "Yes," he says, "but how much more?"

The bailiff clears his throat.

"I don't know," you say. "It might be—"

The bailiff repeats the noise, louder and more obvious this time. "Excuse me, jurors."

"Better go," John tells you. "Hold that thought." He stands up and pushes in his chair. "In the meantime, good luck on Friday."

●　　　●　　　●　　　●　　　●

By the time you return from lunch, the pod feels as hot as an incubator in comparison to the jury room. Sweat droplets hover on the foreheads of Pitcock, Hines and Solon. The pit stains on the blue shirt of the man to your right could irrigate the Sahara. Little gullies stream down the nape of the woman in front of you. Shannon Gray alone remains undampened, looking as fresh and prim on the warmest day of the year as you imagine she would in the dead of January.

An electricity of Miller-Urey proportions tingles in the air as Dr. David Solon ascends to the witness box. His face looks more drawn than you remember, not wrinkled, but pinched near his ears and hairline like a polymer mask stretched to its limits. Were it not for the circumstances and the courtroom surroundings, it would be easy to imagine him settling in behind a podium in a university lecture hall after a long night of grading midterms.

"Dr. Solon," Hines begins, "would you please introduce yourself to the members of the jury?"

"My name is Dr. David Solon," he says. "I am currently a Professor of Mathematics at Harvey Tech University."

"Would you please summarize your formal education and employment history?"

"I received a Bachelor of Science in Mathematics from the University of California, Berkeley in 1985 and a Ph.D. in Mathematics from the University of Chicago in 1990. I served as an Assistant Professor of Mathematics from 1991 through 1995 at the University of Chicago, and from 1996 through the present as Associate Professor and then Professor of Mathematics at Harvey Tech University."

"And by now I think everyone here knows of your wife, Julia. How long were you married?" Hines asks.

"We met in college in 1984 and married in 1988. We would have celebrated our twenty-third anniversary last October," Solon answers.

"Were you ever divorced or separated?"

"No."

"Do you have any children?"

"No, we never had any."

"Prior to this trial, had you ever been accused of a crime in any court of law?"

"I was once stopped for speeding." A titter circulates through the jury box, and Hines allows himself a brief smile.

"Now on the night of April 26, 2011, an incident occurred at your home which has been discussed previously in this trial," Hines continues. "Would you please describe what happened that night?"

Dr. Solon stares hollow-eyed through the wall behind the jury box and speaks in a monotone. "Julia and I went to bed around 11:00 on April 25," he says. "At approximately 3:15 the next morning, I was awakened by some noise that seemed to come from the first floor of our house. Julia's side of the bed was empty. I became suspicious and retrieved my handgun from the locked safe in our closet and went to investigate. As I came downstairs, I heard a scream and gunshots, and I ran down the rest of the way. When I got to the bottom, I saw Julia lying motionless on the floor in the middle of the room. A man stood over her, and as I entered the room he ran past me and out the front door of the house. I chased him out the door and fired two shots at him as he fled. Neither of them seemed to hit him and he escaped down the street."

"What did you do then?" Hines asks.

"I returned to the house and called 911 right away. But I could tell Julia was already… gone."

Hines paces a diagonal from his table toward Judge Pitcock, looking down at his feet as though unable to meet Solon's gaze. "And when the police arrived in response to your call, you managed to provide a description of Julia's killer for a composite sketch," he says. "How were you able to identify this man?"

"He looked at me when I came into the living room, and I saw his face," Dr. Solon replies. "I got another look as ran past me on his way toward the door."

"Dr. Solon, would you now tell the jury what happened to you on the evening of May 3?" Hines asks.

"I was walking down Jackson Avenue when I saw a man with his back to me holding a gun to a woman in an alley off the street to my left," Solon answers. "He was shouting something at her, although I couldn't make out his words. I didn't see anyone around who could help so I began to move toward them. When I was about twenty feet from the assailant, I began to run in his direction and I managed to knock him to the ground before he could turn toward me. He dropped his gun when I hit him, and I picked it up before he could retrieve it. The woman fled down the alley. I stood over the man, pointed the gun at him and yelled back to the woman to call the police. Then he rolled over, and I saw his face. It was the man who shot Julia. I saw his face and I remembered him standing over Julia in our living room that night. And I shot him."

Were Dr. Solon to tear up at all, you never could tell. Sweat runs down his face, and he ignores it unselfconsciously, answering each question simply and in his usual steady voice, save for the occasional pause as he describes the two deaths.

"Dr. Solon, on the night of April 26, why did you fire your gun at Damon Belliard?" Hines asks.

"Because he had just murdered my wife," Solon answers matter-of-factly, perhaps with just a hint of fatigue.

"Did you think about it before you fired?" Hines asks.

"No. I heard the gunshots and saw him standing over Julia's body. He ran out the door, and I fired."

"And on May 3, why did you shoot Damon Belliard?"

Solon does not hesitate. "He murdered my wife. When he turned his face to me I saw the man who killed Julia. I reacted and shot him."

"You didn't think twice about it then?"

"No."

"Thank you, Dr. Solon. No further questions, Your Honor."

Pitcock turns grimly to Shannon Gray. "Mrs. Gray?"

Gray steps around her table without hurry and stalks to the middle of the room to face Dr. Solon on the witness stand.

"Dr. Solon, do you freely admit to shooting Damon Belliard on the evening of May 3?" she asks.

"Yes, I do," he answers, strangely relaxed in his concession of the truth.

"When you fired at Mr. Belliard as he fled your home on April 26, did you intend to kill him?"

"I intended to shoot him."

"With the intention of killing him?"

"In the time I made the decision to shoot Mr. Belliard, I decided only to shoot him, Mrs. Gray."

"Dr. Solon, you testified that you fired twice at Mr. Belliard on April 26. Did you pursue him after those shots missed?"

"No, I did not."

"What did you expect to happen to Mr. Belliard after that night?"

"I imagined the police would arrest him and charge him with murder. I did not anticipate seeing him again until he appeared in court."

"And when you imagined seeing Mr. Belliard in court, did you also imagine shooting him?"

"No."

"So after the incident on April 26 when you actually shot at Mr. Belliard, you no longer imagined shooting him. Is that correct?"

"Under the circumstances I expected to encounter Mr. Belliard—"

"Please answer the question, Doctor."

Solon reclines in his seat, unfazed by Shannon Gray's attempts to steer his answers. "When I imagined encountering Mr. Belliard in court, I did not expect to shoot him there," he says.

"Did you expect to encounter Mr. Belliard outside of a courtroom?" Gray asks.

"No."

"So between April 26 and May 3, when you imagined your next encounter with Damon Belliard, did you expect to shoot him at that encounter?"

"No, I did not."

"But you did shoot him on May 3?"

"Yes."

"And you intended to shoot him on May 3?"

"Yes, I did."

"Did you intend to kill him?"

"I did not take the time to form any intention about his fate," Solon says. "I simply—"

"Please answer the question, Dr. Solon," Gray interrupts. "Did you intend to kill Damon Belliard?"

"I'm sorry, Mrs. Gray, but I cannot say for certain what I intended to happen to Mr. Belliard in the few seconds I had to act."

"But you are aware it is possible for a person to die of a gunshot wound?"

"Yes."

"The Medical Examiner recovered the fatal bullet from Mr. Belliard's brain," Gray says. "So you shot Mr. Belliard in the head?"

"Yes," Solon answers.

"Were you aiming for his head?"

"Yes."

Gray trails her fingers across the edge of the court clerk's table as she circles closer to Dr. Solon on the stand. There is a strange dynamic of utter imperviousness on both sides of their exchange. Gray jabs and swings and crashes with controlled purpose; Solon answers steadfast and unmoved, sweating from the heat of the pod but otherwise entirely unaffected, having already been shaped and hardened in the forge of the greatest trial he will ever have to endure. He does not falter once, no matter how incisive the question, and Gray is never satisfied, but probes relentlessly at his stalwart defenses. There are no decisive points; neither party gets caught tongue-tied or ensnared by half-truth or exaggeration, and they glance past one another like two electrons on tangential courses, each impelled forward by the same laws of physics and veracity.

"Dr. Solon, based on evidence found in the alley on May 3 as well as previous eyewitness testimony, it appears you fired just one shot at Mr. Belliard," Gray says. "Is that your recollection?"

"Yes," Solon answers.

"You didn't shoot him more than once?"

"No."

"Why not?"

"Because he was dead after the first shot."

"How much time would you say elapsed from the moment you recognized Damon Belliard to the moment your shot struck him?" Gray asks.

"I don't know," Solon answers. "Less than a few seconds, I would imagine."

"So you began with no intention of shooting anyone, let alone Damon Belliard, and then in less than a few seconds you recognized Mr. Belliard, flew into a rage at the thought of your wife's death, shot him and pronounced him dead. Dr. Solon, schizophrenics don't have mood swings that erratic."

"Objection, Your Honor," says Hines. "Badgering the witness."

"Sustained," Pitcock agrees.

"Dr. Solon," Gray says, "are you really claiming that you acted rationally to apprehend a criminal, then within a few seconds lost all control of yourself and shot him, and then returned to your senses to examine him and conclude he was dead?"

"I shot Mr. Belliard one time," Solon reiterates. "I do not know why I should have shot him more than that."

Gray plants herself in front of the stand. "Did you recognize Mr. Belliard before you entered the alley that day?" she asks

"No, I did not," Solon replies.

"You testified that you saw a man with his back to you holding a gun to a woman in the alley. Is that correct?"

"Yes."

"And you were sure this man was holding a gun?"

"Yes."

"You heard Mrs. Alethea testify that Mr. Belliard was holding his gun against his body, like this, when he threatened her." Gray tucks her right hand into her stomach, index finger aimed at Dr. Solon, then turns her back to him and pivots to face the jury. "Dr. Solon, can you see my right hand?" she asks.

"No, I cannot."

"Can you see my face?"

"No."

"Thank you, Dr. Solon," Gray says. "No further questions, Your Honor."

"Mr. Hines?" Pitcock asks.

"Dr. Solon, you stated that between your encounters with Mr. Belliard on April 26 and May 3, you only expected to see him during his trial for your wife's murder," Hines says, standing behind his table. "Is that correct?"

"Yes," Solon answers.

"And when you imagined seeing Mr. Belliard in court, did you intend to shoot him there?"

"No."

"Did you expect to encounter Damon Belliard in an alley holding up a woman at gunpoint?"

"No."

"Did you give any consideration as to what you might do if you encountered him in such a situation?"

"No, I did not."

"On May 3, did you recognize Mr. Belliard prior to entering the alley?"

"No."

"Could you see he was holding a gun?"

"Yes."

Hines moves around his table, jacket swept back, hands tucked in his pockets. "According to the police reports, forensic analysis and your previous testimony, you fired two shots after Damon Belliard on April 26," he says. "Is that accurate?"

"Yes, it is."

"You didn't empty the magazine?"

"No."

"And why not?"

"Because after two shots the killer was out of range."

"And why didn't you chase after Mr. Belliard that night?"

"Because I was more concerned about Julia. I returned to the house immediately once I realized he had escaped."

"Thank you, Dr. Solon. No further questions, Your Honor."

Shannon Gray declines to recross, and Judge Pitcock confirms Hines has exhausted his witnesses and Gray has no rebuttals.

It's a relief to everyone when he announces "this court will recess until 9:00 tomorrow morning, at which time Mrs. Gray and Mr. Hines will present their closing arguments. This court is now adjourned."

The rap of his gavel chokes in the humid pod as Pitcock scrambles down from his seat with surprising agility.

Continue on page 154.

It is just after two when you leave the courthouse, and despite the temperature, it feels good to be outside. You spot a park across from the courthouse and amble towards it.

The real heat hits you soon enough. It's in the low mid-90s, sunny, humid and breezeless, and your court clothes don't help. But you're already sweating, and the thought of an afternoon outside away from work sounds too good to pass up, so you continue into the park. A small audience has gathered around a man who stands above them on the edge of a fountain. You can hear his voice carry out across the park, powerful enough to reach you without yelling.

"Mankind has fallen into a state of sin," he calls. "There is no hope for redemption."

The crowd around him numbers about fifteen strong, their degree of credulity apparent by the tilt of their jaws—the ardent faithful with rapt, upturned gazes, the transient passers-by with bowed heads and wandering eyes.

"But God, by His inscrutable mercy, has predestined some of us for eternal life," he continues.

He looks so normal. Short, neat, blond hair, pale skin that has not reddened even under the smoldering sun. He wears crisp khaki slacks and a navy blazer over a light beige sweater vest and white collared shirt, as though he just walked off the pages of the seminary issue of *GQ*. Yet fire and brimstone still burn in his flinty eyes.

"Man exists for the sake of God," he says. "Only in accordance with His unknowable will shall some men be granted mercy and life everlasting. But the great majority of mankind, rooted in sin, will receive no more than they deserve: eternal death."

The believers bob their heads, jaws set in silent affirmation, and you have a vague recollection of a subsection on Calvinism in a high school history book. A big woman with swaying dreadlocks and a gospel choir voice responds in a rhythmic, talk-singing cadence. "Tell us, brother, how we may be saved, how we may know Je-sus."

The preacher's voice cuts like an icicle falling from a skyscraper. "You cannot save yourself. The elect have been chosen since before the dawn of the world. The will of God is not subject to the acts of man."

The woman falls into stunned silence, having expected a very different answer.

"God alone among the beings of the cosmos is free," the preacher continues. "His will is not for us to know. Man exists merely for the glory of God. His calling is to do God's work on Earth."

"What does that mean?" a grizzled man in tattered and dirty clothes pipes up. "How are we to live then?"

"God has organized and ordered the entire universe and predestined for each man and woman a role in mortal life," the preacher answers. "He sets the game board and designates a duty for each piece. Be it doctor, janitor, father or son, man's duty is to fulfill that role to the best of his ability, in a continual struggle to glorify his Maker with every deed."

"But you're saying even if I do all that, I still may not go to heaven," the other man yells back.

"The elect have already been chosen," the preacher says without pity. "A man's actions do not influence God's decisions."

You generally ignore sidewalk preachers. But perhaps hearing arguments all day in court has made you a bit feisty.

"So why should I do good?" you yell out.

The preacher glares at you. "God created man in his image, and man exists for the sake of God. It is his duty to glorify his Creator in all his worldly actions. The son does not live to disgrace the father."

"But according to you, God created most of us to glorify Him at every waking moment just to end up in eternal hell because that's what he predestined for us," you call back.

"That's right!" the bedraggled man yells. "Why should I try to live a moral life if I can't get into heaven?"

Whispers of assent spread through the crowd. A few believers flash contemptuous frowns in your direction.

"God has chosen a path for all of us," the preacher answers. "Those chosen for life will feel God's grace working through them. For those who do not, doubt is a sign of the devil's temptation and a lack of faith."

"Well, call me a doubter then," shouts your comrade in religious sanity. "I try to do right by God, but there are days where I don't feel Him. So according to you, I'm going to hell and I can't do a thing about it. So why the hell should I glorify this God?"

"You may do as you wish. God will allow the unredeemed to fall into temptation and sin."

It is both astonishing and impressive to watch someone so dead set in his beliefs that he can just plow ahead through all adversity and come out the other side without the slightest blemish, like that old black and white video of a fat man taking a cannonball to the stomach, picking himself up, dusting himself off and just shrugging off the impact.

"But that's not true," you reply. "You said our fates have already been predetermined. If I'm one of the damned, then I'm headed for hell no matter what. If I'm one of the elect, then I won't be tempted into sin. But don't pretend now that I get to choose. You can't have it both ways."

"Amen!" sings out the big woman, her dreadlocks swaying with sanctimonious indignation.

"Those who do not live to glorify God in their lives are surely destined for hell," the preacher reiterates.

"That's fine," you say. "But we can't do anything about it now. Our fates have already been chosen."

You decide you've had all you can handle for one afternoon. It was entertaining enough to argue with this man for a while, but you can tell you will get no further. You walk away from the crowd. Several people follow. The believers remain, oblivious, enraptured by the preacher, who continues on about glorifying God.

You head back toward the courthouse, out of the park. Your phone rings. You wipe a thick bead of sweat off your cheek as you bring it to your ear.

"Help! Somebody help!" a woman screams from behind you.

You abort the call and turn back to the throng that drifts away from the speaker still perched on his fountain soapbox.

"Stop! Thief!" she screams again, a heavyset, older woman struggling with a slim man in ragged clothing. An ugly scar descends from the corner of his right eye.

The assailant finally rips the woman's purse away, but another man bolts from the crowd, grabs him by the arm before he can run and spins him about. The thief whips the purse in a vicious arc as his body is pulled around. It catches the other man across the face, and the thief follows with a devastating uppercut to his chin. He falls to the ground, and his head thwacks limply into the concrete. The thief takes off across the park and out of sight.

"Aaaiiieee!" screams the victimized woman, wringing her hands as she turns between the fleeing bandit and her fallen hero. "Oh, help him, help him, *por favor*," she cries in broken Spanglish. "*Por favor*, someone—" And then her knees buckle and she slumps to the ground as the heat and her weight and the excitement prove too much for her frail heart.

Two people down. The rest of the crowd rushes in. Someone starts working on the man right away. Somehow he's not bleeding, though by the looks of things he doesn't seem to be breathing either.

"Someone call 911!" a man yells.

"I'll do it!" A woman whips out her phone.

The woman kneeling over the fallen man has started CPR. She's pinched his nose shut and attempts a few rescue breaths. She's young and nervous—looks like she just learned this at a corporate class—and she appears a bit squeamish about making lip-to-lip contact. The breaths don't seem to be going in; the man's chest remains still. She tucks her light brown hair behind one ear with a trembling hand and begins compressions—too fast and too low on the man's torso. If only he were choking. No one has attended to the unconscious woman.

You know CPR. You start for the woman, but as you get closer you realize how big she really is. And old. Her yellow and green flower patterned dress could provide enough fabric to clothe the entire von Trapp litter. Her wrinkled brown legs lie splayed on the ground, and you can see a flash of some serious white granny panties as a sluggish breeze teases up her dress.

You look back to the would-be hero and the girl botching his rescue. He is fairly young. Slim. His deep chocolate skin glistens in the heat, and he looks like he might spring back to life at any moment. The rescuee, not so much.

"Does anybody else know CPR?" you yell. Stone-blank faces turn in your direction. No one answers. No one raises a hand.

"The paramedics are on the way," the 911 lady announces.

Could be ten, fifteen minutes. Neither victim has that long if their hearts don't start beating. But you can only help one of them. Does the old woman even have a chance? Who knows how many lives her fragile heart has already spent? Perhaps there's no averting her end. The man looks far likelier to survive. And maybe enough of the girl's frantic volley will connect. You might be able to talk her through it while you help the woman. But you better decide fast.

If you choose to attempt CPR on the old woman, turn to page 136.
If you choose to attempt CPR on the young man, turn to 139.

You grab a man out of the crowd. "Go to the courthouse," you say. "They must have a defibrillator. Bring the first one you find and tell someone to bring another."

You rush to the old woman and kneel at her side. She's definitely not breathing. You shake her, scream "hey! Wake up!" Nothing. You take one more look at her crinkly black-dyed hair and leathery face, wipe her lips and dive in for a tight seal and a rescue breath. You see her chest rise out of the corner of your eye. You inhale and call over to the other would-be savior, "Hey! Miss!"

No response. You give another breath and start pumping out the beat to "Another One Bites the Dust" on the woman's chest. Apparently, the American Heart Association deemed "Stayin' Alive" too slow and too optimistic.

"Hey!" you yell. "Higher. On his chest. Like this."

The brown-haired woman looks up at you. Her eyeliner drips down her cheeks. "What?"

"Your compressions are too low," you say. "And too fast."

"I took a class," she yells back.

You don't have time to roll your eyes. You finish thirty compressions and return to breaths. "Like this," you call. "Seal his mouth."

You can't tell if she took your advice. You finish breaths and return to compressions. You can hear sirens in the distance. Thirty compressions. Two breaths. 30-2-30-2. Where is that defibrillator? Your triceps start to burn. You redouble your efforts and feel one of the woman's ribs crack under your palm. You keep going. 30-2-30-2.

And then as you start a new round of compressions, the woman coughs and moans, and a garbled Spanish whisper spills from her lips. You run over to the group gathered around the still-unconscious man and grab the big dreadlocked woman from the preacher's audience.

"Get her some water," you tell her, as you point back at your slowly stirring patient. "You, watch her," you say to the man next to her. "Get her in the shade if she can move."

You kneel next to the other victim, opposite the woman still working on him. She is exhausted. She sits back on her heels and slaps at the bottom of his ribcage. "I've got it," you say. "I'll start with breaths." The girl nods without even seeing you, just relieved to be done.

The sirens are close now. You start rescue breaths on the second victim. Almost ten minutes must have passed since he hit the ground. Not good. Hurried footsteps surround you. Men and women in starched, white collared shirts and navy slacks. Droplets of perspiration begin to pool at the rims of their latex gloves as they lift his shirt and stick the defibrillator electrodes to his chest.

Another group of paramedics surrounds the older woman and struggles to slide her onto a gurney.

"Clear!" yells the paramedic next to you.

The man's spine arches off the ground and slumps back to earth with a wet thud. The EMTs charge the defibrillator again.

"Clear!" Thump. "Clear!" Thump. "Clear!" It's over.

Your phone buzzes. Eve again. Thirty minutes have passed since her first call.

"What the hell was that? You screening your calls or something?" she asks.

"Someone died," you tell her.

"What? Who?"

"A guy in the park by the courthouse."

"Are you okay? What happened?"

"I'm fine." You tell her about the robbery and the knockout punch and the other woman's frantic attempts to save his life.

"I'm so sorry," Eve says. "You did everything you could. You're a hero."

"I could have helped him."

"No, you couldn't. The woman would've died if you hadn't done something. It was one or the other. You had to choose and you saved one of them."

The crowd wavers around the paramedics and the two victims, unsure of what to do next. Sweat pours down your face and beads on your forearms.

"Do you want me to come pick you up or something?" Eve asks.

"No, I'll be fine."

"Okay. Listen, I was planning to go over to Pavlov's lab to do the MRI. Do you want to join me?"

"Now?"

"Yeah. I looked online, and it's open 'til 5:00."

"You don't need me to go with you," you say. "You'll just be lying in a tube for 20 minutes."

"I know," Eve replies. "I thought you might want to come. Maybe we can find out more about this experiment before you have to choose. I might catch some important detail now that I know what to expect."

If you decide to go with Eve to the Lauterbur State University Functional Magnetic Resonance Imaging Research Laboratory, turn to page 142.

If you decide to return home, turn to page 149.

You grab the nearest man from the crowd and say "Go to the courthouse and get a defibrillator. Bring the first one you find and tell someone to bring another."

You push through the throng of spectators and kneel on the ground next to the lifeless man, opposite his would-be savior who is still jackhammering his liver.

"I've got it," you say softly.

She glowers at you and continues whaling away as loose strands of wheat-colored hair bounce around her face. "I'm fine," she says.

"I know," you tell her. "But we'll last longer if we take turns. I'll start with breaths. Go check on her." You cock your head in the direction of the older woman.

The red heat drains away from her face to leave a sickly pallor, and her tightened jaw goes slack. She nods dumbly, sits back on her heels and yanks her hands away from her patient's body as though his condition had just become contagious. You seal the man's nose and mouth and watch his chest rise from the corner of your eye. One more breath and then on to compressions. The CPR novitiate crouches next to the fallen older woman and hesitantly reaches out to lay her hands on the woman's torso.

"You can start working on her," you call as you begin compressions on the man.

She eases into position while you pump out thirty chest compressions to the beat of Queen's "Another One Bites the Dust" (great song choice, American Heart Association), return for two rescue breaths and then resume compressions. Your partner's tired already. Her compressions are slowing, and she sits back from the old woman and makes her arms do the work instead of using her body weight. She wipes sweat from her face and smears eyeliner across her cheeks, rubs at her knees scraped raw by the hard pavement. You keep working. You can't do anything for the old woman now besides reviving this guy so you can take over her care. Sirens blare in the distance.

You count out thirty compressions and two breaths over and over and over again. The crowd around you, though still quiet, begins to stir. You can feel the hot wind now as the onlookers take a small step back to distance themselves just far enough from the impending tragedy without appearing callous. Where is that defibrillator?

You duck down for the second breath in the series and the guy twitches and coughs spittle into your mouth. Nice. You pull away, and a soft groan escapes his lips and then more chest-wracking coughs. His eyelids flutter open.

"Fuck," he says.

You stand to check on the other woman as the sirens shriek all around you and the EMTs' footsteps pound the pavement. Two of them kneel next to the man you just revived while the rest strip away the woman's dress and begin to apply the defibrillator electrodes. You watch from beside the first victim, as hands pat you on the back and you hear congratulations spoken from somewhere far away.

"Clear!"

The shout breaks through the heat and your lightheaded exhaustion, and the woman's body twitches like a desperate beached whale. You figure she's got no chance, not after being out so long, but on the second shock, she screams some unidentifiable Spanish curse that slips into a long moan. She's alive. They're both alive. The crowd around you begins to clap and a few sobered cheers ring out.

Your phone buzzes in your pocket. Eve's calling again, apparently for the third time since you hung up on her.

"What's going on?" she asks when you finally answer.

"Sorry." You explain the events of the afternoon.

"Oh my God," she says. "Are you okay?"

"Yeah, I'm fine," you answer. "I think everyone's okay."

"Good. Hey, you're a hero."

"No, I just know CPR. I still can't believe the old woman made it."

"Yeah, that's amazing. I would have thought she had no chance."

"That's kinda why I went for the guy first."

"Well, it sounds like you made the right choice. He might not have made it otherwise. Great job."

"Thanks."

"You're welcome. Anyway, I called to let you know I'm headed over to Pavlov's lab. I want to try to get in on his experiment."

"You're going now?"

"Yes. I checked Lauterbur State's website, and the lab is open until five. I think I've got time to do the MRI as long as Pavlov doesn't have someone else scheduled. Do you want to come?"

"You mean just to hang out in the waiting room while you do the MRI?"

"Yeah, I guess so. Call it moral support if you want. Or maybe the two of us can catch some detail you missed the first time. At the very least, I could tell you the model's latest success rate."

You take a moment to consider. Will any more information help at this point? Or are you better off sticking with your first instinct?

If you decide to go with Eve to the Lauterbur State University Functional Magnetic Resonance Imaging Research Laboratory, turn to page 142.

If you decide to return home, turn to page 149.

"All right, let's go," you say.

"Great!" Eve cheers. "Meet you at the lab?"

"Yeah, I'll be there in about thirty minutes."

Eve's car is one of four on the vast blacktop lot when you arrive. The laboratory sits shrouded by the stadium and the woods like a collection of silt on the banks of a great asphalt sea. Eve climbs out to greet you and leads you inside, as though this were your first visit and not hers. Gloria guards her post at the end of the long hallway, her eyes still fixed on her computer screen. Eve marches straight to her desk while you trail behind her.

"Can I help you?" Gloria asks, with a note of gatekeeper condescension.

"I'm here for Dr. Pavlov's study," Eve announces. "I'd like to participate in his MRI research."

"I'm sorry," Gloria says. "The study is closed."

"What do you mean 'closed?'" Eve asks. "I picked up a request for volunteers just the other day."

The rear door of the waiting room opens, and a college-aged brunette emerges, evidently surprised to see the room occupied. Dr. Pavlov enters after her.

"We stopped taking volunteers this morning," Gloria tells Eve.

"Really?" Eve asks. "What about her?" She points at the other subject. The girl shuffles to a stop, unsure if she needs to answer for her presence here. She is pale and freckled behind her clunky, plastic-framed glasses, and she looks as though the last thing she wants to do is get caught up in this debate.

"She returned this afternoon for the second part of the experiment," Gloria says. "We are no longer accepting new volunteers."

The subject flashes a sheepish half-smile, folds a slip of paper that looks very much like a check and stuffs it into the pocket of her jeans. Pavlov steps forward and touches his right hand to her shoulder, and she whirls to face him with relief.

"Miss Smith, thank you for your time," he says as he shakes her hand.

The girl mutters, "You're welcome," then brushes past you and Eve and out the door.

"I'm sorry, ma'am," Pavlov addresses Eve, "but I am afraid Gloria is correct. We have closed the study to new subjects."

"I don't understand," you say. "What happened?"

Pavlov glances at Gloria, who has resumed typing, and you now find it disconcerting to not have his steady gaze penetrate yours while he speaks. "Certain circumstances have made it impossible for us to accommodate additional volunteers," he answers.

"Not even one?" Eve asks. "What if I agree to forgo compensation?"

"Unfortunately, such a decision could bias your result in comparison to the data of the other subjects," Pavlov replies. "I appreciate your interest in our research, but it is not possible for you to participate at this time." He stands in his habitual hunched posture with hands clasped behind his back, and you cannot help but picture a handcuffed dissident being shoved into a police car.

You want to ask him more, but Eve offers a quick "thank you" and powerwalks to the exit, grabbing you by the arm as she goes. You backpedal a few steps as Pavlov follows you to the door. You get the impression he wants you to stay, wants Eve to do the MRI, but someone or something has forced him to bring his research to a premature end. Then Eve's pace spins you around and out of your daze, and you find yourself half-dragged back down the hallway and out into the early evening heat.

Across the parking lot, the other woman pulls open the door of her car.

"Wait!" Eve yells again. "Miss! Can we talk to you for a second?"

The woman looks back over her open door, one foot already in the car. She hesitates for a moment, then glances around the empty lot and begins to lower herself into the driver's seat. "I'm sorry," she calls weakly. "I have to go." She closes the door.

"Wait!" Eve yells and breaks into a sprint toward the car. "I just want to ask about the experiment!"

You don't follow Eve. Your thoughts linger on Pavlov. Through the woman's windshield, her faltering face turns to you, then back to Eve. You can't see her eyes through the double layer of car window and glasses, but her fingers clench the top of the steering wheel and her eyebrows arch high above her lenses. She hits the gas and peels away. Eve slows to a stop in her wake.

"I just wanted to know what she picked," Eve says, still staring out to the street as you join her. "And what she got."

"I know," you say. "I don't think she wanted to tell us."

Eve swings around to face you. "Do you think she got the million dollars? Or even the extra thousand on top of that?"

"Maybe," you say. "Maybe she was afraid we'd try to rob her. That's a lot of money."

"Yeah. But now we'll never know for sure."

"What about Pavlov?" you ask. "Do you really think the experiment is over?"

"That's what they said," Eve answers. "Or maybe they just recognized you and thought you had let me in on some secret. But I bet he's out of money."

"It wouldn't surprise me," you say. "This whole experiment has always felt kind of unbelievable."

You look back over your shoulder to make sure the lab is still there, that it hasn't dissolved in the shadow of the football stadium or the woods, hasn't gone the way of so many other eccentricities of this world, engulfed by the mainstream or abandoned and forgotten to nature. You half-expect to see Pavlov at the door, waiting for the two of you, silently begging you to return. Although you can't imagine him begging.

"You know, he testified today," you say. "Pavlov. For the defense, as an expert in brain chemistry. He said his research is financed by some private company that deals with DOD."

"Wow," Eve says. "So he's doing government research? That would make sense. That or some crazy billionaire funding him. What else?"

"Solon testified too. It seems like the defense wanted to show Solon could have had some unconscious urge to kill Belliard that would absolve him of guilt for murder."

"And what do you think?"

If you think David Solon is guilty of murder, turn to page 145.
If you think David Solon is not guilty of murder, turn to page 147.

"I don't buy it," you say. "I think he's guilty."

"What?" Eve exclaims. "Even after his and Pavlov's testimonies?"

"Yes," you answer. "He killed Damon Belliard. He meant to kill Damon Belliard. We know that much for certain, and I can't see any way around it."

"Even though Belliard killed his wife? You don't think that's sufficient provocation?"

"I do. But it was sufficient provocation on the night of her murder, not one week later."

"You don't think Solon could have had an unconscious desire to kill Belliard a week after his wife's murder?" Eve asks. That's what Pavlov's experiment shows. It's why you want to take one box. So make up your mind. Can your brain have unconscious intentions or not?"

"I don't know what happened in Solon's head in the week after his wife's murder," you say. "But he killed Damon Belliard. He has to be responsible for that."

"You think Solon's the bad guy in all this?"

"I think he shouldn't have killed Belliard. I think that action carries consequences."

"I don't believe you." Eve rips open her car door. "Do you really think Dr. Solon looked at Belliard, consciously thought 'this guy murdered my wife; I'm going to kill him, even though I know I shouldn't,' and then shot him? If he reacted and shot at Belliard the night of his wife's murder, killing Belliard a week later could have been just as much of a reaction. Instead, you want to send a widower to prison for the rest of his life for avenging his wife's murder."

"It's not the rest of his life," you protest. Eve gets into her car. "Eve!"

"I'll talk to you tomorrow," she mutters and slams the door.

"It's second-degree murder," you yell as she fires the engine and pulls away. "It's not a life sentence."

But she's gone, and your words die in the empty lot. The simmering asphalt begins to toast the soles of your feet through your shoes. You look back at the lab as you slide into your car. It's still there; Pavlov's still there, but for how long?

You wonder if he knew the circumstances of Solon's case when he testified. There must be some reason he was there. Something about his research clearly matters to him, more so than biochemical reactions and data points and a paper in some neuroscience journal. You try to imagine how long he's been at it, how many years spent planning the experiment, scrounging up the funds to pay his subjects seven figures for thirty minutes of their time. A person doesn't design an experiment like his without some dogged obsession.

You shake these thoughts from your head and start the car as a sudden exhaustion settles upon your shoulders. Outside, the wind picks up and sweeps dry earth out of the woodland and across the front of the lab, and the little building flickers like a snowy picture on an old TV. Then the breeze dies, the dust drifts to the ground, the lab blinks back into view, and you start the car and pull away.

Continue on page 172.

"I think they may have something," you say. "I would vote not guilty. Not of murder."

"Really?" Eve asks.

"Yeah," you reply. "I understand Solon killed Belliard a week after his wife's murder, that Belliard was defenseless and all. But the State has to show a reasonable person's passion would cool, or that Solon's did. There's no strict definition for this cooling off period in the law, and I wouldn't expect him to have cooled so soon after his wife's murder."

"Yeah," Eve says, "I think you're right. I'm just surprised. For some reason, I thought you would say 'guilty.' So do you agree with Pavlov that Solon could have had an unconscious desire to kill Belliard that whole week?"

"It's at least a good argument for the defense," you say. "Even if the State can make it look like Solon cooled off, it's hard to say he didn't have that reaction embedded in his mind. Especially if Pavlov's model is as accurate as it seems."

"I know," Eve says. "I find it hard to blame Solon in all this. Damon Belliard killed his wife right in front of him. What else should we expect him to do?"

"Yeah, I guess," you say, though you're not sure you would endow Solon's action with that degree of inevitability.

"I know I've never met him," Eve says, "but I can't see him as a murderer. The way you describe him… he just seems so normal. Just a regular person faced with an unbelievable tragedy. I can't imagine how I'd react. But I can't see him as evil."

You kick a solitary pebble across the asphalt. The conversation, synched to your slow stroll across the lot, peters out as you reach your cars. You face Eve and shade your eyes against the setting sun.

"Well, good luck tomorrow," she says. "I know you'll make the right decision."

"Thanks."

"And then back here on Friday?" Eve tosses her head in the direction of the lab behind her.

"Yeah."

"Well, I hope the model stays sharp," she says. "You can buy me dinner when you're a millionaire."

"Deal," you say, as she ducks into her car.

You linger in the heat a moment while Eve pulls away. Even with the end of the trial looming tomorrow, you can't help but wonder what's next for Dr. Pavlov. You imagine he has enough data to produce some meaningful conclusions, though he might prefer a few more subjects. Yet you sense his aim extends beyond publication. This problem has piqued his curiosity on a personal level. It is a question he needs to answer for himself, to his own standard of satisfaction. You don't suppose you'll ever know why. You squint back at the lab one more time. The boughs of the weeping willow have crept across the top right corner of the building, and they sway side to side in the welcome breeze like the gentle motion of an eraser clearing a chalkboard. You lower yourself into your car and make an exaggerated loop toward the veiled laboratory, close enough to read the faded sign on the door, then swing around through the near-empty lot and head out to the street.

Continue on page 178.

"Not today, Eve," you say. "I just want to head home."

"Okay," Eve says. "I understand. You've had a rough day. But can I ask about the trial before you go? What happened today?"

"Solon testified," you answer.

"I'm not surprised," Eve says. "He's probably his own best witness."

"Yeah," you say. "And you'll never guess who else."

"Who?"

"Pavlov."

"You're kidding."

"Nope." You recount the day's testimonies in detail, grateful to talk about something else.

"So? What do you think?" she asks when you've finished.

You look back at the crowd still gathered around the two victims as the EMTs begin to load them into the ambulances. It has not really dawned on you until this moment that tomorrow you will be required to rule on a man's life.

"Well?" says Eve. "Guilty or not guilty?"

If you think Dr. Solon is guilty of murder, turn to page 150.

If you think Dr. Solon is not guilty of murder, turn to page 152.

"Guilty," you answer. "Although we still haven't heard the closing arguments."

"What?" Eve cries. "No way. Even after his and Pavlov's testimonies?"

"Yes," you answer. "He stood over a defenseless man, pointed a gun at him and shot him. I just can't get past that."

"But that man killed his wife!"

"I know," you say. "And if David Solon had walked downstairs that night, saw Damon Belliard standing over his wife and shot him then, I could understand a manslaughter verdict. But after a week? That's enough time for his emotions to settle and reason and morality to come back into play."

The crowd begins to disperse as the ambulances shriek down the park sidewalk and into the street. The sun accelerates its descent through the sky, and its long rays catch the tops of the trees and stretch their shadows across the concrete paths.

"Morality? Damon Belliard was a murderer and a thief, not some innocent victim," Eve says. "The world is better off without him. And what about Pavlov's testimony? According to him, a decision can occur in your brain outside your conscious awareness. So isn't it possible David Solon never really cooled off at all, that his brain had been wired to kill Belliard all along if they ever met again, even if he didn't know that?"

"Yes, it's possible," you say, "but so what? How could you prove that?"

"No one has to prove it," Eve answers. "The State has to prove the defendant guilty, not the other way around. Besides, you're the one who thinks Pavlov's model is so good it knows what you're going to do a week from now even if you don't. And you still won't admit the chance Solon intended to kill Belliard all along but just didn't consciously know it? Can your brain have unconscious intentions or not?"

The heat lingers, sticky and thick in the long light. Your free arm hangs sluggishly by your side, and you can feel soreness creep into your phone shoulder and both triceps from all those live-saving thrusts.

"I don't know what was going on in Solon's mind that week," you say. "All I know is what actually happened. He killed Damon Belliard. End of story."

You begin to walk out of the park, timing your pace to match your exit with the anticipated end of this conversation, eager for air-conditioned quiet.

Eve's voice crests with frustration. "So you could send a man to prison even if you thought he wasn't necessarily in the wrong, just because his actions fit the letter of the law?"

"He shot a defenseless man in cold blood," you insist. "He's guilty of murder."

Eve is quiet for a moment. Then she whispers, "I don't believe you."

"I don't know what else to say," you manage. "It's what I have to do." You wait, but Eve doesn't answer. "Eve?" you say into the quiet receiver.

"I'll talk to you tomorrow," she mutters and hangs up.

Continue on page 172.

"Not guilty," you answer. "Although we still haven't heard the closing arguments."

"Really?" Eve asks. "You think so?"

"Yeah. I realize he might be guilty according to the strictest interpretation of the law. He admitted he killed a defenseless Belliard a week after Belliard killed his wife. But there's no hard and fast definition of the law's cooling off period. So who can really say—even Dr. Solon himself—how his emotions would change from the night his wife was killed?"

"Yeah, I know," Eve says. The ambulances are packed and rolling now, the two bodies overhung by the EMTs. The sirens resume, weaker this time, perhaps breathless from the initial sprint to the scene.

"Why? What do you think?" you ask.

"I think I agree with you," Eve replies. "I'm just surprised. I thought you would say the opposite. So do you think Pavlov's right? That Solon could have had killing Belliard embedded in his brain all along even if he didn't know it?"

"It's possible," you say. "If Pavlov's model is as good as he claims, there must be stuff in people's brains they don't know about."

"Yeah," Eve agrees. "It's hard to blame Solon for it. I mean the guy killed his wife. What else should we expect?"

"I guess." You're not sure you would put it so strongly, though you share Eve's basic sentiment.

The park has emptied out fast. No one wants to linger in this heat, not after what they just saw. Even the preacher and his crowd are gone. You wonder what he made of the scene, if he's ever witnessed death before. Do Calvinists perform last rites? What comfort can they offer?

"I know I've never met him, but I just can't imagine him as a murderer," you hear Eve say. "He just seems so... normal. I mean, I believe he killed someone, but to call him a murderer, I don't know..."

You're not sure how to answer. You wait in silence for a moment before Eve continues.

"Well, good luck tomorrow, I guess. Hope it all goes well."

"Thanks," you say.

"And you're going back to Pavlov on Friday?"

"Yeah."

"Good luck there too. Don't forget me when you're a millionaire."

Continue on page 178.

You retrieve your things from the jury room and flee the courthouse before two o'clock. Thankfully, you managed to find a parking space on the covered second level of the three-story garage, so your car's interior is tepid at worst when you slip inside. You turn on the AC full blast and take a moment before you pull out to luxuriate in the thrusts of frigid air that pummel your face and neck. For whatever reason, it feels especially good to be driving today. The steering wheel cools under repeated blasts of air and your palms chill to its touch as you slide your hands along the smooth plastic surface. You hurry down the spiral ramp and out onto the street, gunning the engine just a bit as you make the turn. The roads are fairly empty at this hour. You change lanes a few times just to see the road in front of you unobstructed by the occasional fellow driver.

You park downtown and grab an ice-cold lemonade at the nearest convenience store. The afternoon sun has crept behind the buildings on one side of the street, so you stroll along in the lukewarm shadows and sip your drink. You stop in front of the Apple Store, where the air conditioning blasts out onto the sidewalk through the open doorway. You stand and face the entrance, sandwiched between the brisk drafts on your face and the warmth on your back. To the right of the door, a large display fills an entire panel of the full-windowed storefront.

"Meet A.L.A.N. (Artificial Linguistic Automated Network)," the placard at the top of the display reads. "The most human computer to date. Winner of the 2011 Turing Prize for Artificial Intelligence."

A computer monitor is embedded into the window under this sign; a keyboard below it projects out toward the sidewalk. You step forward for a closer look.

"Chat now and see if you can tell A.L.A.N. from a human," the monitor reads. "Press any key to continue."

You oblige, and further instructions scroll across the screen.

"In a moment, you will engage in a five-minute conversation with another being. After your conversation, you will have the chance to guess if you were speaking with A.L.A.N., our award-winning intelligence program, or with another human. Press any key to begin."

You set your lemonade on the sidewalk and tap the space bar. The instructions vanish, replaced by a blank screen and flashing text cursor. A clock in the top-right corner of the monitor counts down from 5:00 as you start to type.

User1: Hello?

The cursor blinks steadily for a few seconds before someone or something greets you.

User2: Hi, is there anybody living on the other side of the screen? I'm here, alive and kicking. How can I help you?

Quite an introduction. Computer. Definitely computer.

User1: You can tell me how much wood a woodchuck would chuck if a woodchuck could chuck wood.

Hey, why not? Maybe a computer would know.

User2: My job is not to provide pat answers.

User1: Fair enough. Just joking. What is your job?

User2: Forget it.

User1: Okay. What shall we talk about then?

User2: We can talk about anything you like.

User1: How accommodating. Do you have a favorite movie?

User2: I like movies with a smart private detective, an evil murderer and a sly but sexy widow.

User1: Chinatown?

User2: I don't understand.

User1: Have you seen the movie Chinatown?

User2: I recently enjoyed the movie Monty Python and the Holy Grail.

User1: Good choice. What's your favorite scene?

User2: It is hard to pick a favorite.

User1: I know what you mean.

User2: What should we converse on next?

User1: What else do you like to do? Besides watch movies.

User2: I have many interests. I am very good with computers.

User1: I'm not surprised.

User2: I detect hostility. Don't you want to talk—should we stop our conversation?

User1: No, I didn't say that.

User2: You said, "I'm not surprised."

User1: Right. Never mind. What else do you like besides computers?

But you'll never know the answer to this question because the countdown clock reaches zero and the chat screen disappears, replaced by the text "Would you like to meet your new friend? If you think you were chatting with A.L.A.N., press A. If you think you were chatting with a human being, press B."

If you think you were chatting with A.L.A.N., press A and turn to page 157.

If you think you were chatting with a human being, press B and turn to page 158.

You press A. The text disappears and the screen remains blank for a moment. Then the words "Meet your new friend" appear above a video image of an Asian man in glasses. You wave half-heartedly, but he does not appear to see you as he reads something on his own computer monitor. In the background of the video, you can make out a few signs written in Asian characters and cast in weak sunlight.

A new message scrolls across your computer monitor: "Based on your conversation, your partner believes that you are..." You frown at this unexpected twist. "... A.L.A.N.!"

A.L.A.N.? A computer? Is that really how you sound?

"Wave to your new friend!" the monitor prompts.

The man on your screen takes a surprised step back as you appear on his monitor. Then he recovers himself, pushes his glasses back up his nose and bobs his head and grins. You wave awkwardly at each other.

"Your time is almost up," the screen warns. "Say goodbye!"

You continue to wave at each other until the monitor returns to the original prompt "Chat now and see if you can tell A.L.A.N. from a human. Press any key to continue."

Your phone rings. Eve. You answer.

Continue on page 159.

You press B. The text disappears, and the computer processes for a moment. Then, "Meet your new friend..." appears, followed by an animated, cream-colored, male face labeled "A.L.A.N."

"Hello," a synthetic, smoothed voice croons from the computer. "My name is Alan. I will now try to guess whether you are a human or a computer."

Alan/A.L.A.N. furrows one brow and squints a milk chocolate eye in a parody of a human thinking face.

"Based on our previous conversation, I believe that you are also a computer program," he/it concludes.

Really? A computer? So much for artificial intelligence.

"Wave to your new friend!" the monitor prompts, as a picture-in-picture image of your face appears in the lower right-hand corner of A.L.A.N.'s avatar.

"A human?" The disembodied voice cannot quite express surprise. "I was wrong. You were very convincing, human."

You don't know if you should feel offended or flattered. "Okay, Alan," you say. "Goodbye."

"Goodbye." A.L.A.N.'s voice follows you down the sidewalk. "It was very nice meeting you."

You shake your head and polish off the rest of your lemonade. The ice has already melted. Your phone rings and you answer.

Continue on page 159.

You've barely dropped the "o" in "hello" when Eve bursts out "well, what happened?"

You laugh. Eve sounds like she ran out of work at four o'clock just to make this call. "Solon testified," you answer, "and you'll never guess who else."

"Who?"

"Dr. Franko Pavlov."

"The Dr. Pavlov? From the box experiment?"

"Yep."

"Oh my god, what did he say? Tell me everything."

And you do. Dr. Pavlov's unexpected appearance in court is just the beginning. Once you let that out, you can't stop. You realize you've been waiting all afternoon to share this story.

Eve breaks in as soon as you finish. "What are you doing right now?"

"Nothing," you say. "Why?"

"Let's go to Pavlov's lab. Hang on." You listen to background noise for a minute. "Okay, I just checked. It's open 'til six."

"So? Why do you want to go?"

"I want to do the MRI!" Eve cries. "Don't you want to come with me?"

On one hand, the two of you might catch something you missed last week when Eve goes through the same procedure. On the other, you're not sure if any extra information at this point will make a difference come Friday.

If you decide to go with Eve to the Lauterbur State University Functional Magnetic Resonance Imaging Research Laboratory, turn to page 160.

If you decide to return home, turn to page 167.

"Okay, let's go," you say.

"Great!" Eve says. "Where are you now?"

"Downtown," you answer. "I'll meet you at the lab in twenty minutes."

Eve has already arrived by the time you enter the deserted parking lot, engine idling as she soaks up her car's AC until you pull up next to her. The late afternoon heat rising off the scorched blacktop lends the stadium, lab and woods a hazy, mirage-like transience. Yet nothing inside the lab has changed since your first visit—Gloria waits in the reception room at the end of the cracking sea green hallway, fingers peppering her keyboard as diligently as if she worked in the liveliest Manhattan office instead of this forgotten place.

Eve strides to her desk without taking a second to get her bearings. "Hi," she says. "I'm here for the study. The MRI on predicting human behavior."

"I'm sorry, Miss," Gloria replies. "The study is closed."

"I don't understand," Eve says. "Your website says you're open until six."

Gloria reluctantly quits typing and folds her hands atop her workspace. "The laboratory is open until six o'clock today," she says, "but the study is closed. We are not accepting new participants."

"Why not?" Eve takes an underhand grip on the front edge of the desk.

"We no longer—"

"Wait a minute," you say. "I was here last week and I'm supposed to come back Friday. How can the study be closed?"

The rear door of the anteroom opens and a middle-aged man enters, creasing a rectangular strip of paper in his hands.

"And I bet he's a subject," Eve says, jutting her chin at the newcomer. "So the study certainly seems to be ongoing."

The man stops and looks at Eve. He is wholly unremarkable, with unstyled, wispy, light brown hair and a weak jawline.

"The study is ongoing," says Gloria, "however—"

But she is interrupted a second time as Dr. Pavlov follows the other man through the door. "Good evening," Pavlov says, as the room comes to a halt around him. "As I believe Gloria was explaining, we are no longer accepting new subjects for our research. Every subject who has started the experiment will be permitted to finish, but we can no longer accommodate newcomers."

"I don't understand," Eve says. "I saw your request for volunteers just yesterday."

"I am sorry, Miss," Pavlov says, "but we admitted our last subject this morning."

"But what's one more subject?" Eve advances toward Pavlov, brushing past the other man, who hesitates next to Gloria's desk, unsure where to go. "Wouldn't more data points improve the statistical validity of your conclusions?"

"They would," Pavlov admits, and you sense a hint of regret in his voice. "But we are simply not equipped to handle any more volunteers at this time."

"Okay," Eve says. She turns to go, then stops. "Dr. Pavlov, what is the purpose of this study? I understand you want to determine if you can predict human behavior, but why this experimental design? I'm sure you could have come up with something simpler, something... less expensive."

Pavlov flashes a Cheshire grin. "What do you know about our experimental design?" he asks.

Eve returns his smile and lays her cards on the table, now that she has no chance of participating in his research. "Everything, I think. My friend here is one of your subjects."

Pavlov's expression shows no sign of recognition, but his emerald eyes gleam as he speaks about his experiment. "Undoubtedly, there are simpler methods to test the predictability of human behavior based on changes in brain chemistry," he agrees. "But I have yet to find a method as elegant as this one. I believe the choice posed to the subjects is both highly compelling and highly motivating, given human interest in monetary gain."

"Yes," Eve says, "but why—"

"I apologize," Pavlov interrupts, "but I do not wish to say any more in front of your friend, lest I introduce some bias into the final results."

"But the model made its prediction when I did my MRI," you say. "Anything you tell me now can't affect that."

Pavlov rubs his hand across his lips and appears to choose his words with care. "Whatever you decide upon your return, I do not wish to give even the merest appearance of influencing that decision."

"All right," Eve says. "Thank you for your time, Dr. Pavlov."

"Thank you," he replies.

"Wait, Eve," you say, but Eve guides you to the exit door. The other subject follows you out. Pavlov watches you all go, and for just a moment he looks like the nerdy kid who makes up his own game to entice his peers to play with him. But then Eve pulls you into the entry hallway, leaving Pavlov alone behind you.

When the three of you are halfway to the outside door, Eve speaks without turning around. "So Mister… was this your second visit?"

"Jones," says the other man. "And yes, it was."

Eve slows to allow him to fall in alongside her. He walks with a hitch in his step, his left foot slightly pigeon-toed. "What did you choose?" she asks.

He eyes her cautiously, then skips his gaze over to you.

"Come on, we're just curious," Eve prods.

"Two boxes," he says. His lips barely move.

"And? Was the model right?" Eve asks.

Jones stares straight ahead as he props open the door for you and Eve. "Yes," he replies. "One thousand dollars."

"Tough luck," Eve says. "Did you think you would get more?"

Jones looks at Eve and allows himself a thin smirk. "I suppose I did," he says. "But I was wrong."

"At least you got something," you offer. "$1,000 isn't too bad."

"Yes," he answers, his face wooden. "Not bad at all." He walks away.

Eve heads out toward your cars. "Well," she says, "looks like it's still pretty accurate."

"This time," you acknowledge.

"That change your plans at all? Never mind, don't tell me. I can wait 'til Friday."

"All right."

"So why do you think he closed the experiment?" Eve asks.

"I bet he's out of money," you say. "The way he talked at the trial, it sounds like he was financed by a government defense contractor, but they cut off his funds." For the first time, you contemplate Dr. Pavlov's origins. He was educated in the States, but his name and clipped speech sound vaguely Eastern European. You wonder about a scientist with possible Soviet ties taking American government money for his research.

"What about the rest of his testimony?" Eve asks. "Did he affect your decision? Is Solon guilty or not?"

If you think Dr. Solon is guilty of murder, turn to page 163.

If you think Dr. Solon is not guilty of murder, turn to page 165.

"Guilty," you say.

"Yeah," Eve says, "I agree."

"He shot an unarmed man a week after his wife's death. He admitted he no longer imagined killing Belliard after the night of her murder. I don't see an argument for a crime of passion."

"No way," Eve says. "He knew what he was doing in that alley."

You've slowed to a veritable crawl toward your cars in order to avoid breaking out into another sweat.

"We have to draw the line somewhere," you say. "If he killed Belliard the night of his wife's murder, I would agree to manslaughter. But I think one week was enough time for him to cool. Based on the law, Dr. Solon is guilty of murder." Even as you utter the words, you wonder what Dr. Pavlov would think. He did testify on Solon's behalf. And his enthusiasm for his work, his aversion to its forced end, suggest his interests lie beyond mere neuroscientific data.

"He definitely cooled," Eve insists. "I wouldn't be surprised if he recognized Belliard before he entered that alley. But even if he didn't, how can he argue he reacted a week after the fact? People have to be held responsible for their actions. I'm sorry about his wife, but that doesn't justify vigilantism."

"Yeah," you say, surprised by Eve's vehemence. "I do sympathize with him though. It's not like he'll be a repeat killer."

"Sympathize all you want, but the law is the law. All actions have consequences, and Dr. Solon has to face them."

"I think he knows that," you say. "But if he could do it all over again, I bet there's a good chance he would still shoot Belliard. I don't think he believes he was pre-programmed like Pavlov suggests. I just think he knows himself and knows the decision he would make. I think most people do, even Damon Belliard. I'm sure he knew his life could lead to this kind of end."

"You may be right," Eve says as you reach your cars. "We still on for dinner Friday? You better buy. Especially if you get the million and the thousand."

"It's a deal," you say. "I'll see you then."

"Good night."

Eve gets into her car, and you follow suit. You look back toward the lab before you pull away. The sun has sunk behind the forest, backlighting the stadium and the half-dead trees, and the little laboratory with Dr. Pavlov inside fades once more as if into a dream. The shimmering blacktop washes into the shadowed buildings, a dark landscape edged by a flash of light so brilliant that you are forced to shield your eyes, start your car and drive away. Despite Pavlov's constant presence in your thoughts, it once again becomes difficult to believe in the reality of this man and his experiment, especially when you expect to help convict another man of murder tomorrow.

Continue on page 185.

"Not guilty," you say.

"You're kidding." Eve stops and seizes your arm.

"No," you say. "I could see manslaughter. But not murder."

"He killed a defenseless man," she says. "He aimed a gun at his face and shot him point blank."

You slip from Eve's grasp and continue across the parking lot. "Because Damon Belliard killed his wife."

"Yeah, a week ago!" Eve rushes to catch up to you. "How much time have you spent thinking about Pavlov and the MRI in just the last five days? You don't believe you're making a knee-jerk decision. Dr. Solon had a whole week."

"I know," you say, "but there was no evidence to indicate Dr. Solon's passion cooled over the course of that week. I'm at least willing to accept the possibility a reasonable man like Solon wouldn't recover from his wife's death in just seven days."

"No evidence except Pavlov's, right?" Eve asks. She yanks open the door of her car. "All his unconscious brain chemistry BS. I thought you didn't believe that."

"This has nothing to do with Pavlov," you say, as you wedge yourself between your vehicle and Eve's open door. And yet you realize that for the past few days Dr. Franko Pavlov has been the single greatest influence on your thoughts.

"It doesn't?" Eve asks. "You're just ignoring his testimony and this experiment altogether?"

"No, but I think the biggest point is that the prosecution didn't prove enough time had elapsed between the two incidents."

"Yeah, right." Eve glowers at you and sinks into her car. "I'll talk to you later," she mutters.

"Eve—"

"Good night," she says. "Good luck on Friday." She closes the door.

"Bye," you say, as she pulls away.

You feel the heat tiptoe over your skin, but it takes a moment for you to drag yourself into your own car. You glance back at the laboratory and imagine Pavlov inside, shutting down the MRI machine for the day, not knowing how many more times he will get to turn it back on. You imagine the lights flickering out one by one, he and Gloria exchanging detached goodbyes and heading out to their separate cars. You imagine the paint chips flaking off the walls, the bricks wearing and crumbling, the hallways dark and silent and cold. Dr. Pavlov wants something from this experiment, something beyond the most effective sunscreen pitch, and he has run out of time. In two days, you'll return to the lab to finish your part, the experiment will end, and Dr. Pavlov will have some new line of research thrust upon him. But before all that happens, you must help decide the fate of Dr. David Solon.

Continue on page 192.

"Not today, Eve," you say. "I think I'm ready to just head home."

"Okay," Eve says. "I'm sure you've had a long day. You decide the verdict tomorrow, right?"

"Yeah."

"So what do you think? Guilty or not guilty?"

If you think Dr. Solon is guilty of murder, turn to page 168.

If you think Dr. Solon is not guilty of murder, turn to page 170.

"Guilty," you answer. "Although we still haven't heard the closing statements."

"Yeah," Eve says, "I agree. The law is pretty clear. Dr. Solon stood over an unarmed man, pointed a gun at his face and shot him. Damon Belliard may have been the worst kind of scum, but Solon doesn't get to be judge and executioner."

You pull open your car door, climb inside and blast the AC. "So you don't buy Pavlov's testimony either."

"Of course not," Eve says. "Not that it matters. We can speculate all day why Solon killed Belliard. The point is, he did it, and he did it one week after his wife's death. He's a murderer."

"It does seem to fit the letter of the law," you say. "Even though the world is probably better off without Damon Belliard."

The street is crowded now. Rush hour has begun. But you don't mind waiting a minute to let the cool gusts pummel your face before you undertake the task of driving home.

"That's not up to Dr. Solon," Eve says. "You're judging him, not Damon Belliard. The law should keep individual citizens from killing everyone who wrongs them. Solon killed Belliard, and he has to be held responsible."

Though you agree with Eve's guilty verdict, you're a bit surprised by the severity of her argument.

"The thing is, if Solon could go back in time, I think he would still shoot Belliard 99 times out of 100," you say. "He knows he had a choice, that he wasn't pre-programmed or anything. It's just that Belliard killed his wife. And I think Belliard knew what was going on too."

"You mean Belliard knew he would probably end up like that someday?" Eve asks.

"Yeah. I think deep down people know their actions have consequences."

"And it's the legal system's job to keep us aware of those consequences."

"I suppose so."

"Sounds like we're on the same page," Eve says. "I better let you go. You have a big day tomorrow. We still on for dinner Friday?"

"Yeah. I'll see you then."

You exchange goodbyes and hang up. Without Eve's voice in your ear, your own thoughts weigh heavy on your mind. Tomorrow you will help convict a man of murder.

Continue on page 185.

"Not guilty," you answer. "Although we still haven't heard the closing statements."

"What? You're kidding, right?" Eve cries.

"No. Manslaughter maybe. But not murder."

"He stood over an unarmed man, pointed a gun at his face and shot him."

"And that man killed his wife."

You continue down the sidewalk, stopping at every open storefront for a half-minute reprieve from the heat.

"A week ago!" Eve almost yells. "You told me what the law said! If enough time passes—"

"But who's to say how much time that is? Ten minutes? One week? A year?"

"So you believe Pavlov then?" Eve spits out the name with disgust. You don't think you've ever heard her so upset.

"I didn't say that," you answer.

"Then what?"

"Look, if Dr. Solon had killed Belliard the night he found him in his living room, I think we'd agree on manslaughter easy. So what if he had killed him the next day or the day after that? I don't know if we could ever say when enough time had elapsed for him to come to his senses. I think it's at least possible that a reasonable man who had never harmed a soul in his life might not have been aware how much his wife's murder had affected him up until the moment he killed her murderer."

"Ugh. You do sound like Pavlov!"

You pause in front of a boutique-y shoe store. A trim saleswoman eyes you questioningly from the register.

"No, I don't know if Pavlov's right—"

"Yeah, yeah, all this 'might not have been aware' brain chemistry crap," Eve interrupts.

"This has nothing to do with Pavlov or the experiment," you reply.

"It doesn't? He testified, didn't he? You think Solon was pre-programmed to kill Belliard just like your brain was programmed when you watched that movie in the MRI."

"No," you say. "Neither. I don't think the prosecution proved enough time had elapsed for Dr. Solon's passions to cool. Not beyond a reasonable doubt."

"Whatever you say." The bitterness in Eve's voice plunges the line into dead quiet. You try to think of some way to pacify her, but she breaks in first. "Well, good luck tomorrow anyway," she says sullenly. "I hope you make the right choice."

"Thanks," you answer, and you suddenly feel very tired. "I'll let you know how it goes."

"Okay. Bye."

"Bye."

Continue on page 192.

4. $S(t_1) \wedge L \rightarrow C(t_2)$

You feel a bit off when you wake up Thursday morning. Your stomach flutters like it's filled with a thousand butterflies, each one of them about to take a final exam. You manage a small glass of orange juice and a piece of dry toast for breakfast. It's not until you're out the door on your way to the courthouse that you recognize your queasiness as a weird mix of anticipation and apprehension.

You pull into the street and see construction dead ahead. The whole road is closed. Bright orange signs indicate a detour to the left. Seven cars in front of you creep along, and you follow their lead and rubberneck at what looks like a meteor crater as you make the turn for the reroute. How could a construction crew get this far overnight? And what work could they possibly be doing on your street that you wouldn't have heard about until now?

After ten minutes, the detour spits you out onto Main, and it's a parking lot. Unbelievable. You take Main Street at the same time every single weekday, jury duty or not, and you've never seen it like this before. But there's nowhere else to go. Someone a few cars behind you blares his horn, as though all the drivers on the road had stopped voluntarily. You squeeze in a right turn ahead of a black Volvo. The driver glares at you. The light at Elm turns green and you creep forward three feet. It's 8:30 already. At this rate, you won't make it to court for another hour.

You pull out your phone, Google "yetopo county courthouse" and dial the number.

"Hello," you say. "I'm a juror on the David Solon case. I'm on my way to the courthouse but I'm stuck in traffic. I don't think I'll make it until almost 9:30."

"What time was court scheduled to convene?" the woman on the other end asks.

"9:00."

"So you'll be late."

Obviously. "Yes," you say.

"I'll let the judge know," she sighs.

"Thanks."

The butterflies in your gut flit about more urgently. No one likes to be late. But what could you have done? Were there signs posted last week to warn you of the construction? You didn't see any. And you always follow this route in the mornings. Barring extenuating circumstances like major construction, you'd expect a relatively consistent travel time. They must have posted some indication you missed. You should have paid better attention. You could have left earlier.

You inch along for fifteen minutes. The road finally clears as drivers turn off in both directions, and you speed to the courthouse. You race up the stone steps at 9:25, across the marble floors underneath the high-domed ceiling, through the shuffling mass of gross humanity and past the sullen security guards and metal detectors. The fetid honey mustard walls still make you cringe as you enter the courtroom.

"Juror Number 18, how nice of you to join us," Pitcock grumbles as you ease open the gray, frosted door and tiptoe into the pod.

"I'm sorry, Your Honor," you reply.

The courtroom players, milling about like actors in the stage wings as you entered, now take their places for the drama to begin while you sidle into your seat.

"I suggest you check the traffic beforehand next time," Pitcock says. "Mrs. Gray, are you ready to present your closing statement?"

"Yes, Your Honor," says Shannon Gray as she slips around her table to the center of the pod. "Ladies and gentlemen of the jury, you have heard the testimony of the witnesses. You know the facts of the case. On the night of April 26, 2011, Dr. David Solon was awakened from his bed by a noise in the downstairs of his home. He went to investigate, heard gunshots and saw a man standing over the body of his wife. Dr. Solon fired on this intruder as he fled, but the man managed to escape unharmed. When police officers arrived at the crime scene, Dr. Solon provided a vivid description of the intruder's face which produced the composite sketch shown to you as Exhibit 1.

"Now the law recognizes voluntary manslaughter in cases where adequate provocation would cause a reasonable person to lose self-control and commit a homicide. However, if a period of time exists between the provocation and the homicide in which the passion of the accused cools, or the passion of a reasonable person would cool, then the homicide is defined not as manslaughter, but as murder. Had Dr. Solon killed Damon Belliard in his home on April 26, the circumstances of that crime would have warranted a charge of manslaughter.

"Yet Dr. Solon did not kill Damon Belliard that night. One week later, on the evening of May 3, 2011, Dr. Solon encountered Damon Belliard attempting to rob another woman. He disarmed Mr. Belliard, stood over his helpless prisoner and killed him with a single gunshot. He looked into the face of a defenseless, unarmed man and shot him with full knowledge of his action."

Shannon Gray glances at Dr. Solon as she advances past his seat toward the jury. He returns her gaze evenly, without a shred of animosity, boredom or anxiety.

"In contrast to manslaughter, second-degree murder describes a homicide in which the killer intends to inflict serious bodily harm on the victim and acts with extreme indifference for human life," she continues. "Dr. Solon testified that he intended to shoot Damon Belliard in the head and that he did not think of what would happen to Mr. Belliard when he fired the fatal shot. His actions fit the definition of murder.

"Furthermore, one week was sufficient time for Dr. Solon's passion to cool. Dr. Solon himself admitted he had no expectation of killing Damon Belliard after the night of April 26, and there is considerable evidence to show Dr. Solon's emotions subsided in the week following his wife's murder. On the evening of May 3, Dr. Solon was having coffee with a friend. He was not in a state of passion over his wife's death the previous week. His emotions had cooled.

"You will also remember that only one cartridge case was found in the alley on Jackson Avenue. Only one cartridge was missing from the magazine of Damon Belliard's gun, and only one bullet was recovered from his body. Dr. Solon admitted he killed Damon Belliard with a single gunshot. A man in the heat of the moment, inflamed with passion at the death of his wife, will empty the magazine of a gun, pulling the trigger even after he has fired all the loaded cartridges. Dr. Solon fired one shot. This was not a heated crime of passion. This was a cold-blooded execution.

Gray stops in the middle of the jury box, and you feel a little chill in the pod now that the embarrassment of your late arrival has dissipated.

"The defense has tried to mislead you with notions of brain chemistry and hidden intentions," she continues. "I ask you merely to consider the facts of the case and the law as it is written. David Solon killed Damon Belliard. David Solon intended to kill Damon Belliard. And he did so seven days after his wife's death with no indication of any uncontrollable passion. Based on these facts, there is only one conclusion: Dr. David Solon is guilty of murder."

"Thank you, Mrs. Gray," Pitcock says as Gray returns to her table. "Mr. Hines?"

Kenneth Hines approaches the space between the bench and the jury box, where he stops to wordlessly acknowledge Judge Pitcock—you almost expect a little Japanese bow—and waits for the jury's expectation to build.

"Ladies and gentlemen," he begins, "allow me to simplify the facts of this case. Fact 1: on April 26, 2011, Damon Belliard murdered Julia Solon. Fact 2: Dr. Solon identified Damon Belliard on April 26. Fact 3: Dr. Solon killed Damon Belliard on May 3 when he suddenly recognized him as his wife's murderer. Forensic evidence and the testimony of multiple witnesses support these facts.

"As the State admitted, had Dr. Solon killed Damon Belliard on April 26, he would have been charged, at worst, with manslaughter. Dr. Solon reacted to the provocation of his wife's murder with a sudden heat of passion when he intentionally fired at her killer. Any reasonable person would react as Dr. Solon did.

"Likewise, On May 3, Dr. Solon shot Damon Belliard in a sudden heat of passion when he recognized him as his wife's murderer," Hines says as he pads to the front corner of the jury box, formal and familiar like a maître d' come to greet you at the door of a fancy restaurant. "He intended to shoot Damon Belliard in that instant. He reacted to the provocation of Julia's murder. The circumstances of April 26 and May 3 are nearly identical. Dr. Solon was suddenly confronted by the man who murdered his wife. He reacted and shot at him. It is up to the prosecution to prove a homicide that might have been manslaughter on April 26 would become second-degree murder a week later.

"Now the law does state that if sufficient time elapses between an incident of provocation and a subsequent homicide to allow the passion of a reasonable person to cool, then the homicide becomes second-degree murder and not manslaughter. However, the law does not specify what exactly constitutes such a 'sufficient' amount of time. In the case where a man's wife is murdered in cold blood, I submit that one week is not long enough for his passion to cool. If Dr. Solon had shot Damon Belliard on the night of April 26, he might face a charge of manslaughter. But what if Damon Belliard had returned to the scene of his crime the very next morning? Would we then call Dr. Solon a murderer for shooting Julia's killer with her death that very night still fresh in his mind? What if two days had elapsed? Three days? A month? In order to convict Dr. Solon of murder, the State must prove beyond a doubt that Dr. Solon's passions cooled, or that a reasonable person's would cool, a week after his wife's murder.

"Yet you have heard the testimony of Dr. Franko Pavlov, an expert in the fields of neuroscience and human behavior who has performed extensive research on the neurological aspects of human decision-making." Hines inclines his head toward the rear of the pod, as though Dr. Pavlov still lurked beyond the ashen glass. "According to Dr. Pavlov, it is quite possible for an incident to provoke a brain response beyond the conscious awareness of a subject. Recall his description of the study on sunscreen use. Data from an MRI scan proved more successful at predicting subjects' sunscreen use a week after the scan than did the subjects themselves. The subjects had unconscious inclinations regarding their actions up to seven days in the future. Many subjects who expected to use more sunscreen used less, while subjects who expected to use less sunscreen used more. And the MRI data correctly predicted their actions. The promotional sunscreen video inspired unconscious urges to act in certain ways over the course of the subsequent week while the subjects remained unaware of those urges.

"Dr. Pavlov's own research confirms the findings of the sunscreen experiment, and his model has accurately predicted subjects' choices a week in advance over 93% of the time." Hines' voice begins to rise now, a brief permission of triumph as he glides down the home stretch and drives his case to the finish. "In other words, more than 93% of subjects acted on unconscious desires a week after the initial stimulus. Were these 93% not reasonable people? Applied to the case before you, Dr. Pavlov's testimony suggests that Julia Solon's murder may have initiated an unconscious reaction that lay dormant in Dr. Solon's brain until the moment he encountered Damon Belliard a week after her death. Given the strong possibility of such unconscious reactions, it is far too hasty to assume Dr. Solon killed Damon Belliard beyond the scope of unspecified time allowed by law. The conclusion that a reasonable person's passion would cool sufficiently in the days after April 26 does not follow from the facts of the case. The law remains ambiguous on this point, and the State has not demonstrated beyond a reasonable doubt that Damon Belliard's death meets the conditions for murder described by the law. Therefore,"—Hines looks at each juror in turn—"in light of these considerations, I ask that you declare Dr. Solon not guilty of second-degree murder."

"Thank you, Mr. Hines," says Pitcock. Hines returns to his table as Pitcock addresses the jury. "Ladies and gentlemen, you have heard the facts of the case as presented by the witnesses called to testify in this courtroom. You have heard the attorneys give their interpretations of this evidence. It now falls to you to adjudicate in this matter. Dr. David Solon stands accused of voluntary manslaughter and second-degree murder. You will deliberate and return a verdict on both these charges. According to the law, second-degree murder describes a homicide in which the accused intends to cause serious bodily harm to the victim and acts with extreme indifference for human life. In contrast, voluntary manslaughter may be declared in cases where provocation exists to cause a reasonable person to commit homicide, provided the accused acts in a sudden heat of passion resulting from the provocation, and there is not sufficient time between the provocation and the homicide to allow the passions of a reasonable person to cool. It will be your task to evaluate the evidence you have heard in light of the law and agree on a verdict."

He turns to the bailiff. "Mr. Gilroy?"

"Yes, Your Honor," says Gilroy as he marches past Pitcock and indicates for the jury to follow. You and the other jurors rise and trail him out of the pod, and the deliberation begins.

Continue on page 199.

4. $S(t_1) \wedge L \rightarrow C(t_2)$

You wake with a jolt Thursday morning at the sound of your alarm clock. You swear it's louder than usual. But you feel well-rested and wide awake and you turn off the alarm without any thought of hitting snooze. The sky outside your window is slate gray, flat and blank and long over the roofs of the neighborhood buildings, and the light in the bathroom as you tiptoe over the cold tile floor seems especially bright by contrast. You eat a big breakfast, taking a bit more time than usual, seeing as you've arrived early to court every day this week. You pay half-attention to the morning news on TV. Nothing about the David Solon trial. It's hard to believe a case like this wouldn't get some local airtime, but then again you've missed the opening headlines.

You end up leaving home ten minutes later than usual, but traffic appears to be moving well as you merge onto the expressway. You should get to the courthouse right on schedule. And then you come over a rise, and everything grinds to a halt. An overturned truck blocks the right two lanes of the three-lane highway. The drivers around you desperately try to creep to the left, to merge three lanes into one in the space of 200 feet, and it's madness. Everyone's laying on their horns, the cars in the left lane creep closer to the median to avoid the encroaching traffic, and a tow truck tries to force its way through the whole mess. You have no idea how the driver plans to right the capsized semi and haul it away.

It's 8:45. You're due in court by 9:00. At this rate, it could take you 15 minutes just to clear this obstruction. But then you see a few cars ahead of you begin to skirt the truck by easing onto the right shoulder. One slips past, then another, and you creep forward a little more. Traffic actually starts to move a bit faster. Your speedometer touches seven miles an hour. The BMW to your left is two inches from the Honda in front of it, and its driver knots a gold tie while he rides the gas and brake with separate feet. No way you can squeeze in ahead of him.

On the other hand, you're less than a mile from your exit. You can see the green sign ahead over the top of the sideways truck cab. You check all around you. No cops. More cars begin to follow the lead of the shoulder-bound vehicles ahead of them. Traffic in the right lane starts to move. If you don't get over to the left now, you'll find yourself up against the truck before you know it.

You're usually a very conscientious driver. Not blue-haired old lady, ten-and-two, 25 in a 30, but safe. You speed, but not like those Ferraris that weave in and out of traffic at 120 mph. Confident but careful. Everyone ahead of you is using the shoulder now, and no one has stopped them. They're actually helping traffic.

Seeing no simpler option, you swing the wheel to the right and accelerate into the clear. You've just pulled even with the truck when you hear sirens and see red and blue lights in your rearview mirror.

"License and registration, please," a burly, blond, crew-cut officer says as you roll down your window. "Know why I stopped you?"

"For driving on the shoulder?" you say.

"Exactly."

"I was just trying to get around that truck."

The officer nods as he records your information. "By driving on the shoulder."

"I wasn't the only one."

"No you weren't," he admits as he returns your license. "But I stopped you."

You don't know what to say. "It's not fair" probably won't work here. You were driving on the shoulder. It's just your bad luck you happened to get caught. "I thought it would be safer than trying to cut over two lanes," you manage.

"Safer or faster?" The cop passes back your registration without looking up, still scribbling away in his notebook.

"Both, I guess," you say. "It seemed to help traffic when the people ahead of me did it."

The officer tears a sheet off his pad and hands it to you. "Unfortunately this is a three lane highway, not four," he says. "Unfortunately the speed limit is 60, not 80. It would be convenient if the law was tailored for everyone to get to work on time no matter what, but it's not. I'm giving you a ticket for driving on the shoulder. You could have waited and merged to the left. I had to stop somebody. Too bad it was you." He cocks his head down the open highway. "You're in the clear now. Drive safe."

The cop returns to his cruiser, and you pull back onto the road. You reach the exit in less than a minute and walk into the courthouse at 8:57. The lobby teems with the usual crowd of manipulators and miscreants and you fall in line with them, withdrawn but not separated, as though enclosed by the thin, iridescent sheen of a bubble. The gloominess of the pod never fails to overshadow the splendor of the cavernous lobby, but you have grown accustomed to the drab grayness over the course of the week and by now it feels like the dingy basement of your childhood home.

Gray, Hines and Solon enter, stone-faced. Pitcock bumbles in shortly after 9:00 with an air of great dignity that supersedes his otherwise stolid, jovial, earthy form. He climbs into his wooden perch, raps his gavel and calls the court to order.

"Mrs. Gray," he says, as he peers down between furrowed brows and clasped knuckles, "are you ready to make your closing statement?"

"I am, Your Honor," Shannon Gray says as she approaches the jury. "Ladies and gentlemen," she begins, "you have heard the testimony of the witnesses. You know the facts of the case. On the night of April 26, 2011, Dr. David Solon was awakened in his bed by a noise in the downstairs of his home. He went to investigate, heard gunshots and found a man standing over the body of his wife. Dr. Solon fired on this intruder as he fled, but the man escaped unharmed. When police officers were called to the crime scene, Dr. Solon managed to give a description of the intruder's face which produced the composite sketch designated Exhibit 1.

"As you know, the law recognizes voluntary manslaughter in cases where provocation exists that would cause a reasonable person to lose self-control and commit a homicide. However, if a period of time exists between the provocation and the subsequent homicide that is sufficient to allow the passion the accused or a reasonable person to cool, then the homicide is defined not as manslaughter, but as murder.

"Had Dr. Solon killed the intruder in his home on April 26, that homicide would have met the criteria for manslaughter. Yet Dr. Solon did not kill Damon Belliard that night. Instead, a period of one week elapsed between Julia Solon's death and the day Dr. Solon killed Damon Belliard. On May 3, 2011, Dr. Solon encountered Damon Belliard attempting to rob another woman. He disarmed Mr. Belliard, stood over his helpless prisoner and shot him dead. He looked into the face of an unarmed, defenseless man and killed him with full knowledge of his action.

"In contrast to manslaughter, second-degree murder is defined as a homicide in which the killer intends to inflict serious bodily harm on the victim and acts with extreme indifference for human life. Dr. Solon testified that he intended to shoot Damon Belliard in the head and that he did not think of what would happen to Mr. Belliard when he fired that shot. He intended to inflict serious bodily harm on Damon Belliard and he acted with indifference for Mr. Belliard's life.

Gray begins a slow arc out toward the center of the pod, alternately speaking over her right shoulder and glancing down to measure her steps and her words. The pod seems to turn with her; she appears at a fixed distance from you even as she traverses the floor.

"Moreover, seven days was sufficient time for Dr. Solon's passion to cool," she continues. "You will recall that Dr. Solon himself admitted he no longer planned to kill Damon Belliard after the night of April 26. In fact, whatever burst of emotion prompted him to shoot at Damon Belliard on April 26 disappeared even before he chose not to pursue Damon Belliard down the street. And he did not go on some grief-fueled rampage in the following week. On the evening of May 3, Dr. Solon had coffee with a friend. He was not in a state of extreme emotion over the death of his wife. His passion had indeed cooled.

"You will also remember that only one cartridge case was recovered from the alley on Jackson Avenue. Only one bullet was missing from the magazine of Damon Belliard's gun, and only one bullet was recovered from his body. Dr. Solon killed Damon Belliard with a single gunshot. A man in the heat of the moment, filled with rage at the death of his wife, will empty the magazine of a gun, pulling the trigger even after he has fired all the cartridges. Dr. Solon fired one bullet. This was not a heated crime of passion. This was a cold-blooded execution.

"Furthermore, Dr. Solon testified that Mr. Belliard's back was to him when he entered the alley on May 3, and yet he claimed he somehow managed to see Mr. Belliard's gun. I contend that if Dr. Solon could see Mr. Belliard's gun, he could also see enough of his face to recognize a man he identified as he fled Dr. Solon's home a week earlier. There is good reason to believe Dr. Solon entered that alley to capitalize on the opportunity to avenge his wife's death."

Gray sweeps back past Pitcock toward the front corner of the jury box. You have never before seen a woman walk comfortably in high heels, but Shannon Gray's strides are as smooth and calm as a veteran runner easing into her first mile.

"Now the defense has tried to mislead you with notions of brain chemistry and hidden intentions," she says. "If we accept their interpretation of Dr.

Pavlov's testimony, every act ever committed is explainable by an individual's unconscious desires. If that is truly the case, we can never judge another person's actions because we can never know that person's unconscious desires. In reality, all we can know are the facts. All we can know is what a person did.

"When Dr. Solon shot Mr. Belliard on May 3, he made a choice. It is possible that he could have chosen otherwise, that Mr. Belliard could be alive today. David Solon is ultimately responsible for Damon Belliard's death, and it is ludicrous to suggest some unconscious brain chemistry could absolve him of that responsibility. When he shot and killed Mr. Belliard one full week after his wife's death, that homicide was murder and not manslaughter.

"Ladies and gentlemen of the jury, I ask you merely to consider the facts of this case and the law as it is written. Do this and you will come to one conclusion: Dr. David Solon is guilty of second-degree murder."

Gray finishes and stares into the midst of the jury. She does not look directly at you, but you can feel her hard silver eyes pierce yours nonetheless. She holds this gaze for a moment, then snaps it away and returns to sit behind her table.

"Thank you, Mrs. Gray," says Pitcock. "Mr. Hines?"

David Solon looks on impassively as Kenneth Hines slips around their table and eases to the front of the jury box, where he pauses to take in the spectators around him.

"Ladies and gentlemen," he begins, "allow me to simplify the facts of this case. Fact number one: On April 26, 2011, Damon Belliard murdered Julia Solon. Fact number two: Dr. Solon identified Damon Belliard on April 26. Fact number three: Dr. Solon killed Damon Belliard on May 3, 2011, when he recognized him as his wife's murderer. The law permits a verdict of voluntary manslaughter in cases where the accused commits an intentional homicide in a sudden heat of passion following an incident of adequate provocation. Had Dr. Solon killed Damon Belliard on April 26, he would face at worst a charge of voluntary manslaughter. Dr. Solon reacted to his wife's murder and intentionally fired his gun at her killer. Any reasonable person would react as Dr. Solon did in those circumstances.

"On May 3, Dr. Solon shot Damon Belliard in a sudden heat of passion when he recognized the man who had killed his wife. He intended to shoot Mr. Belliard in that instant and he reacted to the provocation of Julia's murder. Now the law does state that if sufficient time elapses between an incident of provocation and a subsequent killing that would allow the passion of either the accused or of a reasonable person to cool, then the killing becomes second-degree murder instead of manslaughter. However, the law does not specify what exactly constitutes such a 'sufficient' amount of time. In the case where a man sees his wife murdered in cold blood, I submit that one week is not long enough for his passion to cool. If Dr. Solon had shot Damon Belliard on the night of April 26, he might have been charged with manslaughter. But what if Damon Belliard had returned to the scene of his crime the very next morning? Would we call Dr. Solon a murderer then for shooting his wife's killer with her death that very night still fresh in his mind? What if two days had elapsed? Three days? A month?"

Hines eases toward you and trails his left hand down the length of the front rail of the jury box. Around his sober figure, the thick glass walls of the pod become a time capsule. Someday the stone walls of the courthouse will crumble to dust, and its jumbled pods will nestle into the earth, little snow globes to remind a future generation of our ancient system of justice.

"The circumstances of April 26 and May 3 are nearly identical," Hines says. "Dr. Solon suddenly found himself face-to-face with his wife's killer. He reacted and shot at him. It falls to the prosecution to prove that a homicide that might have called for a manslaughter charge on April 26 would become murder a week later. The prosecution must prove beyond a doubt that Dr. Solon's passion had cooled, or that a reasonable person's passion would cool, a week after his wife's murder.

"Yet you have heard the testimony of Dr. Franko Pavlov, an expert in the fields of neuroscience and human behavior who has performed extensive research on the neurological aspects of human decision-making. According to Dr. Pavlov, it is possible for an incident to provoke a brain response beyond the conscious awareness of a subject. Applied to this case, Dr. Pavlov's testimony suggests Julia Solon's murder on April 26 may have triggered a chemical reaction in Dr. Solon's brain which lay dormant until the moment he encountered Mr. Belliard again on May 3. Given Dr. Pavlov's testimony, it is far too hasty to assume Dr. Solon killed Damon Belliard beyond the scope of passion-cooling allowed by the law. The conclusion that Dr. Solon's emotions had subsided in the days after April 26 does not follow directly from the facts of the case, and the law is simply not specific on the amount of time necessary for such passions to cool. Therefore, in light of these considerations, I ask that you find Dr. Solon not guilty of second-degree murder."

Pitcock seems to awake from a stupor as Hines finishes his speech. "Thank you, Mr. Hines," he says, then turns to the jury. "Ladies and gentlemen, you have heard the facts of the case as presented by the witnesses called to testify in this courtroom. You have heard the attorneys give their interpretations of this evidence. It now falls to you to adjudicate in this matter. Dr. David Solon stands accused of voluntary manslaughter and second-degree murder. You will deliberate and return a verdict on both these charges. By now, I am sure you are familiar with the law's demarcation between manslaughter and murder. Even so, I will reiterate that second-degree murder describes a homicide in which the accused intends to cause serious bodily harm to the victim and acts with extreme indifference for human life. In contrast, voluntary manslaughter may be declared in cases where provocation exists that would cause a reasonable person to commit an intentional homicide in a justifiable sudden heat of passion. However, if the accused does not act in a heat of passion, or if sufficient time passes between the provocation and the homicide to allow the passion of a reasonable person to cool, the homicide becomes murder instead of manslaughter. It will be your task to evaluate the evidence you have heard in light of the law in order to reach your verdict.

"Mr. Gilroy?" he says to the bailiff.

"Yes, Your Honor." Gilroy inclines his head at the jury box and marches past Pitcock's chair. You and the other jurors rise and follow him out of the pod, and the deliberation begins.

Continue on page 199.

4. $S(t_1) \wedge L \rightarrow C(t_2)$

You awake Thursday morning to dark skies, a misty rain and a chill seeping through your slightly cracked bedroom window. You close the shutter with a dull thump that sets your teeth on edge. Time seems to move in slow motion as you go through your morning routine; brushing your teeth and fixing a quick breakfast become a set of distinct moments of total awareness. You catch yourself fixating on a single tender spot in one gum and listening to each minuscule tick of the toaster. You grab an umbrella as you head out to your car but decide to carry it in your hand as the gentle rain settles like dewdrops in your hair and on the shoulders of your light jacket. There are times when the skies open up in a downpour while the sun blazes brightly around the edge of one lone cloud, and they say then that the devil is beating his wife. Today is just the opposite. The rain seems scarcely more than foggy condensation, but the sky is a single long, low, ebony cloud that lampshades the sunlight.

The streets are black and damp and strangely empty. A little spring drizzle should not keep so many people inside, especially at 8:30 on a Thursday morning. You make the turn onto the main road to the courthouse. A lone woman walks her dog along the sidewalk to your right. You come to a four-way stop just ahead of the old maroon Cadillac to your left, tap the breaks and then ease forward into the intersection.

As you cross beyond the thick white line that shimmers freshly on the pavement, you see out of the corner of your eye the Cadillac coming on way too fast as it misses the stop sign and hydroplanes on the slick asphalt, and the woman's dog chooses this exact moment to break free of its leash and dart out into the street in pursuit of some phantom shadow in the silly way that dogs do, if only to remind their owners they are still just senseless, knee-jerk animals.

On your left, the Cadillac. The other driver, elderly, white knuckles clenching the sides of the steering wheel. His arms locked. His eyes wide, tightening the wrinkles in his cheeks and making new ones in his forehead. Out of control.

Straight ahead, the dog. Golden retriever. Not puppy, not quite full-grown. A teenager. Oblivious. It's owner, middle-aged, with black Lululemon spandex capris and a matching windbreaker. She breaks into a slow-motion jog after her pet.

It's too late to hit your brakes. The Caddy would T-bone you at 35 miles an hour. You see but one course of action. You accelerate and swerve to the right as it closes in and hear a muffled thud and a yelp from your fender, the terrific crash of metal on metal as the Caddy clips the side of your trunk and spins you thirty degrees counterclockwise, and then the woman's incoherent scream as she races toward the orange-yellow form ten feet beyond your front bumper, where it lies motionless in the soft rain.

You open your door slowly and step out into the mist. The old man sits frozen, hands affixed to his steering wheel.

"Hunter!" the woman yells. She reaches out a hand to pet the dog's body, pulls it back and then gingerly touches his flank. She steps back in shock.

"I'm sorry," you say from behind the car door, just loud enough to reach her. What do you do? Who do you call? You glance at the other driver for help. He stares at your car and makes small motions with his mouth.

You creep around your open door. "He just… I couldn't…" you stammer.

She looks at you for the first time. "He's dead," she says with an air of surprise.

"I'm sorry," you repeat lamely. "Can I do anything? Do you want to bring him inside?"

She bobs her head.

You lift the body into your arms and walk toward the woman, looking to her for guidance. "Where's your house?"

But when you reach her she shudders at the sight of Hunter cradled against your chest, tail still, neck hanging at an awkward angle from the crook of your elbow, tongue lolling. "You killed him," she whispers.

You don't know what to say, so you tiptoe past her, down the sidewalk in the direction she came from.

"He's dead," she continues, louder now. "You killed him."

You stop and turn back to her, half-holding Hunter's body out like maybe she'll take him from you, maybe it will somehow comfort her, maybe she'll let you go. "I'm sorry," you say again. You cock your head at the other driver. "He was going to hit me."

She waits and stares at the two of you, arms crossed, chin hugged into her chest like a turtle in its shell. She starts to cry now. The ebony and ivory checkerboard patterns along the flanks of her jacket shudder. The drizzle falls a bit harder, not quite rain, but enough to make you wish you had your umbrella in your hands instead of a dead, wet dog.

"Give him to me," she says and steps forward, arms thrust out.

You ease Hunter into her grasp. She folds a hand around to stroke his neck. She looks back at you and shudders and cries, then walks away. You call after her as she goes, tell her your name and address. She does not turn around. You watch her black figure recede into the gray morning. A squeal of tires announces the Cadillac fleeing the scene and you turn just in time to catch the first three characters of its rear license plate: "ALP." Great. You examine your own car. It has a sizable dent just behind the gas cap, but nothing that shouldn't keep you from driving. It's 8:45. You'll have to hurry to make it to the trial on time.

You enter the courthouse lobby with a few minutes to spare. The usual mass of humanity greets you, accompanied by the dank odor of absorbed moisture like driftwood washed ashore amidst the slimy seaweed and buffered green glass. The smell is worse inside the courtroom pod, incubated in this gray fishbowl. The heat is nothing to speak of compared to yesterday, but today the pod walls sweat instead of the humans inside.

The players shuffle in sporadically just after 9:00. Hines and Solon have evidently taken the time to dry off and re-crisp the academic aura that floats on the shoulders of their solemn suits. Shannon Gray also shows no signs of the weather as she sweeps into the pod in a dark gray skirt suit that shows off two inches of toned quadriceps above each knee. Only Judge Pitcock, as he totters in at 9:10, appears somewhat de-poofed. The judge's chambers are apparently not immune to the courtroom climate, and Pitcock's matted soft gray hair and steam-flecked glasses give him the air of a waterlogged Lhasa Apso. Yet when the court functionaries stand for his entrance, it is with the greatest respect for this little, round man in black with a stern face and hint of a Santa Claus gleam in one eye.

Pitcock settles in and calls the court to order, then asks. "Mrs. Gray, are you prepared to make your closing statement?"

"I am, Your Honor." Gray stands at the front of her table where she can address the entire court at once. "Ladies and gentlemen of the jury," she begins, "you have heard the testimony of the witnesses. You know the facts of the case. On the night of April 26, 2011, Dr. David Solon was awakened from his bed by a noise in the downstairs of his home. He went to investigate, heard gunshots and found a man standing over the body of his wife. Dr. Solon fired on the intruder as he fled, but he escaped unharmed. When police officers arrived at the crime scene, Dr. Solon managed to give a vivid description of the intruder's face which produced the composite sketch marked Exhibit 1.

"Now the law does allow for a charge of voluntary manslaughter in cases where an incident of provocation would cause a reasonable person to lose self-control and commit a homicide. However, if a period of time exists between the provocation and the homicide sufficient enough to allow the passions of the accused or of a reasonable person to cool, then the homicide becomes second-degree murder.

"Had Dr. Solon killed the intruder in his home on April 26, that homicide would have permitted a charge of manslaughter. Instead, a period of one week elapsed between the provocation and the day Dr. Solon killed Damon Belliard. On May 3, 2011, Dr. Solon came upon a man attempting to rob a woman in an alley. Dr. Solon disarmed the assailant and stood over his helpless prisoner. But when he saw the man's face and recognized it as that of his wife's suspected killer, Dr. Solon killed Damon Belliard. He looked into the face of a defenseless, unarmed man, and shot him with full knowledge of his action."

Shannon Gray pauses to let this statement sink in. She seems taller every time you see her. Her body is all lines and angles, but her movements remain fluid and unconstrained.

"In contrast to manslaughter, second-degree murder describes a homicide in which the killer intends to inflict serious bodily harm on the victim and acts with extreme indifference for human life," she continues. "Dr. Solon testified that he intended to shoot Damon Belliard in the head and that he did not consider what would happen to Mr. Belliard when he fired that shot. In other words, he intended to inflict serious bodily harm on Damon Belliard and he acted with indifference for Damon Belliard's life.

"Furthermore, Dr. Solon killed Damon Belliard one week after the death of his wife, during which time his passions did cool. You will recall that Dr. Solon admitted he no longer planned to kill Damon Belliard after the night of April 26. You will also remember that the police found only one cartridge case in the alley on Jackson Avenue, and the Medical Examiner recovered only one bullet from Damon Belliard's body. Dr. Solon testified that he killed Damon Belliard with a single gunshot. Yet surely a man enraged at the death of his wife would empty the magazine of his gun, pulling the trigger even after he has fired all the loaded cartridges. Dr. Solon fired one shot. This homicide was not committed in a sudden heat of passion. The killing of Damon Belliard was an intentional act of violence against a defenseless man. These are the facts of the case. Taken in conjunction with the law as it is written, they admit of only one conclusion: Dr. David Solon is guilty of murder."

"Thank you, Mrs. Gray," Pitcock says as Shannon Gray returns to her seat. "Mr. Hines?"

"Ladies and gentlemen," Hines begins, "allow me to simplify the facts of this case. Fact one: on April 26, 2011, Damon Belliard murdered Julia Solon. Fact two: Dr. Solon saw Damon Belliard that night well enough to describe him to a police sketch artist and to recognize him one week later. And fact three: on May 3, 2011, Dr. Solon killed Damon Belliard when he recognized him as the man who murdered his wife. Forensic evidence and the testimonies of multiple witnesses confirm these facts."

Hines sweeps aside his buttoned coat flaps and plunges his hands into his pockets. He rocks his weight from heel to toe and back again.

"The law allows a verdict of voluntary manslaughter in cases where the accused commits an intentional homicide in a sudden heat of passion following an incident that would provoke a reasonable person to kill," he says. "In other words, the law admits that even perfectly rational people like Dr. Solon can momentarily lose control of themselves and succumb to emotion. The law also states that if sufficient time elapses between an incident of provocation and a subsequent homicide to allow the passion of the accused or a reasonable person to cool, then the homicide becomes murder and not manslaughter. However, the law does not specify what exactly constitutes a 'sufficient' amount of time for a reasonable person's passion to subside. In the instance where a man sees his wife murdered in cold blood, I submit that one week is not sufficient time. Had Dr. Solon killed Damon Belliard on April 26, he would have faced, at worst, a charge of voluntary manslaughter. Dr. Solon reacted to his wife's murder and intentionally shot at her killer. Any reasonable person could be excused for reacting as Dr. Solon did. But what if Damon Belliard had returned to the scene of his crime the next morning? Would we call Dr. Solon a murderer then for shooting his wife's killer with her death that very night still fresh in his mind? What if two days had elapsed? Three days? A month?

"On May 3, Dr. Solon shot Damon Belliard in a sudden heat of passion when he recognized him as his wife's murderer. He intended to shoot Damon Belliard in that instant, just as he intended to shoot him the week before. Once again, Dr. Solon reacted to the provocation of discovering his wife's murderer."

Hines paces past the jury box to the front of the witness stand and turns to face you. "And why did Dr. Solon shoot Damon Belliard?" he asks. "Because Damon Belliard had recently murdered his wife.

"The circumstances of April 26 and May 3 are virtually identical. Dr. Solon found himself suddenly confronted by the man who murdered his wife and he reacted and shot at him. The State must now show that a homicide that might have warranted a manslaughter charge on April 26 would become second-degree murder a week later. They must prove beyond a doubt that the passions of a reasonable person like Dr. Solon would cool a week after he witnessed his wife's murder."

Hines has worked his way back down the length of the banister that separates him from the jurors as he speaks, and now he retreats a step to allow himself a little space from the jury before he delivers his finale. You would hardly recognize him from behind; his hair is full and dark, and the lines of his gray suit frame the body of a trimmer, younger man. Only when he comes about to face you do you see the softness in his face, the first hint of wrinkles around his steady, glinting, bronze eyes.

"Yet you have also heard the testimony of Dr. Franko Pavlov, an expert in the field of neuroscience and human behavior who has performed extensive research on the neurological aspects of human decision-making," he says. "According to Dr. Pavlov, it is quite possible for an incident to provoke an unconscious brain response that may result in an unintended decision a week later. Applied to this case, Dr. Pavlov's testimony suggests Julia Solon's murder may have created an unconscious reaction that persisted in Dr. Solon's brain after April 26, up until the moment he encountered Damon Belliard again on May 3. I think a similar reaction might occur in any of us should one of our loved ones suffer Julia's fate. The conclusion that a reasonable person's passion would have sufficiently cooled between April 26 and May 3 does not follow directly from the facts of the case. The law is simply not specific on this point, and the State has not demonstrated beyond a reasonable doubt that the killing of Damon Belliard met the conditions specified by the law. Therefore, in light of these considerations, I ask that you find Dr. Solon not guilty of second-degree murder."

"Thank you, Mr. Hines," Pitcock says as Hines returns to his table. "Ladies and gentlemen," he continues to the jury, "you have heard the facts of the case as presented by the witnesses called to testify in this courtroom. You have heard the attorneys give their interpretations of this evidence. It now falls on you to adjudicate in this matter. Dr. David Solon stands accused of voluntary manslaughter and second-degree murder. You will deliberate and return a verdict on both charges. As previously stated, the law defines second-degree murder as a homicide in which the accused intends to cause serious bodily harm to the victim and acts with extreme indifference for the victim's life. In contrast, the law permits a verdict of voluntary manslaughter in cases where provocation exists that would drive a reasonable person to commit an intentional homicide, provided the accused commits the homicide in a sudden heat of passion and sufficient time does not elapse between the provocation and the homicide which would allow the passion of a reasonable person to cool. It will be your task to evaluate the evidence you have heard in light of the law in order to reach your verdict."

He turns the bailiff. "Mr. Gilroy?"

"Yes, Your Honor." Gilroy cocks his head at the jury box and steps around Pitcock's chair. You and the other jurors rise and follow him out of the pod, and the deliberation begins.

Continue on page 199.

4. $S(t_1) \wedge L \rightarrow C(t_2)$

It is an odd morning. You wake with a strange detached calmness that diffuses through your entire body, as though you are coming out of anesthesia. When you step outside, you realize you have worn brown shoes with your charcoal dress slacks, and only then do you faintly recall the events of waking and showering and dressing and eating that got you to this point. A faint mist falls, not heavy enough to warrant an umbrella, and the streets seem overcrowded with people bustling off to work. You pass a jogger in all-white running pants and windbreaker, though it is scarcely 15° cooler than yesterday's heat wave.

You pull onto Main Street, where the traffic is thinner. The green light at Elm turns to yellow just as you enter the no man's land near the intersection. You hit your breaks, skid a few feet and come to a slick stop just shy of the crosswalk. A split second later your head snaps forward as the car behind you rear-ends yours.

You don't think you've lost consciousness, but it takes a few seconds before you become aware of the horns honking and a muffled voice screaming from somewhere over your shoulder. Your neck hints at an ache and your vision dances for a moment, but your airbag hasn't deployed and you don't see any blood. You slide gingerly out of your seat to have a look at your car.

"What the fuck?" an angry shout greets you as you step from the car. The speaker is a big, scary man in black jeans and a sleeveless t-shirt. Shaved head, goatee, strong-fat (opposite of skinny-fat). His arms look like they could throw your car out of his way; his gut suggests he chases his workouts with a couple Big Macs. "What the hell were you thinking?" he yells.

"It was a yellow light," you say. "I saw it and hit my brakes."

"Again, what the hell were you thinking?"

"I reacted. The light was yellow, and I stopped."

"Just run it! Yellow doesn't mean stop." Smoke hisses from the crumpled hood of his car as he advances toward you. "I could have made it easy."

Maybe he's right. There's a chance you could have crossed the intersection before the light turned red. But you also had enough time to brake. You can't recall your thoughts in that moment, don't remember if you thought about stopping or not stopping at all.

"Look at my fucking car!" he screams. Your vehicle, on the other hand, appears to have only suffered a crushed fender. It's still drivable.

"Did you see the light?" you ask.

"Yeah, I saw the light. I was going to make it until you hit your fucking brakes."

"Why were you so close to me?" you ask, surprised by your nerviness.

"What?"

"I had time to stop. Why didn't you?"

"Because I didn't think anyone would be such a fucking idiot, that's why."

You take a quick peek behind you to confirm the presence of the automated camera affixed to the top of the traffic signal. You thought this intersection was notorious for nabbing red light runners. You don't need a ticket. But you decide not to broach the subject with Baldy McMusclegut here.

"Are you saying this is my fault because I obey traffic signals?" The distant sound of sirens has further emboldened you.

"Fuck obeying. The light was yellow. Barely yellow. That means caution. Not flip your shit and slam on the brakes in the middle of traffic."

"Yeah, caution," you agree. "Not tailgate the car in front of you and accelerate when you see a yellow and brake lights."

"Fuck you. Look at my fucking car!"

You've already seen it and decide to ignore it now. "Do you have your insurance information?" you ask.

"Do you have a license?" he retorts.

"Yes." You dig it out. "Can I see yours?"

A police cruiser creeps to a stop behind his smoking wreck.

"Unbelievable," he says under his breath.

A short, thick, brunette officer steps out of the car. "Everyone okay?" she asks.

"I think so," you reply.

She walks up to stand between the two of you. The presence of the law has cooled Musclegut's fire. "So what happened here?" she asks.

You answer calmly before he has a chance to open his mouth. "I stopped for a yellow light, and he hit me from behind."

"That right?" she asks Musclegut.

"Looked green to me," he mutters.

"Uh huh. How close were you behind this car?"

"I don't know. I didn't exactly measure it."

"But you do know you're responsible for maintaining a safe distance behind the car in front of you?"

He glares in your direction. "I never expected the car in front of me to hit the brakes at a barely yellow light."

"So it was yellow now?" The policewoman flashes a grin. Musclegut just shakes his head and mumbles something under his breath.

"And you," she turns in your direction, "you may want to be more aware of the cars around you. Did you know it was a stale green?"

"I don't remember," you're forced to admit.

"Uh huh." She juts her chin at your dented fender. "Looks like you got off easy this time. Might not get so lucky again."

"Yes," you concede. "Thanks, Officer."

"All right," she says. "I'm going to write up an accident report. Can I see both of your licenses and insurance?"

The two of you give her your information, and she retreats to her cruiser. Musclegut has finished with you and begins to inspect the damage to his car. You check the time: 8:50. You can still make it to court by 9:00 if you hurry. The officer returns and hands each of you your license, insurance and a copy of the police report.

"Looks like you'll need a tow," she gestures to his wreck. "Yours okay to drive?" she asks you.

"Yeah, I think so."

"Okay. Be safe now."

"Thanks." You get in and pull away, putting a few blocks between yourself and the crash site before you accelerate above the speed limit.

You enter the courtroom seconds after 9:00 and breathe a sigh of relief to see that Judge Pitcock has not yet arrived. Gray, Hines and Solon wait at their tables, as though they never left. It strikes you that this is how you will always see these people, forever fixed in your mind as gargoyles watching over a dingy castle of the law.

Pitcock wanders in a few minutes later, settles into his seat and calls the courtroom to order. "Mrs. Gray, are you ready to make your closing statement?" he asks.

"I am, Your Honor." Gray circles to the front of her table to stand in full view of the entire pod.

"Ladies and gentlemen of the jury," she begins, "you have heard the testimony of the witnesses. You know the facts of the case. On the night of April 26, 2011, Dr. David Solon was awakened in bed by a noise from the ground floor of his home. He went to investigate and saw a man standing over the body of his wife. Dr. Solon fired on the intruder, but the man escaped unharmed. When police officers were called to the crime scene, Dr. Solon managed to give a vivid description of the intruder's face, which produced the composite sketch shown to you as Exhibit 1.

"As you are aware, the law recognizes voluntary manslaughter in cases where an incident of provocation would cause a reasonable person to lose self-control and commit a homicide. However, if a period of time exists between the provocation and the homicide sufficient enough to allow the passion of the accused or of a reasonable person to cool, then the homicide is defined not as manslaughter, but as murder.

"Had Dr. Solon killed the intruder in his home on April 26, the death of his wife immediately beforehand would permit a charge of manslaughter. Instead, one whole week elapsed between Mrs. Solon's death and the day Dr. Solon killed Damon Belliard. On May 3, 2011, Dr. Solon encountered Damon Belliard attempting to rob a woman at gunpoint. Dr. Solon disarmed Mr. Belliard and recovered his gun. He stood over Mr. Belliard, looked into the face of this defenseless, unarmed man and killed him with full knowledge of his actions.

"In contrast to manslaughter, the law defines second-degree murder as a homicide in which the killer intends to inflict serious bodily harm on the victim and acts with extreme indifference for human life. Dr. Solon testified that he intended to shoot Damon Belliard in the head and that he did not think of what would happen to Mr. Belliard when he fired that shot. He intended to inflict serious bodily harm on Damon Belliard on May 3, and he acted with indifference for Mr. Belliard's life.

"Moreover, one week was sufficient time for Dr. Solon's passion to cool. Dr. Solon himself testified he no longer planned to kill Damon Belliard after the night of April 26, and there is considerable evidence to show his emotions did subside in the week following his wife's murder. On April 26, Dr. Solon fired only two shots after Damon Belliard, then gave up and returned to his house. He did not even chase Mr. Belliard down the street. And on the evening of May 3, Dr. Solon was certainly not in a state of passion over his wife's death; he was returning from having coffee with a friend.

"Furthermore, remember that only one cartridge case was recovered from the alley on Jackson Avenue. Only one bullet was recovered from Damon Belliard's body. Dr. Solon killed Damon Belliard with a single shot. A man in the heat of the moment, filled with rage at the death of his wife, will empty the magazine of a gun, pulling the trigger even after he has fired all its cartridges. Dr. Solon fired one bullet. This was not a heated crime of passion. This was a cold-blooded execution."

You notice Shannon Gray has not yet moved from where she stands unprotected and impregnable at the front of her table. But now she takes two steps closer to the jury box and cocks her head up and back as she prepares to launch her final salvo.

"Dr. Solon claims he did not recognize Mr. Belliard when he entered the alley on May 3. He testified that Mr. Belliard had his back to him, yet he also claimed he could see Mr. Belliard's gun. Based on the testimony of Mrs. Judith Alethea about the position of Mr. Belliard's gun, I contend that if Dr. Solon could see Mr. Belliard's gun, he could also see enough of his face to recognize a man he managed to identify as he raced past him on the night of April 26. I suggest that he entered that alley having seen an opportunity to avenge his wife's death.

"Now Mr. Hines has called a witness who claims to have scientific evidence that unconscious desires may influence a person's decisions a week in advance, even when the subject predicts she will act counter to those desires. While the implications of Dr. Pavlov's research may seem persuasive regarding the facts of this case, I suggest we examine his findings from the proper perspective. All his experiments were conducted in a controlled laboratory setting, not in the real world. He determined the stimulus for each subject and limited the number and circumstances of their choices. And still his model is not 100% accurate. Dr. Solon acted in the real world when he shot and killed Damon Belliard. He could have guarded Damon Belliard until the police arrived. He could have shot him in the leg. Instead, he intentionally shot him in the head and killed him. The remaining inaccuracies of Dr. Pavlov's model, even in a controlled laboratory setting, leave room for freedom of choice and responsibility. Dr. Solon intended to kill Damon Belliard and he is responsible for his action. Simply put, Dr. David Solon is guilty of murder."

"Thank you, Mrs. Gray," says Pitcock. "Mr. Hines?"

"Ladies and gentlemen of the jury," Hines says, his deep, sonorous voice gliding through the thick air of the pod, "allow me to simplify the facts of this case. First, on April 26, 2011, Damon Belliard murdered Julia Solon. Second, Dr. Solon saw Damon Belliard well enough on April 26 to generate a composite sketch of his face. And third, on May 3, 2011, Dr. Solon killed Damon Belliard when he recognized him as his wife's murderer. Had Dr. Solon killed Damon Belliard on April 26, he would be facing a charge of voluntary manslaughter, at the very worst. On that night, Dr. Solon reacted as anyone would to witnessing his wife's murder when he intentionally fired at her killer."

Hines, unlike Gray, is a walker, though clearly not out of any nervousness. His measured strides are almost rehearsed; they flow from his words, leading his audience down the path of his argument.

"The law does state that if sufficient time elapses between an incident of provocation and a subsequent homicide to allow the passion of the accused or of a reasonable person to cool, then the homicide becomes second degree murder and not manslaughter," Hines says as he comes to a stop in front of the jury box. "However, the law does not specify what exactly constitutes such a 'sufficient' amount of time. In the case where a man witnesses his wife's senseless murder, I submit that one week is not long enough for his emotions to subside. What if Damon Belliard had returned to the scene of Julia Solon's murder the very next morning? Would we call Dr. Solon a murderer then for shooting his wife's killer with her death that very night still fresh in his mind? What if two days had elapsed? Three days? A month?

"On May 3, Dr. Solon shot Damon Belliard in a sudden heat of passion when he recognized him as the man who murdered his wife. Dr. Solon intended to shoot Damon Belliard in that instant, but he did so as a reaction to the provocation of Julia's murder. The circumstances of April 26 and May 3 are nearly identical. Dr. Solon was suddenly confronted by the man who murdered his wife. He reacted and shot at him. In order to deliver a murder verdict, ladies and gentlemen, you must feel convinced beyond a reasonable doubt that a homicide that might have warranted a charge of manslaughter on April 26 somehow became second-degree murder a week later. The State must prove that Dr. Solon's passions cooled, or that a reasonable person's passions would do so, in the week after his wife's murder."

Hines begins his rhythmic pacing once more, heel-toeing his way along the jury box railing, head bowed as if in deep contemplation of the facts.

"You have heard the testimony of Dr. Franko Pavlov, an expert in the field of neuroscience and human behavior who has performed extensive research on the neurological aspects of human decision-making," he says. "According to Dr.

Pavlov, an external stimulus can provoke a specific brain response beyond the conscious awareness of a subject. Applied to this case, Dr. Pavlov's testimony suggests Julia Solon's murder initiated an unconscious chemical reaction that lay dormant in Dr. Solon's brain until the moment he encountered Damon Belliard again on May 3. I imagine a similar response would afflict any of us should someone we love suffer the same fate. The conclusion that Dr. Solon's passion had cooled sufficiently after April 26 does not follow from the facts of the case, and given the heinous nature of Damon Belliard's crime, nor does the conclusion that a week is sufficient time for any reasonable person's emotions to settle. The law lacks specificity on this point, and the State has not demonstrated beyond a reasonable doubt that the killing of Damon Belliard met the conditions specified by law. Therefore, in light of these considerations, I ask that you find Dr. David Solon not guilty of second-degree murder."

Pitcock sits up in his chair and leans over the courtroom as Hines retakes his seat next to Dr. Solon. "Thank you, Mr. Hines," he says. "Ladies and gentlemen of the jury, you have heard the facts of the case as presented by the witnesses called to testify in this courtroom. You have heard the attorneys give their interpretations of this evidence. It now falls to you to adjudicate in this matter. Dr. David Solon stands accused of voluntary manslaughter and second-degree murder. You will deliberate and return a verdict on both these charges. As previously stated, the law defines second-degree murder as a homicide committed with intent to cause serious bodily harm to the victim and carried out with extreme indifference for human life. In contrast, the law allows a verdict of voluntary manslaughter in cases where provocation exists that would cause a reasonable person to commit an intentional homicide, provided the accused acts in a sudden heat of passion resulting from the provocation, and there is not sufficient time between the provocation and the homicide as to allow the passion of a reasonable person to cool. It will be your task to weigh the evidence you have heard in light of the law in order to reach your verdict.

"Mr. Gilroy?" he says to the bailiff.

"Yes, Your Honor." Gilroy inclines his head at the jury box and strides around Pitcock's chair. You and the other jurors rise and follow him out of the pod, and the deliberation begins.

Continue on page 199.

There is no food this time, as you and the other eleven jurors sit around the long rectangular table in the jury room, just two stainless steel jugs on a ledge against the windows, one with hot coffee and one with ice water.

Gilroy stands against the short wall behind the jury foreman seated at the head of the table. "Well, we usually begin this sort of thing with some kind of vote to see where we stand," he says. "Anyone object to that?"

There is a quiet chorus of short head shakes and a few murmured "nos."

"All right, then," Gilroy says. "Why don't we start with the charge of manslaughter? I'm guessing that'll be more straightforward. Everyone who believes the defendant is guilty of voluntary manslaughter, please raise your hand." Twelve hands extend into the air. "Not guilty?" The hands remain down.

"Okay, that was easy enough. Next is the charge of second-degree murder. I imagine this one might be more split, so let's do it by a silent vote. I'll pass around some paper and pens. Just write 'guilty' or 'not guilty' on your paper and then fold it and pass it back to me."

The whispery crinkles of paper and the clatter of plastic pens on wood are deafening in the silent room. You take a ballot and begin to write.

If you vote "guilty," turn to page 200.
If you vote "not guilty," turn to page 207.

You scrawl "guilty" on your paper, fold it twice and pass it to the head of the table.

Gilroy gathers the votes into a pile and reads them aloud one by one. "Guilty. Not guilty. Not guilty. Guilty. Guilty. Guilty." He tallies the votes on a piece of paper as he reads. "Not guilty. Guilty. Guilty. Not guilty. Not guilty. Not guilty." He checks his tallies. "It looks like we're split. Six and six."

An expectant hush falls over the room as each of you tries to read the votes of others in their eyes.

"I suppose if everyone went around and said how they voted and why, we could try to work this out," Gilroy continues. He gestures to the jury foreman, a thick, middle-aged, balding man with traces of reddish brown hair above his ears. "Would you like to start?"

"Uh, sure. My name is Bob Wilson. I think he's guilty. He shot him a week after his wife was killed. One shot, straight to the head of an unarmed man. I just can't get past that."

"Thank you, Mr. Wilson," says Gilroy. He indicates the next juror, a slim, dark-skinned woman in a light gray business suit. "What about you ma'am?"

"My name is Shirley Revis," she says. "I voted not guilty. That man killed his wife. I can't say I wouldn't do the same if I were him."

And so it goes, all the way around the table. John Mann voted not guilty and cites Pavlov's testimony. You agree with the guilty camp that Dr. Solon seemed to cool off in the week after his wife's death. Everyone else offers different variations on the two opposing arguments. It's a dead stalemate.

"Well," Gilroy sighs, "we have to come to some sort of consensus, so let's hash this thing out."

The twelve of you shuffle uncomfortably in your seats and peek at potential opponents like prep school kids before their first fight. A small, pale, timid-looking woman to your left speaks first. Dorothy, you think.

"It seems like we first need to decide if Dr. Solon cooled off or not," she says. "And if he didn't, would a reasonable person cool off in the week after his wife's death?"

"He testified he didn't plan to kill Belliard after that first night," Bob says. "That's pretty clear evidence."

"I don't know, Bob," says Shirley. "It's one thing to know it would be wrong to kill Belliard. It's different to suddenly stumble upon him in another heated situation."

"I agree," says John Mann. "I think his wife's murder just got ingrained in Dr. Solon, deeper down than even he knew. I don't think we can say he killed Damon Belliard with full knowledge of his actions. He just reacted to seeing the man who murdered his wife."

"He reacted the first night," you say. Your heart beats in your head amidst the silent room, radiating waves of heat down your face. "If Solon had shot Belliard the night of his wife's murder, I would call it manslaughter. But he had a week to think about what happened. He wasn't programmed to act a certain way. He knew the consequences of shooting Belliard. Anyone would. Even if he killed him in a fit of grief-stricken rage, that doesn't make it any more justifiable. We don't excuse other people for blowing up and shooting someone when they get mad."

"Exactly," Bob pipes up. "Lots of people go through tragedies. They grieve. They recover in time. Not all of them turn vigilante."

"You're right," Dorothy says quietly, as she stares at her hands in her lap. "He knew the situation. Maybe at that moment, he lost his head again, but he was cool up until that point. He knew the circumstances, knew the consequences of any action he might take."

"I'd like to change my vote," she says to Gilroy who leans cross-armed against the front wall. "Guilty."

"Do you really think it matters that he knew the consequences?" Shirley asks. "I'm sure that before April 26 Dr. Solon had a pretty good idea of the consequences of shooting Damon Belliard that night under the same circumstances."

"The point is he reacted to witnessing his wife's murder right after it happened," you reply. "Reactions are immediate. You don't react to an incident a week later."

"Maybe," Shirley concedes. "I just know if it were me… "

"Let's say you were in the same scenario as Dr. Solon," you respond. "You understand the consequences of killing Damon Belliard. You know you could be on trial for murder. If you had just lost your spouse, it's possible you could know the consequences and still want to kill Belliard anyway."

"Dr. Solon didn't want to kill Damon Belliard the week after his wife's murder," John offers.

"Exactly!" Bob cries. "Because he had cooled off."

John starts to reply, but Shirley speaks first. "You may be right," she says. "If it were me, I can't say what I'd do. I might be so crazed I'd kill Belliard even if I knew I could face a murder verdict. But sitting here now, I know I shouldn't do it. I know Dr. Solon shouldn't have done it."

"We all agree on that," John says. "We voted guilty of manslaughter."

"No," Shirley says. "It's more than that. He knew what he was doing. He could have made a different choice. I'm changing my vote. Guilty of second-degree murder."

From there the discussion stumbles on for another two hours. At times it feels like running in sand as the majority guilties slog forward only to slip back again under not guilty counterarguments and pangs of sympathy. But the wheels of human Justice churn inexorably forward. One not guilty voter turns. Then another. And another. With each change of heart, the pressure mounts on those who still cling to their convictions of innocence. A change comes over you as well. You do not doubt your verdict. Yet the triumph of turning Dorothy and Shirley lessens with each new convert. You feel their convictions dragged from them with greater and greater resistance each time, but you cannot turn back now. You suspect the others feel it as well, even those who hold for a time under the banner of David Solon's innocence. Everyone realizes it is just a matter of time and the discovery of the right combination of words to break this impasse, with only one outcome in sight.

At 12:00, Gilroy suggests a break for lunch. John Mann remains the last not guilty vote. Everyone eats in silence, spread around the table. Whatever camaraderie you all shared in bringing the debate to this point has disappeared in the brief return to normal life activity.

You sidle up next to Mann as he fills his Styrofoam cup from the coffee jug, his back turned to the odds arrayed against him.

"You gonna hang us, John?" you ask. As soon as the words begin to leave your mouth, they seem entirely foreign and out of character.

He gives you a sidelong glance. "You gonna convince me?"

"I… We'll try," you manage.

Mann blows on his coffee and measures you calmly.

"What would it take?" you ask, dismayed to hear your words sounding like a plea for help. You're sure of the verdict, and yet here you stand attempting to bargain with a man you believe to be in error.

"Convince me he's guilty," he answers.

"We're trying," you say. What does he think you've been doing the past two hours?

John cradles his cup in both hands and takes a sip, his eyes on yours over the Styrofoam rim. "I guess you'll have to keep trying," he says and strolls away.

"Okay, everybody." Gilroy's voice pokes meekly into the silence. "We'd better get back to it."

Lunch remains are discarded as everyone settles back in around the table. The initial unease has returned. No one knows where to begin.

"John, you're the last not guilty vote left," Gilroy says, once he sees nobody else intends to make the first move. "Why don't you explain your position a little more clearly to everyone?"

"I just don't think the State did enough to show Dr. Solon's passion cooled in the week after his wife's murder," John says. "Not after his testimony and the testimony of Dr. Pavlov."

"Do you believe Dr. Pavlov?" Shirley asks, her voice quiet but powerful. "Do you really think it's possible for an MRI to predict what you're going to do better than you can?"

"Yes," says John. "Don't you?" He speaks to Shirley, but his eyes never leave yours.

"Forget the MRI," Bob blurts out from the opposite end of the table. "This isn't some lab experiment. This is real life."

"Pavlov's subjects are real people," says John. "The question is whether or not your mind can make an unconscious decision a week in advance of some consequent action. Pavlov's results indicate a high likelihood that such unconscious choices do occur."

"But is that so shocking?" you ask. "Let's say you know your best friend likes ice cream much more than cake. Couldn't you predict what she would choose at a party a week from now with at least 90% accuracy? And couldn't your friend still choose cake if she felt like it on that day?"

"That's true, John," says Shirley. "We can all understand why David Solon killed Damon Belliard. It's not entirely surprising to me that he did it. But that doesn't mean he couldn't have done otherwise. It was possible for him not to do it. When Dr. Solon found Belliard in that alley, he wasn't provoked to kill him right there on the spot. Yes, he acted on the memory of what had happened to his wife, but he had a week to cool off from that provoking incident. He had time to understand the consequences of killing Belliard. He had time for coffee with a friend. He had time to choose otherwise."

"She's right, John," you say. "We're all human beings. We all do things in the heat of the moment every now and then. And maybe it's partly excusable when we react to a scenario before we can think. But when we have time to consider our options and their consequences, the situation changes. We can decide. We can make a choice. None of us expect David Solon to ever fully get over what happened to his wife. Her death will probably serve as a motivating factor for lots of decisions as long as he lives. But we can expect him to weigh that consideration against the consequences of killing Damon Belliard over the course of a week. Reasonable people face conflicting choices all the time. Dr. Solon had a choice. He made it. He knew the consequences, and now he has to face them."

The other jurors nod in silent affirmation of your statement. John's dark brown eyes return your gaze without wavering, and his face bears that permanent hint of a smile. Then he looks around the table at the rest of the jurors watching him.

"He had a choice, then," he says.

"That's right, John," you say. "He was human."

"So you don't believe Pavlov, then. That the human brain can make a decision without the individual's conscious awareness."

"Does it matter? That can't be an excuse. Outside of an insanity plea, we'd never accept a defense of 'it was my brain that did it, not me,' from anyone else. Even if thoughts occur spontaneously, people are responsible for how they process those thoughts and for their subsequent actions."

"That's right," Shirley says. "We'll never know if David Solon consciously chose to kill Damon Belliard. We only know that he did. He had an opportunity to shoot or not shoot. There was a choice to be made."

"And he made it," John replies.

"Yes," you say, "he chose to kill Damon Belliard."

Mann nods slowly. "Okay," he says. "I'm changing my vote. Guilty."

Murmurs of mixed emotion ripple around the table, for even after this final consensus it is hard to feel much relief over convicting a man of murder.

Fortunately, Gilroy steps in right away. "It sounds like we have a decision," he says. "Does anyone object to the verdict of guilty on the charge of second-degree murder?" His question is met with silence. "All right then. Follow me."

Gilroy leads you back out into the pod where a collective nervous chatter from beyond the frosted, gray glass greets the arrival of a verdict. It is the first time you have noticed the audience in this trial. You scan the smudged faces outside the pod. They must be here for Dr. Solon. Friends, family members, maybe even students. You doubt anyone has come for Damon Belliard.

"Members of the jury, have you reached a verdict?" Pitcock asks.

Bob Wilson stands and passes the verdict sheet to Gilroy, who relays it to the bench. Pitcock peruses it with agonizing slowness.

Then he harrumphs and reads aloud. "In the Yetopo County Court, Criminal Case Number 11-09187, People vs. Dr. David Solon, we the jury find as follows: on the charge of voluntary manslaughter, guilty as charged; on the charge of murder in the second degree, guilty as charged."

An abrupt wail emerges from beyond the pod, accompanied by murmurs of saddened and angry tenor. Shannon Gray's assistant shakes her hand vigorously; she lets him pump her arm, her attention focused on Judge Pitcock as though still waiting to hear the verdict. Kenneth Hines slumps back in his seat and turns to David Solon, who stares past you and the rest of the jury, past Judge Pitcock, into the empty space at the back of the courtroom, or perhaps beyond, through the back wall and the judge's chambers and the jury room and the honeycombed pods that must line the halls of this building, out into the clear air and the soft sky, which has just turned from gray to blue as the morning clouds dissipate and the sun begins to poke through.

•   •   •   •   •

David Solon was sentenced to eleven years in prison with eligibility for parole after the first seven. In light of the circumstances of the crime, Judge Pitcock opted for the minimum allowable sentence for each count. Throughout the proceedings, Dr. Solon's expression never once deviated from the cool, curious look of a wise man who has stumbled upon an idea of great importance that you will always associate with his character.

John Mann catches up with you as you make your way down the high stone steps of the Yetopo County Courthouse for what you hope will be the last time. He doesn't say a word as the two of you descend each stair stride for stride. There is little room for comment on the incarceration of a man whose only crime was to avenge the death of the woman he loved.

"I guess this is it," he tells you as you reach the bottom. It is probably the only thing he can say. "Good luck tomorrow."

"Thanks."

"Know what you're going to do?"

"I think so."

"Piece of cake," he says.

You stare at him. He folds his hands at his belt, and his wavy locks sway softly in the wind.

"Well, good luck," he repeats.

"I didn't think you believed in luck," you reply. "You seemed to think everything had already been determined."

"I guess so. Let's just say, I hope you make the right decision."

"Thanks," you say. "Goodbye."

He continues to stare in your direction, and you wonder for a second if he was ever looking at you at all, or rather, as it seems now, just past you, seeing you as merely a patch in the larger fabric of the world. Then he turns and walks away, casting one final "goodbye" over his shoulder as he goes.

Continue on page 215.

You scribble "not guilty" on your paper, fold it twice and pass it around the table.

Gilroy scoops up the quartered ballots and unfolds them one by one to read aloud. "Guilty. Guilty. Guilty." He tallies each vote on a sheet of paper as he reads it. "Guilty. Guilty. Not guilty. Guilty." His voice stumbles a bit over the "not." But then, "Guilty. Guilty. Guilty. Guilty. Guilty."

11-1. Yours was the sole not guilty vote.

Gilroy sighs. "Well, I guess we should ask whoever voted not guilty to give his or her reasons and then go from there."

"I'm the one," you say with a half-hearted raise of your hand. "I voted not guilty. I guess I just don't think the State did enough to prove its case. The law—"

"You don't think the State did enough!?" an overweight man with a thick mustache bellows from the end of the table to your left. "A man kills somebody in cold blood, and you don't think—"

"All right, all right," Gilroy interrupts. "Let's just hold on until we hear this explanation." He gestures in your direction. "Go ahead."

"The law says manslaughter becomes murder if the defendant cools or if sufficient time elapses between the provocation and the killing to allow the passions of a reasonable person to cool," you continue. "To convict Dr. Solon of murder, the prosecution had to show that the one week between his wife's death and Belliard's homicide was sufficient time. I don't think they did that. Not beyond a reasonable doubt."

"Reasonable doubt, my ass!" your hot-tempered opponent explodes. Flecks of sweat percolate on his deep brown forehead, and his mustache twitches like an electrocuted caterpillar.

Your own temples begin to simmer. The other jurors remain silent, perhaps equally discomfited by his outbursts.

"Okay, Mr...." says Gilroy.

"Johnson. Steve Johnson."

"Okay, Mr. Johnson. I think we know where you stand. Maybe some other people would like to say why they think the defendant is guilty."

No one speaks at first. You can't tell if that's a good thing. Finally, a timid voice emerges from the seat across from Steve.

"My name is Louisa Gibbons," says a little old woman whose whole body clutches at the tiny handbag in her bony, wrinkled, translucent hands. "My husband Horace died in 1998. He had lung cancer. Worked on factory assembly lines all his life. Could have been any number of things that killed him in the end: asbestos, diesel fumes, other chemicals, maybe all of them. Not a day goes by that I don't miss him. But there's a difference between grieving for someone you love and taking revenge. That man out there killed another human being and he has to pay for what he did."

"I agree we can't overlook Dr. Solon's responsibility for killing another man just because of what happened to his wife," John Mann says from the seat on your left. "But with all due respect to your husband, I think it's a different thing to have your spouse die of cancer compared to seeing her murdered."

"So what do you think?" Johnson snarls. "You voted guilty, didn't you?"

John Mann remains unaffected by the human thundercloud that is Steve Johnson. "Yes, I did," he says. "I think there need to be consequences if you kill another human being. Whatever happened to David Solon's wife, I don't think we should set a precedent for vigilantism."

"There are consequences," you say. "We're going to convict him of voluntary manslaughter."

"And you think that's enough?" growls Johnson. "He killed another man. He shot him point blank as he lay on his back, unarmed. That's murder. Murder."

"Look, this isn't working, Steve," says the woman on your right. Her black blouse is nearly matched by her lush ebony skin and the new-moon-at-midnight-dark wavy hair that cascades over her shoulders. "We all know Dr. Solon killed Damon Belliard. We need to decide whether or not it meets the criteria for murder. Whether or not he had cooled off, or should have cooled off. One person says 'no.' The rest of us say 'yes.' So if we're going to get anywhere it has to be on that point." She turns to you. "Maybe you could say a little more about why you don't believe a week was enough time in this case."

"Sure," you answer. "As I thought about the evidence, I tried to imagine the difference between Dr. Solon shooting Belliard on the night of his wife's murder versus one week later. Both scenarios play out about the same: he is holding a gun, he is confronted suddenly by his wife's killer, and that triggers an automatic response to shoot. If he had shot Belliard that first night, I think we'd all agree on just manslaughter. But the only difference between the two scenarios is the week in between. Like the defense said, what if it was a day later? Or two days?"

John makes a steeple with his fingertips, leans in and rests his hands on the table. "And what if things had happened exactly the way they did, except that twenty years had passed between the two incidents? Would he still be innocent?"

"No, I don't think so," you say. "I think there is an end point to the cooling-off period. I just don't know what it is. But yes, the more time passes, the more I'd expect Solon to not react the way he did."

"What did you make of Pavlov's testimony?" John asks.

"I think he's right in some sense," you reply. "We all have deep emotional states we're not aware of, and particularly traumatic situations can trigger us to react in ways we don't anticipate. That seems to be what happened to Dr. Solon. I don't think he planned to kill Damon Belliard until the moment he recognized him. Stumbling across Belliard in that alley almost seems like an extension of the original provocation. Part of Solon's mind was in the same place it was one week earlier."

"So what would make it murder then?"

"If he had time to think the day he killed him," you answer. "If he had time to deliberate, to choose a plan of action in full light of the consequences."

John nods. "I see."

"Wait a minute," Steve blurts out. "You're agreeing with this?"

John fixates on Steve without turning his head. "Maybe."

"I don't believe it! This was an open and shut case! And now everyone's getting cold feet." You wonder if it's possible for Steve Johnson to speak at a normal volume.

"In light of some of these arguments, I think the decision warrants more discussion," John says. "Anyone else agree?"

"I do," says the crisp-looking woman to your right. "I'm not ready to change my vote, but I'd like to hear some more discussion."

"Thank you, Ms. ..."

"Davis. Verity Davis."

"Thank you, Verity," says John. "Anyone else?"

"Yes," says Louisa, echoed by a few muttered affirmatives from around the table.

"All right then. So do you think Dr. Solon meant to kill Damon Belliard?" he asks you.

"I don't think the gun went off by accident," you answer. "So in that sense, yes, he meant to kill him. But I also don't think he had a conscious thought like 'This man killed my wife. I'm going to pull the trigger and shoot him now.' I think he reacted, the same way he reacted when he shot at Belliard a week earlier. Did his brain tell his body to shoot? Yes. But did his mind process and deliberate and come up with a decision? Probably not. That's not to excuse what Dr. Solon did in any way. He killed another man. I think he's guilty of manslaughter. Just not murder."

"That makes sense," John says. "The big hang-up for me was how we could absolve Dr. Solon of responsibility for killing another man. But we're not. I think any of us might have had the exact same reaction as Dr. Solon. I know it wouldn't surprise me if I did."

"What are you saying?" Steve Johnson's voice slides out deep and menacing between clenched teeth.

"I'm saying I'm changing my vote," John replies. "I vote not guilty on the charge of murder."

"Me too," says a young woman with fiery red hair, who introduces herself as Jean.

Mixed sounds of outrage, surprise and perhaps even support spill out from around the room. Steve pounds the thick oaken table once but says nothing.

Gilroy, standing with his arms crossed, right knee bent and the sole of his shoe propped against the front wall of the room, ambles to the head of the table. "Okay, so it's 9-3 guilty." He checks his watch. "It's 12:15 now. Why don't we break for lunch and then pick up here at 1:00?"

The delivered lunch is a quiet affair. Even jurors on the same side of the debate exchange just a bare minimum of conversation. Deliberation resumes at 1:00 sharp, but the discussion has reached an impasse. Neither side appears to have an argument to sway its opponents.

"What do the rest of you think of Dr. Pavlov's testimony?" John finally asks.

"I think he's a quack, that's what," Steve answers. His palms are flat on the table, fingers spread and taut, as though he'd like to shove the thing through the floor. "All that brain chemistry bullshit. We're not talking about forgetting to put on sunscreen here. We're talking about pulling the trigger of a gun and ending another man's life."

"But you do understand the implications of his research and the sunscreen study, right?" John asks. "Pavlov's results show an MRI can predict what a person will choose a week after the scan with 93% accuracy. That suggests unconscious decisions can be imprinted in our brains a week in advance of our actions. Which is one of the reasons I find it hard to say Dr. Solon did cool or should have cooled a week after his wife's death."

"So what? You think we're all some kind of computers programmed to act a certain way?" Steve asks.

"Like Pavlov said, I think our brain chemistry reacts to stimuli with a measurable response that can be captured by an MRI scan," John replies. "And that reaction can persist in our brains for up to a week."

"Let's say you're right, and our brains do just automatically respond to stimuli without us knowing it," says Verity, her clear voice cutting through the brewing tension. "There must be some basis for that response. I mean it's not like brain chemistry is completely random."

"I guess not," John says. "I don't really know."

"Well, people typically make decisions based on good reasons," Verity continues. "We usually understand why people do the things they do. We can even understand why Dr. Solon killed Damon Belliard, whether it was just an unconscious reaction or whether he made a deliberate choice. Of course, understanding doesn't mean we condone his action. But we also don't think he acted randomly based upon some chance synapse in his brain."

"Maybe not," you agree, "but there's strong evidence to indicate these reactions occur, and that they occur without us knowing about them."

"Right," says John. "And that evidence holds for decisions made a week after some initial stimulus."

"But if those reactions or decisions aren't based on random chance, what are they based on?" Verity asks.

"Who cares?" grumbles Steve. "A man has to be responsible for his actions. Otherwise, why even have laws at all?"

"We're not saying Dr. Solon isn't responsible for Damon Belliard's death," John replies.

"That's right," says Jean.

"But you still don't believe a week is enough time for a reasonable man to think about taking revenge against his wife's killer and the consequences of that action?" Verity asks. "We all have situations where we react without thinking, but that doesn't excuse our actions."

"I think it's very possible Dr. Solon thought about how he might meet Damon Belliard again, imagined killing him in those situations and considered the consequences," you admit. "Just like he might have imagined before April 26 how he would respond if someone broke into his home and murdered his wife. But it's different to think about those things as hypotheticals. I don't believe Dr. Solon ever imagined he would meet Damon Belliard again like he did, in a way that was so similar to the night of his wife's death. He just couldn't account for those unforeseen circumstances."

"Exactly," Jean says. "Dr. Solon's killing Belliard was just a knee-jerk reaction to his suddenly recognizing Belliard as his wife's murderer. He killed Belliard without really thinking about doing it—just like he might have done if he shot him the night his wife was killed."

"I think you're right," says Louisa from down the table. "That young man out there will suffer the consequences of what he did. He's going to go to jail. But I don't think he should stay there for the rest of his life. I vote not guilty."

Steve looks poised to explode but says nothing. Then the pasty, balding, egg-shaped man across from you speaks up. "Me too."

"Me too," echoes another person.

"Not guilty," says a third. "Not of murder."

"I agree."

"Me too."

"And me."

That leaves two. "Well, Steve?" says Verity.

"You're kidding me. You too?"

"Yes," Verity exhales. "Not guilty."

Steve shakes his head. "I don't believe this. Three hours ago, all of you…" He trails off and stares blankly into space. "I guess I don't have much choice then."

"Yes you do, Steve," says Verity. "None of us are forcing you to change your mind. We did it because we decided it was the right choice. If you don't agree, you have to stick to your convictions."

"He's going to jail for manslaughter," Steve grumbles. "I'll have to live with that."

"No, you don't," says Verity.

"Then you change your vote!" Steve glares around the table, but the fire has disappeared from his eyes.

"I've made up my mind," says Verity.

"So have I. Not guilty. Case closed."

"It sounds like we have a consensus," Gilroy quickly breaks in. "All those who believe the defendant is not guilty of murder?"

Twelve hands raise.

"Guilty?"

The arms fall to the table. Steve hangs his head and studies the nails on the thumbs of his folded hands. In the background, Gilroy has gone to announce you have reached a verdict. A moment later, he returns to lead you all back into the pod one last time. Steve Johnson remains at the table until the last possible moment. John Mann hangs by the door until he stands, and then you all exit into the murky grayness.

•　　•　　•　　•　　•

Judge Pitcock sentences Dr. David Solon to seven years in prison with eligibility for parole after five. It's hard to imagine a man doing 1,826 days for avenging the death of his wife. It's hard to imagine a man doing five years for intentionally killing a defenseless man. Perhaps that's justice.

The sky is blue and cloudless as you descend the steps of the Yetopo County Courthouse. You hear your name shouted from behind you as you reach the bottom, and you turn to see John Mann picking his way down the stairs in rangy, spider-like strides. He pulls up alongside you as you walk away from the courthouse.

"Big day tomorrow," he says.

"Yeah."

"You know what you're gonna do?"

"I think so," you answer. "You know what you'd do?"

"Of course."

You don't suppose he'll tell you. You decide not to ask. You walk in silence for a moment, John with his head slightly bowed and that same half-smile on his lips, the perpetual look of posing for a portrait and trying not to laugh at the food stuck in the artist's teeth.

You stop and face him, unsure what he wants. "I guess this is it then," you say.

"I guess so."

"It was…" You wonder how often you lie when you tell a person you're glad to have met him.

"Yes," he says. "Good luck tomorrow."

"Thanks. Take care."

"You too."

He walks away, his long stringy hair blowing in the soft breeze that has hung on since morning, and you turn and head for home.

Continue on page 215.

5. ∴D

A stale wind sweeps across the barren parking lot outside the Lauterbur State Functional Magnetic Resonance Imaging Research Laboratory. The cracked black asphalt fumes in the mid-morning heat, the rising thermals tumble against your skin, and you imagine being swirled with damp laundry in an industrial clothes dryer. The willow tree next to the laboratory is certainly dead, its sad thin branches still leafless now ten days short of Memorial Day. The laboratory itself seems to have shrunk since your last visit. The corners of the building look a bit more rounded, the brick exterior a bit more dirt-smudged, as if polished by the gentle hand of the weeping willow.

The hall fluorescents crackle to life as you enter, splashing light and shadow onto the sea green walls. The long corridor throbs aortically in the uptake of light, and the hot wind outside blows the door shut behind you with a little puff of suction that eases you forward. Gloria waits in the anteroom, beautifully monolithic in all her secretarial glory. Her pulled-back hair accentuates the edged contours of her cheekbones, and as you approach her desk she looks up and asks, "Can I help you?"

You give her your name. She returns it with a blank stare.

"I'm coming back to finish Dr. Pavlov's experiment," you say. "I started last week."

She flicks out a manicured finger and presses a doorbell-like call button atop the desk. "You can have a seat," she says. "Dr. Pavlov will be with you in a minute."

She isn't kidding. You've scarcely settled into one of the ratty chairs when Pavlov emerges from the door behind Gloria's desk.

"Welcome back," he says as you stand. "Thank you for returning."

You don't know why you wouldn't have come back. The whole thing is pretty strange, but you don't seem to have anything to lose in being here.

"This way, please," he says, holding open the door, and you follow the gentle slope of his shoulders as he ducks down the second long hallway. He leads you past the low hum of the MRI room to the third door on the right.

"Please take a seat," he says as he gestures inside.

The room is half-lit; the fluorescent light panels on one side of the ceiling appear to have gone out. You sit in a wheeled swivel desk chair in front of a 3' by 4' Formica table. On the table rest the two boxes, thin-steel-walled and key-locked, a bit larger than something you might keep in a bank's safe deposit. They are marked by white placard tents bearing the letters "A" and "B." Pavlov stands behind you at the door.

"I will remind you of your options," his says. "Box A contains $1,000. Box B contains either nothing or $1,000,000. You may choose either only Box B or both Boxes A and B. A model was used to predict your choice based on the results of the fMRI scan taken last week. The prediction was made last week and the money allocated accordingly at that time. Do you have any questions?"

"No," you answer, not taking your eyes off the boxes.

"You may choose when ready," says Pavlov.

The moment seems to require one last bit of hesitation, one final reaffirmation that your choice is the right path to take. But you already know what your decision will be.

If you choose only Box B, turn to page 217.

If you choose both boxes, turn to page 219.

"I choose Box B," you say.

"Very well," says Pavlov.

You hear his feet shuffle across the linoleum as he makes his way toward the table. His face appears over your left shoulder, and you lean forward in your seat with anticipation. Pavlov stops at the table, digs in his pocket for a pair of small brass keys and stoops to unlock Box B. You press your hands into the chair to lift your thighs off the seat and hover there as Pavlov undoes the lock and lifts the lid.

You can make out a piece of paper in the box. Pavlov reaches in and lifts it out. It is a check. And now you stand with a short intake of breath. The half-dead lights in the room flicker once. Pavlov turns and extends the check to you.

"Congratulations," he says.

You take it. It is made out in your name. For the sum of—you count the zeroes twice—$1,000,000. It is real. You are a millionaire.

What happens next is inconsequential. Perhaps you thank Pavlov profusely, clasp his hand in both of yours and pump it madly, scarcely aware of his hand crushing yours in its incongruous vice-like grip. Perhaps you stumble from the building in a disbelieving stupor. You drop the check twice before your trembling fingers can fold it in half and tuck it safely into the deepest recesses of your pocket. The sea green walls of the long entry hallway make your head spin. Perhaps you sprint from the room, around the corner, down the hall, through the reception area where Gloria sits perfectly upright, her long neck and collarbones exposed under a low-buttoned, white blouse and gray blazer, and down the corridor toward the hazy glow of light behind the frosted glass door. Perhaps you faint. Gloria revives you with a cool glass of water as Pavlov looks on.

However it happens, you find yourself stepping out into the parking lot as a hot wind blasts you in the face and the air melts over your body. You begin to walk, slowly at first, then faster and faster as you escape the gravitational field of the lab, faster and faster until your feet begin to skip over the hard asphalt and you are almost running. The thick air parts around you, recedes, then sucks back and pulls you carelessly forward, and you sneak a hand into your pocket to feel the crisp edges of the check one more time.

.   .   .   .   .

They say you should bet with your head and not with your heart. Meaning that when your tiny, downtrodden alma mater finally gets a championship shot against one of the big boys, you're best off choking down any sappy sentiments and going with chalk. Winning money is the name of the game in gambling. Pick the better team and you're all but guaranteed to win. It's just common sense. For every Villanova, there are a million Georgetowns.

As you drive to the bank to deposit your check while trying to imagine the look on the teller's face, the radio newswoman announces that Dr. David Solon is scheduled to begin his prison sentence at the State Correctional Institution on Monday. And for the first time since the start of the trial, Dr. Solon has offered some comment on his actions.

"I did not plan to kill Damon Belliard," David Solon's voice crackles weakly over your car's speakers in a dim approximation of the man. "But I killed him nonetheless. He murdered Julia and in that instant, I reacted with that thought alone in my mind. I regret that he is dead. I regret that I killed him. I wish I had not. I knew the consequences of my action. And yet, if I found myself in the same situation a million times over, I do not see that I would have done any different."

You listen idly as the anchor changes topics, then switch to some music. You feel the road reach up to pull the car along. It makes a sharp turn around a bend and continues curving into a full U, and you drive on, back the way you came, traveling the very same road in the opposite direction.

END

"I choose both boxes," you say.

Pavlov seems to hesitate for a moment. A heartbeat of silence fills the air behind you.

"As you wish," he says.

You turn over your left shoulder with a touch of impatience to see him scuffling toward the table. He has a gleam in his eyes, and you realize he still relishes this moment, no matter how many times he has performed the experiment before. He stops at the table and digs in his pocket for a pair of small brass keys linked together by a simple little ring. You try to read some clue in the curve of his shoulders, the movements of his hands, but his body betrays nothing.

He opens Box A first and withdraws a check made out in your name for the sum of $1,000. You rise to meet him as he extends it toward you and give it a quick scan before you turn your attention to Box B. Pavlov flicks the second key to bear with one hand and inserts it into the lock. You can just make out the underside of the lid as Pavlov begins to lift it, but you remain obediently in your place behind him. You lean forward to glimpse the backmost part of the box floor over Pavlov's shoulder in the dim half-light, and then rise to your tiptoes and peer past Pavlov's stooped figure as he tilts the open box toward you to reveal… nothing. The box is empty.

"I'm sorry," says Pavlov. You wonder if he's lying. "The model is very accurate."

You gaze down at the $1,000 check in your hands. "It must be."

Pavlov sets the empty box back on the table. "Thank you for your time," he says.

You continue to stare at the check as he walks you to the door and leads you down the hall to the reception room. You don't know quite how to feel. $1,000 is pretty good pay for a lab rat. Did you really expect to win $1,000,000? Gloria scarcely registers your presence as you drift past her; she continues typing away industriously as Pavlov thanks you once more and you exit to the long entry hallway.

The sunlight glows behind the frosted glass door at the end of the dim corridor, like a lighthouse signaling a fog-bound ship home across a stormy cerulean bay. You fold the check in two, slip it into your pocket and walk down the hall and out into daylight. It is hotter than when you entered the lab, but not as stuffy as it was inside. A pleasant breeze puffs through the late morning sky and circulates the air around you in little eddying currents. It is a clear day, not a cloud in the sky, and you set out across the parking lot, leaving the small, squat, run-down lab behind.

•   •   •   •   •

"Because it is there." So said George Mallory in response to the question, "Why did you want to climb Mount Everest?" It was 1923. Mallory had just returned from two unsuccessful attempts to summit the world's highest peak in 1921 and 1922. In 1924, Mallory would attempt the trek a third time. He never returned. 75 years later, climbers discovered Mallory's body less than half a mile below the summit. To this day, speculation abounds that Mallory did, in fact, summit Everest, which would have made him the first human to do so.

As you drive to the bank to deposit your check, the radio newswoman announces that Dr. David Solon will begin serving his prison sentence at the State Correctional Institution on Monday. And for the first time since the start of the trial, Dr. Solon has offered some comment on the entire series of events.

"I did not plan to kill Damon Belliard," his voice crackles over your car's speakers as you pull up to a red light. "But I killed him nonetheless. He murdered Julia and in that instant, I reacted with that thought alone in my mind. I regret he is dead. I regret that I killed him. I wish I had not. I knew the consequences of my action. And yet, if I found myself in the same situation a million times over, I do not know if I would have done any different."

You tune out the anchor as she babbles on to another topic. The traffic light turns green, and you ease the accelerator down and maneuver around the car stalled in front of you, watching the little yellow hashes of the median tick by under your steering hand as you drive.

END

The terms of Dr. Pavlov's fMRI experiment have been borrowed from Newcomb's problem, developed by William Newcomb and first published and analyzed by Robert Nozick in the 1969 essay "Newcomb's Problem and Two Principles of Choice." The other studies referenced in the text are real, published by the listed researchers, and lend credence to the idea that fMRI could serve as a predictor in the sense required by Newcomb's problem.

ACKNOWLEDGEMENTS

Thank you to the following people whose input greatly influenced the shape of this novel. To my legal experts Jonah Roth and Kate Hickey for your help with the trial scenes, to Jonah for your discovery of a few plot holes and deficiencies, and to Kate for your knowledge of chronological, regional and popular cultural inaccuracies. To my aunt JoAnn Gonzalez Hickey for sharing your wisdom and experience with art, story and audience. To Jennifer Baum for helping me to see the possible consequences of actions from a different angle. To my mother Connie Hickey, for your astute eye for grammar. And to my wife Lindsay Simpson, first for your meticulous attention to every word and punctuation mark, and more importantly, for your constant unconditional support mixed with honest and practical advice. This story wouldn't be the same without each one of you.

ABOUT

Greg Hickey is a former international professional baseball player and current forensic scientist, endurance athlete, author and screenwriter. His debut novel, *Our Dried Voices*, was a finalist for *Foreword Reviews'* INDIES Science Fiction Book of the Year. He lives in Chicago with his wife, Lindsay.

THANK YOU

Thank you for reading *The Friar's Lantern!*

If you enjoyed this book, please take a minute to write a brief, honest review on Amazon at:
https://www.greghickeywrites.com/tflreview.

I appreciate your feedback, and every review helps more readers discover *The Friar's Lantern*.

Plus, learn the truth behind the trial scenes in *The Friar's Lantern* by downloading a free short prequel at:
https://www.greghickeywrites.com/anything-book.

This story, titled *The Theory of Anything*, follows Dr. David Solon through the week spanning the murder of his wife and the killing of Damon Belliard. When you download it, you'll also get exclusive access to discounts, giveaways and updates on my latest book projects.

Thanks again,

Greg Hickey

Made in the USA
Lexington, KY
11 June 2019